FINAL REST

Nelligan stepped into the bedroom and whistled two notes. A huge, brass canopy bed dominated the room, its frame draped with shimmering silk, the bedcover bearskin. Heavy red-and-cream drapes covered the window. Two ornate candelabra, unlit, sat on night tables on either side of the bed. Opposite the window hung an oil painting with garish, swirling bands of crimson and black in sensual and unsettling patterns. The rest of the furnishings matched the beautiful brass bed, with no extraneous household items visible and nothing out of place except for the corpse in the middle of the plush shag-carpeted floor.

Bantam Books offers the finest in classic and modern American murder mysteries. Ask your bookseller for the books you have missed.

PERPETUAL CHECK

Conrad Haynes

BANTAM BOOKS

TORONTO · NEW YORK · LONDON · SYDNEY · AUCKLAND

To Don, Shirley, Landy, Lee, Tim, Maryssa, Mary and Tyler on the one hand, and Barbara, Susan, Jared, Scott, Tami, Matthew, Casey, Ed and Carol on the other hand. To Peggy for everything. And to Bill Lewis, a good friend and an admired scholar, but who was never Harry Bishop.

PERPETUAL CHECK

A Bantam Book / April 1988

ISBN 0-553-26943-7

Published simultaneously in the United States and Canada

Bantam Books are published by Bantam Books, a division of Bantam Dou-
bleday Dell Publishing Group, Inc. Its trademark, consisting of the words
"Bantam Books" and the portrayal of a rooster, is Registered in U.S. Patent
and Trademark Office and in other countries. Marca Registrada. Bantam
Books, Inc., 666 Fifth Avenue, New York, New York 10103.

PRINTED IN THE UNITED STATES OF AMERICA

KR   0 9 8 7 6 5 4 3 2 1

ONE

✛

"Ladies and gentlemen . . . my very good friends . . . welcome to another exciting year at John Jacob Astor College!"

There was a spattering of polite applause. College President L. Charles "Chuck" Eckersley smiled a smile from an orthodontist's dream and waved. Almost the entire staff and undergraduate and graduate faculties of John Jacob Astor faced him, filling the curved, rising rows of plush seats in the arch-ceilinged Karl W. Kneibel Room. President Eckersley stood behind an oak rostrum, dressed as always in a $800 Savile Row suit and $90 tie, and flanked by the various deans and vice presidents of the institution.

It was September 14, the day fall term began. By tradition, the first Monday of the term was also the date of the president's State of the College address to the staff and faculty. It was an affair not taken lightly: in an average academic year, most employees of the college glimpsed L. Charles "Chuck" Eckersley only once or twice. Some faculty claimed to go the whole year without hearing from the president, which was odd, because he rarely missed a day of work. At nine-thirty every morning, Monday through Friday, L. Charles "Chuck" parked his dark blue Seville in the stenciled parking place in the shadow of the brick-and-mortar administration building and walked briskly to his enormous paneled office, his Italian leather attaché case clasped firmly at his side. And every afternoon promptly at three, he stepped out to his car and departed. That much everyone knew. What he did in the interim was anyone's guess.

But Day One of fall term was another matter. The State of the College address was one of only three events each year wherein one could place good money on seeing the president. The others were graduation commencement (L. Charles "Chuck" in his black robe and mortarboard, his Yale tie and gold tie pin gleaming at his collar), and the Homecoming Varsity-Alumni game (L. Charles "Chuck" in his wool sweater, calfskin coat with fur trim, and monogrammed leather gloves).

Now, Eckersley straightened his perfectly straight tie and cleared his throat. He adjusted the stack of three-by-five cards before him and beamed around the crowded auditorium. "We're anticipating, I think it's safe to say, and I'm sure everyone here will agree with me, a terrific year for John Jacob Astor," he intoned, and waited for the obligatory—if slightly delayed—applause. When that came, he nodded solemnly and continued.

"I think it's safe to tell all of you that I just had breakfast with the chairman of the board of trustees, and he shares with me, and with all of you, of course, and our students, both those here now and those who have elevated themselves to the rank of alumni, the great feelings about the year to come, which shall be a stand-out year for this institution, as I'm sure you'll agree, and I wanted to be sure the board is aware of this as well. They are."

Virtually three quarters of those present thought *They are what?* and began sifting through the twisted wreckage of syntax to recover the subject.

"In fact, I think we can sum up this exciting and, yes, I don't think it's overstating things to say, truly exciting year behind us, and, in point of fact, in front of us. The one word that, to my mind, epitomizes this year to come would, of all the possible superlatives that, naturally, equally apply, would have to be—"

A deafening crash reverberated in the back of the auditorium; a series of rhythmic thumps followed. Every eye turned to see a three-foot high, barrel-shaped ash can rolling down the wide, carpeted stairs. It rolled slowly, propelled by the slight tilt of the room, and thudded dully on each step, until it banged to a halt against Eckersley's podium. Eckersley looked down at this, his handsome gray eyes following the trail of ashes and squashed cigarette filters back up to the top row and the exit.

Professor Henry Bishop stood by the exit door and smiled shyly. In his right hand he carried a much abused blackstone bag and a much-too-heavy pile of textbooks. Under his left arm was a folded copy of the morning newspaper, and the fingers of his left hand were curled around a brown lunch bag and a red thermos decorated with bright Yosemite Sam decals. It had been the doctor's bag that had banged against the ash can, as Professor Bishop—Harry, to his friends—had tried to sneak in.

President L. Charles "Chuck" Eckersley cleared his throat. He flipped through the note cards, visibly struggling to remember which pearl of wisdom he had been about to impart.

Harry eyed a seat, three rows down and midway between the aisles. He would have vastly preferred to slip out quietly, but that was impossible now. Instead, he began to crab-walk down the rows of seats, mumbling "excuse me . . . thank you . . . pardon . . . excuse . . . thanks." His crumpled bag lunch brushed through the hair of everyone in the next row forward. His doctor's bag whacked the knee of an elderly associate biology professor who grunted and bit her lip to avoid swearing.

Harry finally reached the empty seat and plopped down, the blackstone, lunch bag, newspaper, thermos, and texts on his lap. Up front, Eckersley droned on, his metaphors tossed like a salad.

It was going to be another one of *those* terms at John Jacob Astor, Harry thought.

TWO

❖

The shanty was about the size of the average American bathroom. Its walls and roof were a hodgepodge of cardboard and plywood and a handful of two-by-fours, nailed together at some joints, connected by twine or barbed wire at others. The walls hung at eccentric angles, like a house in a Dr. Seuss story. There was no door: one of the two narrow sides was open to the elements.

Someone had recently daubed peanut butter onto the inner walls and fat, black flies had ventured in to investigate. In front of the shanty a wooden post had been driven into the lawn. A crude sign on the post read "WELCOME TO SOWETO. POPULATION 2 MILLION. YOUR TUITION DOLLARS AT WORK."

Harry sat at a table in the college cafeteria, staring out at the shanty on the western lawn. His narrow chin rested in his palm and his disheveled gray hair hung over the collar of his tweed jacket. He was a tall, painfully thin man with hollow cheeks, tired eyes, and, despite Portland's near-record dry spell that summer, no tan whatsoever.

Lee Connar set down a plastic tray, loaded with a tossed salad and tall iced tea with lemon wedge for himself and a microwaved Danish and coffee for Harry, and sat down opposite him. "By the way, Harry, I loved your entrance today."

Harry groaned. "I'd hoped no one noticed."

"That's like not noticing Mount St. Helen's, or our charming new protest, out there," Connar said cheerfully. He nodded toward the shanty.

Harry grinned and ripped open a pink packet of sweetener. "I don't know, Conny. I sort of like it."

"Oh, good. I'll tell our esteemed president. He'll be mightily relieved."

Harry poured a second packet of granules into his ceramic mug, followed by three containers of nondairy creamer. "I take it L. Charles 'Chuck' has seen yon shanty?"

"Oh, yes. He called a special meeting this morning, before the big speech, with all us deans and vice presidents in tow."

"And the provost and assistant deans and department directors?"

"Plus division heads, program directors, and degree coordinators."

"Conny, old salt, do you ever feel as if John Jacob Astor College is a tad top-heavy?"

"No. Never."

Harry sipped the light gray morass and winced. He set the mug on the table. "There's no caffeine here."

"Anyway, L. Charles 'Chuck' Eckersley himself summoned us together in the early hours and asked all seven thousand administrators why there was a shack on the western lawn."

"This coffee is decaffeinated, Conny."

Connar carefully forked together lettuce, a mushroom, slice of cucumber, and a dollop of Thousand Island. "We explained to His Eminence that this shanty—not a shack— had been erected to make a statement, probably by one or more unnamed student protest groups."

"Excuse me." Harry stood and shuffled away. Connar, a nondescript man in his late forties with perhaps the only pair of black plastic horn-rimmed glasses left in Oregon, had nearly finished his salad when Harry returned, his mug newly filled. He repeated the sacred coffee ritual. "Anyway, His Officiousness was none too thrilled, I take it?"

"None too. In fact, he expressed his fervent wish that said eyesore be removed by lunchtime, today."

Harry looked out the tall window at the structure, then back to the dean of faculty. "This is lunchtime."

"For me it is, because I eat wisely. Is your Danish cold?"

Harry touched the lump of prepackaged dough with a long, narrow finger. "As a stone."

"There *is* justice."

"Why is the shanty still up?"

Connar pondered the question. "Because I sort of like it."

Harry grinned. "You scoundrel, you."

"I deny I said that. I deny denying it. I'm not even here."

"Fair enough. And why, dean of my heart, are you telling me all this?"

Connar removed his glasses and rubbed his eyes. "Because the subject will undoubtedly be on the agenda of the board meeting this afternoon."

"True." Harry's tone was disinterested.

"By the way, did I tell you Dr. Westhaven broke his leg and shattered his kneecap yesterday?"

"'By the way'? Clever segue, Conny. Who's Dr. Westhaven?"

"Anthro. department. Pudgy, no neck."

"Bad hairpiece?"

"That's him. Seems he was on a dig in Eastern Oregon, in the Malheur Reserve. According to his wife, poor Westhaven will be laid up for some time."

"That's a shame."

"Certainly is."

There was a disconcerting air of serenity about the dean which Harry knew, from long experience, boded ill for him. He took a nibble of the Danish and regretted it. "Why do I keep sensing a primrose path flashing by?"

"Funny you should ask. Seems Westhaven was scheduled to be faculty liaison with the board of trustees this term."

"Oh?"

"And now he can't."

"Ah."

"So the rotation has been moved up, and the professor scheduled for winter term will have to be liaison for fall."

"Um."

"And do you know who was on tap for winter term?"

"Me?"

"Yup."

Harry removed his faded leather wallet and counted out his paper money, folded the bills lengthwise, and slid them across the table. "Sixteen dollars, Conny, and there's more where this came from."

"Chicken feed. I'm dean of faculty at a respected, private liberal arts college. I cannot be bought cheap. You'll love being faculty liaison to the board, Harry."

Tucker Nelligan tapped in the final paragraph. The green liquid light letters flashed across the dark screen. He finished the last sentence with the word *group*, thought about it for a moment, then deleted it and inserted *committee*.

Nelligan took a sip of his tepid Diet 7-Up, sighed, and leaned back in his chair. Around him the daily din of the *Portland Post*'s newsroom echoed off the walls, issuing from everyone and heard by no one. Nelligan shook his head and retraced the cursor. He swiftly replaced *committee* with *organization*.

"Tuck, you done?" Joann Dembrow rested a slim hand on Nelligan's shoulder and squeezed.

"Hmm. Just about."

"Length?"

"Ten and a half, eleven column inches."

Dembrow made a note on her run sheet. "What do you suggest for a headline? Will the commission make a final report this week or what?"

Nelligan erased *organization* and tried *commission*. "No. As usual, they're stalled on whether drugs should be a federal or local issue, and who pays for what. The mayor's people want the FBI and DEA to take the point on this, and the attorney general's reps see it strictly as crime prevention. They also don't fancy the idea of Feds running operations within state borders."

The city editor jotted the information down in her own brand of note-hand, a homegrown combination of shorthand squiggles and personal memory codes. The war on drugs had been crawling along all year and although there had been no significant changes, they had heard lots of red-hot rhetoric. She set down the clipboard and slumped into the chair by Nelligan's unnaturally tidy desk, stretching her long legs out and tucking her plaid skirt around her thighs. "The way I see this, the mayor's drug team is going to meet every other day for the rest of autumn and end up with a thousand-page report that says 'Drugs are bad' and not much else besides. True?"

Nellian tried *team.* "True." He scowled at the screen.

"I'm desperate to find something to keep the summer internship people busy for the last two weeks of their tour. I'd like to take you off the story and give it to one of them."

The young man sighed. "Okay. I want to do a follow-up anyway on this guy I heard about who's running industrial-strength marijuana to military academies around the country. You let the Junior Woodchucks take this story, and I'll get started on that."

Dembrow studied the reporter, whose attention never wavered off his VDT. At thirty-one, Nelligan was ten years younger than she, with a strong profile under short, sandy hair. When he had first joined the *Post*, three years earlier, Dembrow and nearly every other female employee had fallen instantly in lust with Nelligan's Irish good looks, boyish charm, and cocky demeanor. Even after word of his sexual preference got around, she had remained attracted to him. Dembrow shook her head and ran a hand through wavy, black-with-silver hair. "Let's let the marijuana story sit for a while. I want to give you something different."

The glowing square devoured *team* and spat out *unit,* then quickly reversed itself and spelled out *agency.* Nelligan grimaced. "Like how different."

Like a casual, heterosexual fling flashed unbidden through her mind. Dembrow shook her head and scanned the run sheet. "Let's see. I think we need to give you a breather from crime beat."

"No, thanks. I like cop-shop."

"Spice of life, Tucker. It's policy, you know that. You've still got good contacts at Astor College, right?"

"Yeah, but—"

"Student protests over college investments in South Africa are heating up. I'd like you to do a piece on that."

Nelligan swiveled around in his chair and looked at her for the first time. "Come on, Joann. No one gives a damn about student protests. The school administration doesn't. The board of directors or trustees or whatever won't. P. W. fucking Botha won't. It's Romper Room politics. Let me stick with crime, all right?"

"Look, Tucker, I was at the University of Illinois in sixty-eight. Don't tell me no one cares about student protests. *We* made a difference."

"Yeah, right." He turned back to the bothersome last sentence.

The fatigue of the twelve-hour day suddenly caught up with the city editor and she scribbled Nelligan's initials on the sheet beside the story. "This is your article, Tuck. Put a lid on the cynicism, will you? You're way too young for it. Try *group.*"

He tapped out *agency* and entered *group.* "Yeah. Student protests, huh?"

"Yes. Get started, okay. I've already got a shooter up there, so don't worry about photos. Twenty, twenty-five inches, max."

Nelligan shunted the story to the mainframe so the copy editor could retrieve it. He shut down his terminal. "No problem, boss. The reaction of JJAC's white-bread student body ought to be real pertinent. I'll try to catch Biff and Buffy while they're out polishing the ceramic colored jockey on the front lawn, and ask 'em how they feel about apartheid."

Dembrow stood. "You're one damned fine writer, Tucker Nelligan. But a little of your attitude goes a long way. Just write the copy, will you?"

"I've talked to Bledsoe. He's going to take your federalism class, if he can, or reassign it if not. That'll leave you just senior seminar, right?"

Harry cringed. The thought of Lyman Bledsoe, Jr., political science department head and all-around nebbish, running his beloved federalism class was nauseating. Harry and Connar were strolling down a meandering cobblestone path, past the library. Students flew past, laughing and chatting. The cross country team jogged by in mute file formation. Harry and Connar carried their suitcoats over their arms and licked ice cream cones—chocolate chocolate chip and butter pecan, respectively.

"So. I'm faculty liaison to the board. How can I get out of it?"

"You can't."

"I mentioned the jury duty, didn't I?"

"Again, Harry? That's three times this month."

Harry mentally sorted through his favorite excuses for one a bit less shopworn, but came up empty. "What do I need to know, then?"

Connar licked melted ice cream off the knuckle of his thumb. "Well, of course, South Africa will be topic numero uno. After that, who knows? Getting funds for a new football field press box is a hot topic."

"Be still my beating heart."

"And Geoffrey Eriksen's campaign to lower the percentage of tenured faculty will probably come up."

"He's still on about that?"

"Yes, and Eriksen's still chairman, so—"

"Chairperson."

"Chairperson, so we shouldn't take it lightly."

"Fine. What about South Africa?"

"Well, your old buddy Cordelia Applebaum is leading a lonely fight to divest from the Common Fund, from what I gather."

Harry grinned. "Dear Cordelia: last of the fighting FDR liberals. Who's with her?"

"Practically no one, from what I hear. In Oregon's depressed economy, most of the board is scared stiff about hobbling investments. Reverend Avenceña is with her, and he brings considerable clout. A couple of the old-timers still long for the days when Astor had official ties to the Presbyterian church. If Avenceña's fervent enough on this issue he might be able to swing the Colossus Sisters."

"Whom?"

"You remember them, Harry. Mmes. Feingarten and Fenscher. Been on the board since forever. Scuttlebutt has it they first came to the Northwest while following the migrating mastodon herds across the Bering Strait."

"Yes, I believe I remember them. Who's primary opposition to divestment?"

"Look out!" Connar grabbed Harry's arm and pulled him back out of the way as three students, dressed in suits and ties, with elbow and knee pads and mirrored sunglasses, whisked by on skateboards.

"Well, Irena Shoenborn-Eriksen, old Geoffrey's wife. Do you know her?"

"No."

"She's a lot like her spouse. Tough and aggressive. Born to Big Money. Anyway, she thinks apartheid is none of our business and during the summer session meetings let it be known that she'll lobby hard to keep Astor in the Common Fund. Standing with her, albeit quietly, will be Geoffrey, who likes to look neutral on these issues. And of course Richard Llewelleyn."

"I don't know him either." Despite the ice cream, Harry was perspiring. He was thankful that the humidity had remained low, but the hot weather that had dominated July and August was tiring. The grounds crew had worked diligently throughout the summer to keep the fabled, sprawling campus lawns sylvan. Harry wondered who on the grounds crew had been suborned by the student protestors to keep the sprinklers off the shanty.

"Well, Llewelleyn is sort of a twit," Connar continued. "He's a junior partner in that financial planning company owned by Big Sam Broderick, who's also a trustee. The firm is Broderick, Somebody, Someone, and So-and-so. I forget. Anway, Llewelleyn is some kind of financial wizard, I hear, but a little too slick for my taste."

"If he's a financial wizard, Llewelleyn should know divestment wouldn't seriously hurt the college."

Connar popped the end of the cone into his mouth and fastidiously licked his fingertips. "Times are tough, Harry. The endowment campaign could be going better. I've got to admit, I see their point."

"And the injustice of apartheid?"

"At ease, Harry. On the board, you're an observer. Period. Promise you won't stir things up today."

"Me?"

"Promise, Harry! You have an amazing talent for taking any difficult situation and making it worse."

Harry's face was serene. "Conny, your lack of faith in me is astounding. I *hate* controversy. You know that."

"Uh-huh." The dean sounded far from persuaded.

Harry finished off his cone and pouted. "I believe you've hurt my feelings, Conny. All right, I'll be good."

"Promise?"

"Promise."

"On your honor?"

"No."

"Okay. Fair enough."

THREE

❖

It was going to be yet another beautiful autumn day in Portland; the west winds sweeping in off the Pacific and over the opulent homes and vast array of radio and television towers in the West Hills carried no hint of impending winter. Nelligan left his jacket in the office when he stepped out for lunch.

"You're pissed," Martin Kady observed when Nelligan had crossed the street to him. Kady was standing beneath the rainbow-striped umbrella of a hot dog cart, paying the vendor for two dogs, a bag of Fritos, and two diet 7-Ups.

"Yeah. Fritos for me?"

"No, they're for me. The sodium you don't need."

Kady, a lanky man in pinstripes and perfectly knotted tie, handed Nelligan his lunch, squeezing the reporter's hand gently in the exchange. They crossed back into the Park Blocks and selected a redwood bench beside one of Portland's innumerable fountains.

"So?"

Nelligan munched on the hot dog and scowled at a pigeon. "So, Joann put me on some sort of stupid student protest story because she says I need a break from cop-shop."

"She's right. You do."

Nelligan shot an acid glance at the other man, a decade older and five inches taller. Unflustered, Kady grinned back.

"Do not."

"Do too. You've been more irritable than usual, which is considerable."

"Yeah, well, it's not because I've been on the police beat too long, it's because this stupid town is so boring."

"Portland's boring?" Kady asked mildly.

"Marty, please, you're a lawyer. You know how clean the city government is. The only thing you can accuse the cops of is being idiots, and that's not indictable."

"All Portland cops are idiots?"

"Certainly." Nelligan's reply was devoid of humor. Kady nodded and offered him some corn chips.

"No good juicy murders recently, I take it."

"No. And now this student protest bullshit. Who cares?"

"Someone, I suppose, or no one would be protesting. Portland State?"

"No, Astor."

"Oh? Going to see Harry?"

Nelligan finished the dog and licked mustard off his fingers. "If he's around."

"Well, tell him to drop by. We haven't seen him in weeks. Tell him to bring Kate."

"Kate's in D.C., on sabbatical."

Kady raised one eyebrow and frowned. He had a receding forehead and too-large ears, and Nelligan told him he looked like a basset hound when he did that. "I don't see what you're so upset about, Tuck. This time of year, JJAC's awfully pretty. It'll be nice to see Harry, won't it?"

"Yeah, but I mean, who cares about a bunch of rich white kids screeching about South African domestic policy? No one. It's throwaway copy. Joann should have one of the interns doing this."

"But not Clark Kent, mild-mannered reporter for a major metropolitan newspaper?"

"And what's that supposed to mean, counselor?"

Kady shook his head and finished the soft drink, refusing to be goaded. "I've got to go. Ton of stuff on my desk."

"Waitwaitwait. Marty, now *you're* pissed. What's wrong?"

"What's wrong? You're what's wrong. You're the most cynical, sniping individual I know."

"Cynical?" Nelligan sounded amazed. "I'm not cynical."

"Ha! Tucker, you make Machiavelli look like a candy-striper."

"I don't know what you're—"

"Tucker, you're treating these student protests like you treat everything in life—not weighed against the subject's intrinsic value or its social cost, but on how many column inches you get out of it and whether or not it's front-page material."

"Oh, fine. Now you're angry because I'm good at my job."

Kady stood. "I've got to go."

"Fine. Bye."

"Tucker, believe it or not, not everything in life revolves around your byline. These students could have a valid point. Maybe they see an injustice and are trying to do a little something about it. What's wrong with that?"

Nelligan got to his feet and started backing away. "Right. You got it. Couple dozen rich white kids attending an expensive liberal arts school paid for by daddy have decided to pool this week's cocaine allowances and buy pickets. If this doesn't topple the Botha regime, I don't know what will." Fifteen feet from Kady, he turned and marched off.

"Meshugah," Kady said softly.

Harry poured a fingerful of middle-of-the-road Scotch: not hooch, not Pinch, but something in between. He drank it down in a gulp, sighed, and refilled his thick, lopsided mug.

It was three in the afternoon and if the city was warm and breezy, Bishop's Closet, as he called his office, was hot and musty. His window faced the brick wall of the history department faculty office building, and no breeze ventured down the narrow corridor between the buildings. At three o'clock, he was supposed to be in the Karl W. Kneible conference room, meeting and reacquainting himself with the trustees of Astor College. At 3:05 he polished off the whiskey, popped a Tic Tac in his mouth, and locked up the office.

An hour earlier he had been in the classroom assigned to him for Senior Seminar: History of American Radical Politics. Being a seminar class, there were fewer than ten students signed up for it. The room assigned for the class was an auditorium, seating 250 with a slanted floor, projection booth in the back, and electric-controlled chalkboards and film screens, both of which retracted into the ceiling.

Harry and the eight students had clustered at the back of the room, staring at each other. When someone spoke, the voice echoed off the far walls.

"This will never do," Harry informed them. The students had agreed. Harry handed out tentative class schedules and first week's reading assignments, then informed the group that he would arrange for a new classroom and post its location on his office door before the afternoon was over. With that, he dismissed the group.

His next step was to go see Lyman Bledsoe, Jr., department chair for poli. sci.

"Lyman," Harry began, "you've given me Radio City Music Hall for a seminar class of eight people."

Bledsoe, a tubby little man who bore an uncanny resemblance to Humpty Dumpty, glared at Harry from behind an offensively immaculate desk. "There's nothing I can do about it, Henry. The class list was assigned months in advance."

"Well, would you try to find an empty classroom somewhere else?"

"Ha! Let me remind you, Henry, that classroom space is no mediocre commodity at Astor. There are no other classrooms. You're in Lecture Hall Three."

"Lyman, please, it's a *seminar* class. We're supposed to *discuss* political theory. I can't hold it in a zeppelin hangar."

The little man had turned a deeper shade of fuchsia. "The registrar's office was furious about the change in teaching assignment for Federalism 312. I'm certain they won't soon step out of their way to help our department again."

"Yes, well, I trust you explained to them it wasn't our fault Westhaven broke his—"

"How is it you always do these things to me, Henry? You don't realize, of course, that you've thrown the entire fall political science schedule into a turmoil. The timing couldn't be worse. It couldn't."

Lyman Bledsoe, Jr., used a schedule the way some paralytics use an iron lung, clinging to the predictability of his itinerary and calendars and course outlines as if drawing life from their rigid lack of surprises. Anything that upset his carefully drafted plans spelled apoplexy for Bledsoe.

Harry assumed the soothing voice one uses when speaking to a man standing on a window ledge. "Lyman. I didn't sign up to be the winter term liaison; it was assigned to me. I didn't break Westhaven's leg. I don't want to be liaison this term. I don't want you to handle my federalism class. I am, as you are, a victim of happenstance. Will you please find me a reasonable room for seminar?"

"No."

"No?"

"No. I realize you have no respect for schedules and proper procedure, Henry. None at all. This may serve as a lesson to you."

"A lesson."

"Yes. Remember: an ounce of—"

"Lyman, please. No clichés, I don't think I could handle it sober."

Since there was no point in arguing with Bledsoe, Harry had returned to his own, much smaller, office. It took him two phone calls and less than ten inspired minutes to find a space large enough for the seminar class, yet small enough to provide a feeling of intimacy. He scrawled the notice on a piece of college stationery, folded it in half, and taped it to his door, along with a plea to his seminar students to keep the new class location a secret.

Everything handled. QED. But he was annoyed now. One more problem stacked atop everything else. Harry didn't consider himself an employee of the college or a member of the professor's union, but a teacher. He didn't want anyone else handling his classes. Normally, when this sort of nonsense reared its ugly head, he would turn to Kate Fairbain of the economics department for solace. He and Kate had been academic rivals since they had met, friends for the last few years, and romantically interested—if not yet involved, more's the pity, Harry felt—for the past several months.

Kate shared Harry's love for the education of politics and antagonism for the politics of education. But two mornings earlier, he had driven her to the airport. She was spending fall and winter term in Washington, D.C., where she planned to finish her fifth book on the future of capitalism.

Trudging past the administration building, Harry kicked a wayward chrysanthemum by the cobblestone path and watched the petals fly. He was still sulking, but it made him feel a bit better.

The panicky look Harry received from Lee Connar as he entered the Student Union Building's auditorium at a quarter past the hour reminded Harry that he was, as always, late. The room was cavernous (though not, he noted sullenly, much larger than Lecture Hall Three), with sloped, semicircular seating and lectern in front with a mahogany moderator's desk in the center. The desk had been shoved back against the far wall and four heavy oaken tables were jammed together into a rectangle in the center of the raised floor. High tracklights blazed on the dais, leaving the rows of plush folding seats in semishadow.

Here were gathered the august members of the Astor Board of Trustees. Mostly male, mostly Harry's age or older, mostly white, mostly wealthy, they sat around the table or stood in small groups, drinking coffee or iced tea and chatting. The meeting had not started on time. Already in position around the tables were President L. Charles "Chuck" Eckersley and his entourage: deans of students and the faculty, vice presidents for academic affairs and administrative affairs, provost, chancellor of the graduate school. Dean of Faculty Connar made a great show of pushing back his coat sleeve and scrutinizing his wristwatch when Harry entered.

Harry made directly for the refreshment table near the tall, leaded windows with their sweeping views of the campus. As he poured iced tea into a glass, he peered out at the western lawn. Nearly fifty students stood around the shanty, waving pickets and singing heartily. He couldn't name that tune through the thick panes.

Harry shook his head in awe. He must have walked right past the protestors without noticing them. *I'm getting senile.*

"Hi." A brisk voice snapped Harry out of his reverie. He turned to face a man who stood nearly a foot shorter, with narrow shoulders and a narrow waist. The little man grinned up at Harry and thrust out a slim hand. "Richard Llewelleyn. Pleased to meet you."

"Hullo, I'm—"

"Noticed the kids, did you?" Llewellyn steamrolled over the rest of the introduction. "Amazing. All up in arms about something they don't understand in the least. Makes you wonder what we're teaching these days, doesn't it?"

"I think they may have a good point."

Llewelleyn chuckled and slapped Harry on the arm. "Sure. The world's an unjust place. They don't want to sully their own hands, but they want a full sports program and a bigger budget for student government and that joke of a newspaper, plus they want their damned dorms remodeled. Kids. Listen, I'm glad you've joined us; I've wanted to meet you for some time."

"You have?"

"Hell, yes! It's a real pleasure to have you aboard. Hey, have you met Geoffrey?"

"Once or twice, some time ago."

"Hold on." Harry's new acquaintance expertly caught the eye of a gentleman on the far side of the conference room and waved energetically. The man broke away from the group and headed in their direction.

"Noticed your accent," Llewelleyn said, turning back to Harry. "You're English."

"Scots, actually, but I was raised in England. You're from New York?"

"Yeah. Still got my accent. Been twelve years out here in the west, though. God's country."

"Really?"

"Sure. Hey, Geoffrey, thanks for joining us. I understand you know Elliot O'Malley here."

Harry and the newcomer glanced from the little man to each other with a touch of embarrassment and decided to make the best of an awkward situation.

"Geoffrey Eriksen." The newcomer beamed and offered a meaty hand.

"Henry Bishop."

"What?" Llewelleyn's double take was classic.

Smoothly, Eriksen said, "Richard, this is Professor Bishop. Ah, political science?"

"Yes."

"The professor here is our faculty liaison this term."

Harry nodded. "Yes. Sorry about the confu—"

"Right. Excuse me." Curtly, Llewelleyn nodded and moved away. Eriksen, a big, square Swede, grinned, watching him wend his way to the table. "Forgive Richard, professor. He thought you were someone rich."

"Oh?"

"Yes. New board member, O'Malley. I'm afraid our Richard is a bit enamored with gold. It's a pleasure to see you again, professor."

Where Llewelleyn had been brash and abrasive, Eriksen was warm and demonstrative. He spoke with a thick Northern European accent, although Harry guessed he had probably lived thirty years or more in the States. Like Henry Kissinger, some people strive to hold on to their home accents, as part habit, part nostalgia, part stage-acting. Eriksen wore a crew cut, the hair as bristly as a horse brush. His head was almost a perfect cube, with pale blue eyes and a nose that had been broken and poorly reset at least once. Although his three-piece gray pin-striped suit was far too warm for the weather, he appeared perfectly comfortable.

Eriksen rested a thick hand on Harry's arm. "We're running a bit late. Many of our members took the summer off and felt the need to compare vacations. Ladies and gentlemen?" This last bit burst forth in a basso profundo. Magically, all conversation ceased. "Shall we get down to business?"

It was a command, couched as a question. As one, the board members and college personnel surged toward the tables.

Harry's eye was caught by a fluttery motion. An elderly woman in a flowery dress waved enthusiastically and cleared a large straw handbag from the padded chair to her left. Harry stooped to kiss her powdery cheek and sat. "Cordelia."

"Hello, Harry. I heard they'd dumped us in your lap. Poor thing."

At age seventy-one, Cordelia Applebaum weighed perhaps ninety pounds. She and Harry had been friends since the mid-seventies, when she resigned from the JJAC English Department faculty to run, with Harry's assistance, for a seat on the Portland city council. Looking at her beaming face now, Harry mentally kicked himself for not calling on her more often.

"How have you been keeping yourself?" he asked.

"Oh busy, busy. I'm on the board at the Metro zoo now, you know."

"No, I hadn't heard."

Cordelia bowed her beautifully coiffured head closer and whispered, "Easier dealing with *that* livestock than *this* livestock. 'Fraid you've got to put up with us till Christmas break."

"Ah well. It's a bear we all have to cross. Join me in a drink after the meeting?"

"We'll see how long this goes. At my age, a body needs her rest, you know."

"Translated: You have a hot date."

She patted his arm, pleased. "Something like that."

At the head of the four tables, Eriksen rapped a massive signet ring against the oak. "Ladies and gentlemen, this meeting is called to order. Welcome to another sound year for John Jacob Astor."

A group of twenty students chanted "Out of Africa! Out of Africa!" beneath the windows of the Karl W. Kneible conference room. Others waved banners. Someone in the center of the activity tried to start a round of "We Shall Overcome" but it didn't take and faded after one verse.

Nelligan stood well back, leaning against an oak that probably predated the Lewis and Clark Expedition. He had taken a handful of quicky quotes from irate students and faculty. He had also located the staff photographer to let her know he was around. It was really none of his business which shots the shooter chose to take, so long as she got the primary interview subjects. In this case, that meant the members of the board, among others.

Someone who knew him well had once referred to Tucker Nelligan, accurately, as an information predator. By instinct, he had scanned the crowd for key players: instigators and opponents of whatever the primary action seemed to be. Protagonists and antagonists. He had also noted his competition, to see what they got or missed. Nelligan thus caught the attention of a fellow journalist and waved.

Sandi Braithwaite, editor in chief of the college newspaper, grinned and jogged over to the oak. She and Nelligan had met and worked together one year earlier, during the investigation of her predecessor's, David Wasserman's, murder.

"Hey, Tucker!"

"Hi, kiddo. Looks like you've got your front-page story for this week."

Sandi's cheeks glowed and her brown eyes sparkled. "Yeah! Great, isn't it?"

Sandi was plump but not fat, with the boundless energy of a fusion reactor. Her messy brown hair was pulled back and held in a ponytail with a rubber band, and as always, she wore baggy jeans and a polo jersey in JJAC's colors, many sizes too large. A Minolta camera hung from a strap around her neck. "Is the *Post* covering us?" she asked breathlessly.

"Yeah." Nelligan seemed somewhat less thrilled. "Slow news day."

"What do you mean? This is exciting, don't you think?"

"Right. Exciting."

Sandi had a natural ability to judge people, and understood Nelligan's dominant cynicism. She shrugged and asked how he'd been.

"So-so. How's school?"

"Très crappy. I'm a senior, which means I've got my thesis as well as the newspaper. Hey, I've got Bishop this term. Senior Sem."

"How is old Harry?"

"I dunno. We had class for all of two minutes this morning. He's faculty liaison with the board this term, you know."

Nelligan's face lit up. "No, I didn't. Is he in there now?" He jerked a thumb over the heads of the protestors and their pickets, to the high leaded windows.

"Yup."

"All right. A friendly face."

"Look, Tucker, I never got to thank you for that letter you sent to the AP. That had to've been the best summer internship in the world. I really owe you."

Nelligan threw an arm around her plump shoulder, causing her heart to stutter. "No problem, Sand. I started filing the wire with an internship, about four hundred years ago."

"Oh yeah. The Old Man of the Wire. Listen, do you need to know names of student leaders or anything?" she asked, hopefully

"No, thanks. I got 'em. I'm half tempted to head in there, so I can get back to the office and home by a decent hour."

"Executive session, Tucker. No press allowed."

Nelligan eyed the girl. "Oh yeah? What'd they do if I sneaked in? Shoot me?"

"C'mon, Tucker. You know the rules. This school's a private institution, and not governed by the Open Meeting Laws."

He rubbed his eyes and stifled a yawn. "Yeah, yeah. No offense, Sand, but this story isn't really my speed. How long do these board meetings usually last?"

"Couple hours."

"God. Okay, I'm going to head over to the cafeteria and grab a sandwich or something. Want to tag along?"

"I'd love to, but I'm waiting for my photo editor to get out of class and finish this roll of film for me. I might catch you later, though."

"Okay, kiddo. See you." Nelligan squeezed her arm, then headed off for the far side of the Student Union Building. Watching him, Sandi's heart did a fast fandango.

"Hi, Sandi." A student in thongs and a stylish Ralph Lauren sweatshirt strolled over and jerked his chin in Nelligan's direction. "Who's he?"

"What? Oh, hi, Makoto. How do you say 'beefcake' in Japanese?"

"A proper young woman doesn't say 'beefcake' in Japanese."

"How does a proper young woman say 'screw you'? Want to take some photos out here?"

"Sure. Who do you need?"

Sandi pointed out the prime interview subjects to her photo editor and handed over the camera. "Where you headed, chief?"

"Inside." She nodded toward the conference room windows.

Makoto shook his head somberly. "Off limits."

"Mak, what are they gonna do?" she asked. "Shoot me?"

FOUR

❖

"Good. Anything else?"

Geoffrey Eriksen scanned the faces around the table. "No? Fine. On to new business."

Reverend Geraldo Avenceña had entered late and, with an apology, sat beside Harry. Now he nudged his old friend with an elbow and Harry's head snapped up. Avenceña leaned over and whispered, "You awake? The fireworks are about to start."

To Harry's right, Cordelia Applebaum raised a dainty hand clutching a lace handkerchief. A low mutter eddied around the table. Someone groaned. Everyone knew or guessed what subject she would bring up.

Eriksen's pale blue eyes scanned the assemblage, passing over Cordelia. "Yes, Richard?"

Llewelleyn stood—not standard practice for trustees with the floor, but before Harry had drifted to sleep earlier he had noted a recurrent theatrical vein in the little man—and waved to the balding, bespectacled man sitting across from him.

"Friends, I'd just like to take this opportunity to introduce our newest trustee and a member of the great Class of Fifty-four, Elliot O'Malley!"

There was a polite round of applause, even from Geoffrey Eriksen, whose job it was, as chair, to introduce new members. Harry studied the stocky Swede and noticed more than a hint of anger. Clearly, Eriksen had planned to handle the formal introductions after the meeting.

Geraldo leaned over again. "Do you know O'Malley, Harry?"

Harry shook his head.

"Me neither. But I can tell you now, he's loaded, or Richard the Shark wouldn't give him the time of day."

Harry suppressed a grin. Geraldo had been resident minister of the on-campus Presbyterian chapel for a half dozen years, even though the college and church broke official ties in the early seventies, in order for the school to retain certain federal funds. Before the rift, the ministers had always been board members, and Geraldo had been offered a position on the board out of a sense of tradition.

Avenceña was a monumental man, a former All-American football player with bristly black hair receding off a dark brow, thick eyebrows, and a beard and mustache the consistency of a Brillo pad. Harry had little use for organized religion, but found Geraldo, with his liberal theological views, background in education, and sense of humor, refreshing.

On the other side of the reverend sat Sam Broderick, a man who actually introduced himself as "Big Sam." Harry had met the man at a few trustee/faculty events in years past and had a vague recollection that Broderick owned one of the Northwest's most prestigious accounting firms. He was also the senior partner of the firm for which Llewelleyn worked.

When Harry switched from civil service to education, the day after Richard Nixon's first presidential swearing-in ceremony, it had taken him some time to get used to the Sam Brodericks of the world. The man had no college education and no understanding of economics. He knew how to turn a dollar, to be sure, and was righteously convinced that every school ought to be run on the principle of profit-making. Broderick was a pleasant enough fellow, but somehow he rubbed Harry wrong. He was fat. Not chubby or plump or overweight. Sam Broderick was fat, with massive rolls of flesh between his head and collar, waxy, pale skin, and rubbery lips. He grinned incessantly, showing yellow, uneven teeth. The skin covering his hands was a dull yellow, as if his blood had long ago given up the trek from that overworked heart to the extremities. Instead, it had all settled in his face, which was puffy and red. Broken veins lined his nose. Even that was fat. Harry noticed that Big Sam had a propensity to laugh out of context. A strange man.

To Broderick's left sat Llewelleyn and the Colossus Sisters, Mrs. Feingarten and Mrs. Fenscher. Harry didn't know which was which, and it didn't really matter. Like Rosencrantz and Guildenstern, they were interchangeable. Mmes. Feingarten and Fenscher were large women, with a taste for radioactively bright colors and plumed hats and extremely unusual, sometimes silly, suggestions for the well-being of Astor College. They were considered comedy relief by most people, but Harry noted that they attended college theater productions and concerts and sporting events with conscientious diligence. A bit fuzzy headed, to be sure, but clearly they also cared deeply about the school.

Next to the Colossus Sisters sat the administration members. Lee Connar was drawing what appeared to be sailing ships on his napkin. Geoffrey Eriksen came next, with an attractive woman in an austere business suit to his left. Probably his wife. To her left sat Donal Patrick Cavenaugh, one of Astor's most famous alumni. Cavenaugh had been a nationally renowned sculptor for a few years, in the late sixties, and the tabloids had been filled with his creative élan and near-endless series of sexual encounters with beautiful women. But something—time and too much cocaine, or so the rumor went—had dulled Donal Patrick Cavenaugh's muse, and he was reborn as a celebrity, at least on the local level: a man famous for having been famous. Harry had always liked the works of the Irish artist, though he couldn't remember seeing any new sculptures for some time.

Between Cavenaugh, who slumped low in his chair, arms crossed belligerently across his chest, thick eyelids nearly closed, and the prim, alert Cordelia Applebaum was the new man, O'Malley, looking considerably uncomfortable amid the strangers. Harry wondered what quirk brought O'Malley to this group. It was clear he was not relishing the overlong introduction from Llewelleyn.

"—so I'd like to say, on behalf of us all, welcome to the John Jacob Astor Board of Trustees!" Llewelleyn began clapping even before his own panegyric was concluded, and the rest of the group dutifully followed suit, as if the newest trustee was a combination of Nelson Rockefeller and Armand Hammer.

"Who is he?" Harry asked Cordelia, *sotto voce.*

She leaned closer. "I really couldn't say, dear. I think he's in timber or some such." She raised her hand again and placidly locked her vision on Eriksen.

The chairperson may have been opposed to divestiture, but he understood Robert's Rules of Order well enough. He rapped his ring once on the table. "Cordelia?"

She smiled politely around the room. "I think we need to discuss the subject uppermost in the minds of the student body: divestment from the government and businesses of South Africa, and all U.S. businesses doing business in that country."

Half a dozen voices chimed in, some deriding, some joking. None supporting. Harry made note that neither Donal Patrick Cavenaugh nor Elliot O'Malley chimed in. The first seemed too bored, the second too confused. Eriksen rapped the gold signet ring against the table.

"Very good, Mrs. Applebaum, I agree," the chairperson intoned. "If I may, I'd like to suggest we turn the floor over to the chair of our financial advisory standing committee. Is that all right with you?" He addressed Cordelia, who nodded.

"Irena?"

Eriksen motioned to the woman beside him. She was tall and slim, and her age was tough to determine, Harry thought. Just turned forty? Fifty? She wore her blond hair up in a conservative bun that matched her business suit, leather note pad, and gold Cross pen.

"Thank you, Geoffrey." Irena Shoenborn-Eriksen flipped through a manila folder until she found the financial statements she wanted. In a clipped, Northwestern accent, she began to describe the economic situation of John Jacob Astor: a picture she clearly found none too rosy.

Harry stared out the window, unseeing. The board traditionally painted the bleakest of pictures, and yet miraculously managed to raise millions, year after year, in never-ending endowment campaigns. He had rarely seen any department go without, his own included. Still, Harry was nothing if not a political animal. His instincts said there was a fight brewing, and he wanted to see how it would be played.

Shoenborn-Eriksen was thorough. She had been chair of the finance committee for some time, and clearly knew how to read a spread sheet. To Harry, economics was an art closely related to voodoo or Druidic rituals. Whenever he heard anyone lapse into that particular jargon, he recalled Arthur C. Clarke's law: Any form of science, properly advanced, will be indistinguishable from magic.

"In conclusion, Astor is heavily dependent on tuition—too dependent, I think we'd all agree. Oregon has yet to feel the national recovery, and now there are hints of a recession on the horizon. If there was ever a time when we needed a rock-solid investment profile, it is now. Any attempts to divest from the Common Fund would be disastrous. Geoffrey?"

"Thank you." Eriksen beamed at his wife, his gaze shifting down anticipatorially to Cordelia.

"Who the hell are you?" Richard Llewelleyn's nasal voice piped in before Cordelia could speak. Every eye in the room shifted first to Llewelleyn, then followed his gaze outward to the rows of seats. A student sat in the first row, a clipboard and white legal pad on her knee.

Harry groaned.

"Hi!" Sandi Braithwaite waved breezily at the gaping administrators, ex-officios, and trustees gathered before her. "Um, I'm Sandi Braithwaite, editor in chief of the *Pathfinder*. Don't mind me."

The ruckus broke out again. Eriksen gaveled the group to silence with his ring, then half turned in his high-backed chair. "Young woman, this is a closed meeting. You have no right to be here."

"Oh?" Sandi asked. She blinked her big brown eyes and Harry cleared his throat to cover a laugh.

"I'm sorry, everyone. This is my first time covering the board, and I didn't realize. There aren't any signs up, you know."

"For Christ's sake!" Llewelleyn jumped to his feet, his face dusky with rage. "Get out! Now! And leave the notes!"

"What?"

Llewelleyn leaned on the table, his hand outstretched. A gold chain with thick links glittered on his wrist. "Your notes. You have no right to be here. We could have you arrested, little lady."

"No you couldn't." To his utter astonishment, Harry realized the contrary voice was his own. Lee Connar rested his forehead in his palm and groaned.

Llewelleyn turned a cold eye on Harry. "Excuse us. You're here as an observer, professor. We'd all appreciate it if you'd just shut up, okay?"

Harry loved anonymity and, except in the classroom, scrupulously shunned the spotlight. Still, the words were out of his mouth before he could think. "Mr. Llewelleyn, this is an executive session meeting, and indeed, the press has no right to be here. However, Sandi's presence is not a criminal offense. I don't think you ought to be threatening one of my students with something you can't back up."

"Richard"—Eriksen's voice was serene but the slicing edge of hostility lurked behind it—"please calm down. Miss Braithwaite, we cannot allow you to remain here. In the future, if you want to be a journalist, I suggest you learn to check before you simply storm into a meeting—"

"And lurk in the dark," Llewelleyn shrilled. "That's shitty, kid."

Eriksen turned a frosty eye upon the furious little man. Big Sam Broderick, Llewelleyn's employer, was clearly not happy with the situation, and his pasty face burned a dark red. It was not in Harry Bishop's nature to dislike anyone too fervently. Idiots and the self-righteous annoyed him, but annoyance was about the extent of his negative feelings toward his fellow human. Richard Llewelleyn was an exception. "Tell me," Harry whispered to Cordelia, "is that little fellow always such an ass?"

Cordelia patted his arm like a maiden aunt. "Yes, dear. Incessantly."

Sandi had played a gutsy hand, but she knew now that a timely exit was called for. "Well, listen, sorry to disrupt your meeting." She scooped up her notebook and smiled vacuously.

"Oregon's Open Meeting laws don't apply to private institutions, miss, so you cannot publish a word of what has been discussed here. You understand that?" Eriksen asked crisply.

"Sort of." Harry gave Sandi an A-plus for her stage frown. She looked as if the concept were too abstract to grasp. "You're Mr. Eriksen, right? Is it all right if I call you later to clarify this?"

"Certainly. Now, if you'll excuse us . . ."

"Sure. Bye, professor." She waved to Harry and he heartily returned the gesture. Once Sandi had disappeared through the great double doors, Eriksen rapped the table for order.

"Richard." The chairperson spoke softly, reining in his bass voice. "Do not ever objurgate a student or college employee like that again, please, or this body will have to request your resignation. We are trustees, not prison wardens. I believe that once this meeting is adjourned, you owe an apology to that young woman and to the professor."

It was an order, not a request.

Some people are natural leaders, and maintain a personal, magnetic resonance in their voices and actions that is difficult to disobey. Geoffrey Eriksen was that sort, Harry concluded. Thus, he was more than a little surprised by the look of defiance on the pinched face of Richard Llewelleyn. "It's letting these kids walk all over us that's got this school in such bad financial shape, Geoffrey. There was a time when we used a little discipline to get things accomplished."

"Discipline is an important part of education. Temper tantrums are not. Please learn to control your emotions."

Llewelleyn straightened his tie and ran a hand through his hair. "Fine. You're still chairman around here. But there'll be an election at the end of the term, and I think many of us agree a new direction is what's needed."

Eriksen rapped his ring thrice, in slow, steady cadence, his eyes never leaving Llewelleyn. "New business?" the chairman asked the gathering.

"Hey, Tucker!"

Nelligan had located the last remaining copy of that Sunday's *New York Times* in the college bookstore and was sipping tea in the cafeteria and reading James Reston when Sandi plopped down opposite him. The Douglas Fir Room was fairly quiet at that hour, and Sandi had had no trouble locating him.

Nelligan peered over the top of the paper and winked. "Hey, kiddo. How's—Sand? What's wrong?

Sandi's face was flushed and her breathing irregular. Her hair, never at the best of times what one would call coifed, was more unruly than usual. She stuck out her lower lip and blew an errant strand off her forehead.

"I got into the board meeting," she announced, sitting forward on the edge of the plastic chair.

Nelligan promptly folded away the newspaper. "No!"

"Yeah!"

A grin of appreciation slowly spread across his handsome face. "How'd you do that?"

"There're two doors on the second floor that open up at the top of the seating area. I just waltzed in, all nonchalant and cool, and sat down right in front."

"I love it. And they kicked you out?"

"Sure, eventually, but not before they opened the topic of divestment."

"What happened when they spotted you?"

Reveling in her moment of triumph, Sandi spoke in conspiratorial tones. "Well, this one guy, a real jerk, stands up and starts screeching at me and everything. He says I gotta hand over my notes, and they might call the cops."

"Are you kidding? What guy?"

"Richard Llewelleyn." Llewelleyn's harangue had clearly failed to intimidate. "So I acted all innocent like and apologized. Then Eriksen, the chairman, told me I couldn't print anything I'd heard and I told him I sort of understood that, but could I call him later and discuss it?"

Nelligan offered a hand and they shook. "So you got an interview with a guy who otherwise wouldn't've given you the time of day, and you've got him underestimating you. Sandi, m'love, that was sneaky and underhanded."

"Thanks," she said, blushing. "Another thing! Guess who jumped to my defense? Professor Bishop!"

"Right. True to form. Harry looks like the guy who invented Flubber, but he's got a Galahad complex a mile wide." Nelligan dug into his light linen jacket, hanging over a third chair, and produced pen and pad. "All right, kiddo, so who's on which side, concerning divestment?"

Sandi sat back, stretched out her legs, and smirked. "Ha! You wish!"

"What?"

"Tucker, I'm not telling you jack. You wanna know, read tomorrow's *Pathfinder*. Speaking of which, I'm way past deadline—"

"SandiSandiSandi." Nelligan rested a hand on her arm. "C'mon, pal. Give. You know I've got superior resources at the *Post*."

"So?"

"So, you want the true scoop to come out, don't you?"

She blew the strand of hair off her forehead again and frowned. "Yeah, sure."

"And you're already past deadline, which means you're going to have to do a rush-rush job to get this in this week's issue. And it's the first week of classes, so who has time for that sort of hassle?"

"True, but—"

Nelligan deviously dredged up his most intimate smile. "Look, you and I have worked well together in the past, right? Let's call this a two-pronged attack. You and me, the Dynamic Duo. Tell me how it went down in there and the *Pathfinder* and *Post* will pull a one-two punch on 'em. What say?"

Sandi considered it for a moment. "Well . . . you're not just saying this because you don't want to hang around here for another hour or so, are you?"

"Hell, no! I just want the truth." He squeezed her forearm.

Sandi placed her hand atop his, leaned close and winked. "Tucker Nelligan, fuck you and the horse you rode in on."

Giggling, Sandi stood and jogged out of the cafeteria.

Harry dug a mushy Mars bar out of his coat pocket and sat back, admiring Geoffrey Eriksen's form.

Parliamentary procedure is an arcane craft, and not every chairperson knows how to use it effectively. Eriksen was a rich, conservative industrialist, founder and chief executive officer of Cascade Electro, which manufactured computer chips and software for, among others, the military. Thus, he was deeply opposed to anything which ran contrary to U.S. foreign policy.

Still, he permitted the subject of South African investment to be brought to the table, and allowed Cordelia Applebaum her opportunity to speak. He had allowed his wife, chair of the standing finance committee, to set the economic mood for the trustees, deftly handling the interim

intrusion of a student and Richard Llewellyn's unexpected
tantrum. Now, he sat listening amiably to Cordelia's high-
minded, lofty rhetoric. Eriksen had no way of defending
apartheid, nor had he the interest in doing so, Harry
thought, so he allowed Cordelia to make her speech, knowing that she would sound flighty and spiritual and none too
business-minded. The chairperson had deftly moved the
argument from the playing field of morality to that of economics: from emotion to the pocketbook.

Harry and Geraldo Avenceña exchanged glances. Cordelia's heart was in the right place, but her style did the
cause as much harm as good.

". . . so I urge my fellow trustees to turn away from the
racist policies of the Botha administration by withdrawing
all college investments in businesses that operate in South
Africa. I believe that's all. Thank you."

Eriksen nodded as if her eloquence had forced him to
reevaluate his position on the matter. "Thank you, Cordelia. Your points are well made. I open the floor for discussion. President Eckersley?"

The college president, looking suave in his Savile Row
suit, dark blue silk handkerchief peeking out of his breast
pocket, stood and smiled the truest, whitest smile imagina-
ble.

"Mr. Chairman, Geoffrey, thank you for this opportunity to address you, the board of trustees of this great
liberal arts college, on this most momentous of subjects, divestment from, or rather, a proposed charge to not invest
in, the South African government or companies of this
country, or companies of this country, the United States of
America, doing business with those companies of South Africa or the South African government, as our mutual
friend, the good Mrs. Applebaum, so perfectly summed up
here for us today.

"My friends, as college president, which I am, it is not
my place to make policy for the board of trustees or even, as
I now find myself asked to do here, today, to even offer my
personal opinion on this subject which, needless to say,
finer minds than my own meager one have slaved over, both
on the local levels as well as nationally, and, yes, internationally as well, for the past few years. Still, you do me the
honor of asking my opinion on this topic of great interest,
not only to trustees, such as yourselves, and administrators,

including my associates here with us and others as well, but students, staff, faculty, alumni, and staff of this great college, as demonstrated today by this disturbing display of protest on the western lawn, which you may or may not have noticed as you arrived, depending, of course, on whether you parked in the administrative parking lot, which is your right as trustees, despite the lack of available space there, or in the visitor parking area to the rear of this very building, which is closer and, thus, more convenient.

"Having stated my position, allow me simply to add that, of course, in this as in all matters, we employees of John Jacob Astor, including those of us in the undergraduate school, school of graduate studies, and our rightly famous doctoral programs (for which, like so many things here, we have *you* to thank), have utmost faith in your intelligence and perseverance to see this matter through in its logical and acceptable resolution. Thank you."

L. Charles "Chuck" Eckersley flashed a dazzling smile, nodded his thanks, and sat. The trustees and administrators sat in stunned silence. Lee Connar popped two Tums and washed them down with iced tea.

"Yes. Thank you, Charles." Eriksen produced a wan smile. Harry had never heard a soul refer to L. Charles "Chuck" as Chuck. Eriksen took the floor without asking for further input. "Well, having heard the arguments for and against divestment, and the opinion . . . ah, of the administration, I suggest we mull over the situation and table any further discussion until the next meeting, in three weeks' time. Comments or motions?"

"Yes." Cordelia spoke up. "Listen!"

The group obediently hushed, and in their silence the chanting protestors outside could be heard. "This is a burning question. I recommend we do something formal today, and not wait. I move we create an ad hoc committee to examine the situation."

To Harry's surprise, Donal Patrick Cavenaugh, who had said nary a word since the meeting began, promptly seconded the motion. Harry wondered how Eriksen would parry this new thrust.

"Wonderful." He beamed across the table at Cordelia. "Would you be willing to chair this group?"

Cordelia was as surprised by the invitation as Harry. She accepted.

"Fine. Volunteers?"

Irena Shoenborn-Eriksen flicked her wrist and waved a pen before the word had fully formed. Harry repressed a smile. Eriksen had foreseen Cordelia's zeal and had a loaded deck on hand.

"Fine, Irena. Richard?"

Llewelleyn flinched slightly. It was not so much an offer, as an opportunity to mend fences for his earlier outburst. "Sure. I'll sit on the committee," he mumbled.

"Thank you. Perhaps, Mr. O'Malley, this would be a fine time for you to enter the fray, as it were." With a soft smile, Eriksen maneuvered the newest trustee into "volunteering." Harry mentally applauded. Without overt threats or compromises, Eriksen had stacked the new committee with two opponents of divestment and one man who, in all probability, would feel uncomfortable bucking a majority. Cordelia stood alone.

"We're a small group, so I think four members should be sufficient. Comments or questions?"

Geraldo raised an arm like a tree trunk. "Yes. I traveled to South Africa, two years ago this summer. I'd like to sit on the ad hoc committee, too, if Mrs. Applebaum doesn't mind."

"Not at all." Cordelia knew a lifesaver when she saw one.

Eriksen accepted this setback with an impassive nod. "Good. If there is no further new business—is there? No— then I would like to remind everyone of the banquet tonight at our home. This is always a good way to begin the year, we've found, and I invite everyone to attend. Administration as well. Oh, please do come, Professor Bishop. We're hoping to see you all. Do I hear a motion to adjourn?"

Adjournment was moved and seconded and the meeting gaveled to a close. Maps to the Eriksens' home were passed out to those who had not been there before.

Harry sat back and breathed a sigh. "My. He *is* good."

Geraldo nodded and Cordelia patted Harry's arm. "Geoffrey is the master coalition builder. Geraldo, thank you for leaping to my aid. Your input on the committee will be invaluable."

"Least I could do," he rumbled. Geraldo had a voice like a polar bear and generally spoke in a near-whisper to offset its power. "I'm with you all the way, Cordelia."

"Well, I'm afraid this time I'm tilting at another windmill. The others have no intention of divesting."

Harry cupped her tiny, veined hand in his. "As memory serves, you took no-win situations a time or two on the Portland city council and came out on top. I've great faith in your ability to twist arms and count coup."

Cordelia's hazel eyes twinkled. "With my muscle and Geraldo's political experience, how can we lose? Could you hand me my bag, dear?"

Harry reached behind his chair and picked up the wicker bag, painted with reds and greens in a Mexican design. He glanced into the bag and shook his head.

"Cordelia, you wrote two of the finest books about Emerson I've ever read, as well as the final word on Dylan Thomas."

"Thank you, Harry."

"How is it, then, you can read a book called *Summer's Savage Lusts*?"

The lady was unabashed. "Prurient but delicious fun, Harry. Judge not. I seem to remember you telling me your master's thesis was on the sociological aspects of *Terry and the Pirates* and *Steve Canyon*."

"I'll defend to my death Milton Caniff's impact on American political thinking and popular support for foreign policy. In the meantime, may I interest you two in a wee dram?"

Geraldo bowed out, citing unfinished work at his chapel office. Cordelia also declined, but promised to see them both that evening at Eriksen's first-of-the-year soiree. "And Harry—do find a suit bought in this decade, won't you?" she pleaded, standing on tiptoe to feel the worn collar of his gray tweed and *tsk*ing.

FIVE

✤

When the board meeting adjourned at a little past five, a noticeable chill had settled over the campus. The protestors were gone. There was no doubt that fall and the rains were creeping in.

Harry and Geraldo Avenceña strolled down into the heart of the campus, discussing Harry's Radical American Politics class. "It took some guts to call the class that," Geraldo chided Harry. "I know the admin. wasn't too happy about it. Astor gets a lot of heat from conservative think tanks as a liberal-leftist haven as is."

Harry felt a bit of tension in his arthritic knee and wondered if it signaled rain or an increase in humidity. "Well, it's good policy to shake things up from time to time. The faculty senate nixed my idea for a class on Reagan's Pro-Terrorism Policies."

The sound of Geraldo's laughter boomed off the chemistry building's brick façade.

"Say, Geraldo, won't change your mind about a quick sip, would you? I could use the moral support before tonight's banquet."

"You don't like social events, do you?"

"Not much, I'm afraid."

"Sorry, Harry, I've got tons of things to do before the party, and I'm meeting with Richard Llewelleyn in a few minutes."

Harry shuddered. "Charming fellow. I don't usually speak up like that, but I didn't want to see him yell at Sandi.

She's a good student and a fine writer. She may well have stepped over the boundary a bit today, but there was no call for his threats."

"I'm glad you spoke up. I almost did, and it wouldn't have looked good. I still answer to the church, you know. They would have been very unhappy if I'd pinched his head off."

"Subtle, yet elegant. What business have you with him?"

Massive shoulders shrugged, stretching black cotton dangerously. "Physical Plant Committee. Business as usual. By the way, be careful with Llewelleyn. He's a conniver."

They stopped outside the political science office building to allow a trio of students on rollerskates to whiz by. "A conniver?"

"Yes. He's only been on the board a year or so and, to be honest, he's completely Eriksen's toady."

"Really? Didn't look like that today."

Geraldo nodded pensively and kicked at a tuft of grass growing between cracks in the walkway. "True. I've never seen him speak up without permission or challenge Eriksen like that. I'm sure he's going to run for the chairman of the board next term."

"Ghastly thought."

"Oh well. You are coming tonight, aren't you?"

Harry pouted. "Yes. Lee Connar has threatened my life if I don't show up."

"Parties are supposed to be fun, Harry."

"Tell that to the Montagues and Capulets."

"The food will be good."

"I cook a mean Swanson's TV Dinner."

"The booze will be free."

"Things are looking up."

A piece of steno-pad paper, slipped under his office door, read: *HB. Missed you. Covering protests. Yawn. Call me a.s.a.p. Who voted how and why??? See you. Marty says hi. TN.*

Harry smiled. He hadn't seen Nelligan in a few weeks. With Kate in D.C., it might make a nice change of pace to have dinner with Tucker and Martin.

Kate! Harry grabbed his dilapidated blackstone bag and jammed in a few folders and texts. He had meant to drop by her place for the past two days, to water her plants. God only knew if they had survived. The only plants Harry had ever owned were the cacti his daughter, Caroline, sent to him on his birthday every year. Presumably Caroline had inherited her keen sense for picking just the wrong present from her father.

Harry hurried to his car and found another note, this one in his own handwriting, attached to the steering wheel. It said: *stop store.* That morning, on his way to work, he had obviously realized he needed something, but now, as he stared at his note, he had no idea what. To stay on the safe side, his first stop upon leaving campus was a liquor store where he knew both attendants by their first names and they, by his. He bought a fifth of Scotch whisky, just in case that's what he needed at home. A typhoon could swing out of the Sea of Japan at any minute. Why take chances?

He had reached his apartment before he remembered he had once again forgotten Kate's plants. He cruised past his apartment and wound his way into residential Lake Oswego, a bedroom community for Portland's rising upper middle class and rich.

Kate Fairbain was a fully tenured professor and author of no small note, which explained the spacious condominium overlooking the lake. The condo stood a good forty feet off the street, surrounded by a copse of cedar. There were five townhouse units, each spaced well apart and provided with privacy and a small backyard surrounded by a tall, redwood fence.

Harry took five minutes sorting through his considerable collection of keys until he found Kate's spare, dabbed with fingernail polish. A subtle, professional shade. Just her style.

Harry Bishop was not a man with an interest in horticulture, but it was his opinion that plants seemed to grow better in the Pacific Northwest than nearly any other place he had lived. It rained a lot in the Pacific Northwest. Thus, there is a direct correlation between the amount of water a plant receives and its ability to grow. Simple. He filled a copper kettle and walked through the condo, filling each planter he saw to the brim. He made three more trips to the kitchen for refills, ignored the water he sloshed on the sills, then shut off the lights, locked up, and headed home, to change for the trustees' banquet.

Nothing like the feeling of a job well done.

SIX

✤

Harry handed over the reins to a young Philippino and then stood pensively, biting his lower lip, as the young man expertly jockeyed the battered and chipped Datsun into a glove-tight slot between a new-looking Saab and newer-looking Mercedes.

Geoffrey Eriksen and Irena Shoenborn-Eriksen lived in what Harry would label a mansion. The house was maybe fifteen years old, probably younger, and designed to look Colonial. The three Philippino attendants were carefully but efficiently stacking cars on the manicured front lawn, green as emeralds and edged with military precision. The grass was matted and, in places, churned up by the rough treatment. No matter, Harry assumed, the (Shoenborn-) Eriksens would just buy new sod. Too many guests? No problem: simply rip out the sculptured hedges and, come morning, have new ones installed.

Harry walked in through the open, double doors, into a foyer with an Oriental rug and tasteful wallpaper. Humans were clumped together in the foyer and front room (*parlor?* he wondered) like seaweed on the sand after a terrific storm. He recognized most of them as trustees or administrators. A young woman in an abbreviated black and white maid's outfit whisked by and Harry impressed himself by gauging her velocity and vector, matching it, and whisking a drink off her silver tray. The drink was bourbon, not his usual, but top-of-the-line stuff. He inhaled the aroma, savoring it, before the first luxurious sip.

"Professor!" Geoffrey Eriksen burst upon him from nowhere, pumping Harry's hand like an old friend. The chairman of the board stood a good five inches shorter than Harry, but had the shoulders and chest of a stevedore. He wore a light sweater, dark blue shirt collar peaking out around his thick neck, and rough corduroy slacks. "How do you do, Henry? May I call you that?"

"Of course." Harry wasn't Harry to just anyone.

"And I'm Geoffrey, eh? Henry, we had about given up on you. You're late."

"Sorry. Had to feed the cat."

Eriksen laughed his deep, throaty laugh (why, Harry wasn't sure). "Well, you're here now and you have a drink. Good! I mistrust a teetotaler. I'm also pleased to see you didn't dress up. Some of us here look like we're on our first date, eh?"

Harry glanced down at the better of his two gray suits and best of three gray ties and was crestfallen.

Taking him by the arm, Eriksen led him to the buffet table. They walked with arms linked and Harry was reminded of his childhood in Scotland and London. He couldn't remember the last American male he had seen do that. The host was more jovial and animated than he had been at the board meeting, but not a bit less the natural commander. His Northern European accent was less pronounced tonight, and Harry wondered how much of it was an affectation.

"I noticed your accent," Eriksen said in a chillingly psychic comment. "We're fellow expatriots, you and I. You're . . . London, England, with a touch of . . . Ireland? No, Scotland. City-Scotland, not highland. Am I right?"

"Why, that's remarkable, Geoffrey. Spot on. Edinburgh, to be precise. I'm afraid I haven't your skills with accents. You're Swedish, I'm told."

"Yes. Karlstad, originally, and later Stockholm, but I've been an American since the war. You missed World War Two, I suppose. Some cheese?"

"Thank you. Yes and no, about the war. Yes, I was too young to serve, but no, I didn't miss it. We had front-row seats in the London Underground."

"Ah. The Blitz." Eriksen nodded ponderously. "I was in a different underground, eh? Free French. The stories I could tell!"

Yes, well please don't, Harry thought and smiled politely.

"The Americans landing in France: I was only a few days away, and the news spread through the villages like the plague. I remember seeing the American GIs like it was yesterday. The big guns, firing over the Siegfried. The fires. It was an amazing time."

"Yes." Harry loathed the esprit de corps of old war stories. His own memories of serving with U.N. forces in Korea usually centered on great food in Seoul and his one, brief bout with malaria. He vaguely remembered throwing up on a lieutenant colonel, whose nationality escaped him now.

"Anyway, Henry, mix! Mix! I'll see you." His host disappeared into the fray, his rich laugh echoing back to Harry, as Cordelia Applebaum appeared at his elbow.

"Hello, Harry. Tried the fondue yet?"

"My, people do come and go awfully quickly around here. How are you, my love?"

A young man started up a Gershwin number on the piano, a few feet away, and Mrs. Applebaum, looking quite charming in something mauve, spoke up. "I'm quite all right, Harry, but I've been lobbying for divestment since I arrived."

"And?"

She shook her head and sipped a champagne cocktail. Despite the light, social atmosphere, Harry knew from her days on the city council that Cordelia Applebaum was a political creature. For her a party was nothing more than fertile lobbying ground. It rankled her to stand almost alone on an issue she cared about so deeply.

Harry put an arm around the shoulders of the woman who could almost be his mother and smiled reassuringly. "Well, you've got Geraldo. That's something."

Cordelia looked somewhat cheered. "Yes, and he's popular. Mrs. Feingarten and Mrs. Fenscher may be willing to switch votes, if he talked to them."

"And our sculptor, Donal Patrick Himself Cavenaugh?"

"No, Harry, I doubt Donal Patrick Himself will switch votes. He almost invariably votes with Geoffrey. That leaves me Geraldo, possibly a few others, and, of course, you, dear."

Harry stopped loading his plate with cheese and pâté and cast a cowled look at his friend. "Cordelia, *cara mia*, leave me out of this. I'm only an observer, not an actor."

"Yes, yes, Harry. Do try that bread and crab salad. It's wonderful."

Harry let it slide, and chatted with Cordelia about Portland Mayor Bud Clark and the latest city hall turmoils. As he finished his second glass (Scotch, this time) Lee Connar and his wife, Penny, sidled by. Connar reminded Harry of his moral obligation to mingle, and Harry secretly decided to slowly mingle his way to the door and escape before anything more was demanded of him.

He had barely gotten five feet from the buffet table before he was accosted by the Colossus Sisters. Mmes. Feingarten and Fenscher had about a hundred and twenty years of life between them and twice as many pounds each. They were dressed identically, in flowery dresses the size of tent canvas and hats: one with a purple plume, the other with a short, black lace veil. Harry had no idea which was whom, but was fairly sure it didn't matter.

"Ah, hello, ladies. Lovely evening." Harry smiled lamely.

"Yes, indeed. We've been meaning to speak to you," said purple plume.

"Oh?" Harry swallowed whisky to stifle the panic.

"Yes, indeed. Why, Olivia and I were just yesterday discussing a plan for the college that we feel would be mutually beneficial."

"Mutually?"

"Oh, yes!" gushed lace veil. "Beneficial for the college and for Oregon Health Sciences University, where we are also quite active, you know."

"Ah, of course," Harry lied, and looked from one plump, grinning face to another. He remembered seeing the megalithic stone lions in front of the New York Public Library for the first time when he was about fifteen. This felt much the same.

"The point is, we feel John Jacob Astor should offer a brand-new graduate school of professional studies," said lace veil.

"Yes," confirmed purple plume. "It is a college's job to fulfill the needs of its society, true?"

"Of course."

"Oh, professor! We knew you'd agree!"

"Er, what sort of professional studies are we talking about? Education?"

"Forensic medicine," declared purple plume.

"Forensic medicine?" echoed Harry.

"Yes." Lace veil nodded. "We were reading just the other day that this country is suffering from a shortage of morticians and coroners. Did you know that?"

"Ah, actually, no."

"Well, there you are."

"There, indeed." Harry finished off the drink.

"So you see," continued purple plume, "Astor should begin such a program, in conjunction with the Health Sciences University, which has lots of money, and also faculty who are doctors."

"Helen," intervened lace veil. "Our faculty at Astor are doctors, too, don't you know?"

"Well, yes, certainly, but they're *doctors*. Not *doctors*. Professor Knight knows what I mean, don't you?"

"Bishop, actually, and I believe it's a wonderful idea."

The Colossus Sisters gushed in unison. It was not a pleasant sight.

"In fact," Harry continued, his eye longingly following the lovely young maid with the drinks tray, "I suggest you take this to a specialist."

"Specialist?"

"Certainly. If I may be so bold, you need a professional administrator in your corner. I believe this is Dean Connar's purview, actually. He's most interested in dead things and undertakers and that sort of business. He's frequently told me so."

"Dead things?" Purple plume's bosom swelled in excitement.

"Yes, indeed. You ladies have heard of 'Day of the Dead' and 'Dawn of the Dead'? We like to think of Lee Connar as 'Dean of the Dead.' Everyone says so. I'm sure Lee would be most pleased to entertain this idea. He'll carrion so."

"Do you really think so?" giggled lace veil.

"Dead certain. Say, isn't that him, over by the piano?"

Lee Connar had worked with Harry Bishop long enough to be constantly on his guard whenever Harry was near. When he glanced across the room and saw Harry pointing him out to the Sisters, Lee made a vain attempt to hide behind his wife. But too little, too late, and the Sisters cut a swathe through the crowd like icebreakers racing for the north pole.

Harry was now close to the accordian-shaped doors which led to the covered brick patio in the rear of the house, so he followed the sound of laughter outside. Here, most of the guests stood in semicircles, their conversations muted. Diminutive Richard Llewelleyn dominated one group, his voice raised in the telling of an off-color joke.

Standing alone beside a stone fountain was the latest board member, looking uncomfortable and bored. Harry snatched a new drink from a tray and approached him, hand outstretched.

"Mr. O'Malley, isn't it?"

The pudgy man smiled sheepishly and shook hands. "Yes. You're . . ."

"Henry Bishop, political science. I'm faculty liaison this term."

Elliot O'Malley said how do you do. Harry commented on the beauty of their hosts' home. O'Malley agreed, and mentioned what a lovely night it was. They stood in uneasy silence for a few minutes.

O'Malley finally glanced at his wristwatch. "Well, I really ought to be going. Tomorrow's a working day."

"Not for most of us, I suspect."

"The idle rich, you mean, professor? Yes, I agree. Some of us still work for a living, though."

"What do you do?"

"I'm in sales, more or less. My company underwrites timber sales." He blushed a bit. "It's all pretty boring."

"Like hell it is!" Richard Llewelleyn swooped down upon them like a hunting falcon, clapping O'Malley on the back. The little man wore his tie loosened and top shirt button undone, and the sharp color in his cheeks suggested a bit too much liquor.

Bad taste, getting soused at a colleague's banquet like that, Harry reflected and finished off his whisky.

"Mr. Llewelleyn." O'Malley smiled weekly in greeting.

"*Richard!* Please!" Llewelleyn turned to Harry and flashed a quick on/off smile. His eyes remained unfocused and distant, as if hunting for the next, elusive client. "Professor, I owe you an apology for spouting off this afternoon. Sorry about that. No hard feellings. Elliot, I understand you're finagling a deal to sell Oregon lumber to North Korea. True?"

Harry's acceptance of Llewelleyn's vague apology was almost out of his mouth before Llewelleyn spirited away the perplexed Elliot O'Malley, leaving Harry by the fountain, mouth agape, empty glass in hand. He felt a bit like Wile E. Coyote, trying to figure out where the Roadrunner went. One problem at a time, he reminded himself as he deftly replaced the empty glass with a fresh one.

He stood by the fountain and watched his hostess step out onto the brick patio and approach the odd duo of O'Malley and Llewelleyn, now in deep conversation. Irena Shoenborn-Eriksen was dressed in a cream silk blouse with puffy sleeves, the collar turned up, maroon slacks and shoes with very high heels. Once again, Harry had difficulty guessing her age, but thought she was closer to forty than fifty.

"We're so happy you've joined the board," Shoenborn-Eriksen assured O'Malley, her voice at once both powerful and feminine. "I understand you got your master's from Astor in business administration?"

"Yes, I—"

"Yes, well, things have changed," Llewelleyn blurted out. "Most of these kids are too busy taking toenail painting and Early European Bullshit to know from business. I'm handling the finances for the Eriksens right now, you know."

The non sequitur appeared to catch O'Malley as off guard as it did Harry, who felt like he was eavesdropping (which, of course, he was), so he polished off the drink and headed back inside.

"Harry." He almost bumped into the monumental Geraldo Avenceña.

"Oh. Hullo, Geraldo. I didn't see you earlier."

"I just got here," the giant said. He scanned the crowded living room, his thick eyebrows almost meeting in a scowl.

Harry touched his forearm. "Geraldo, is everything all right?"

"Hmm?" Still he didn't look at Harry.

"Yoo-hoo. Geraldo? Tall, dark, and ecumenical? Is everything all right?"

"Oh. Yes, Harry. Everything's fine. Have you seen—"

"Geraldo, thank goodness you're here!" Mrs. Applebaum stepped between them. The contrast in sheer mass between hulking Reverend Avenceña and petite Cordelia Applebaum was a little shocking. Her well-coifed silver hair was barely as high as his chest. Geraldo breathed in deeply, expelled it, and nodded once, as if to convince himself of something. "Mrs. Applebaum, I've been looking for you. Something's come up."

"It certainly has!" Cordelia chimed in. "You know our resident *arr-teest*, Donal Patrick Cavenaugh? What an absolute swine!"

"What happened?" Harry noticed Geraldo was barely listening to Cordelia's tale.

She took a sizable swig of her cocktail before continuing. "I was speaking to him about divestment, when the little twerp informed me he was far too busy to deal with the focus of my mid-life crisis. For heaven's sake, I'm seventy-one years old! My mid-life crisis coincided with that simpleton's first teething! I told him so, mind you. Egoist!"

"Cordelia—" The minister spoke softly.

"Just like that, he smiled sweetly, the way one does to a doddering great-aunt, and left. Said he had an appointment! Appointment. Harry, if you loved me, you'll find the blackguard and hit him."

"I don't love you that much."

"Oh. That's right. Geraldo, if you love me, you'll find the blackguard and hit him."

Geraldo swallowed with difficulty. "Ma'am, I'm afraid I'm going to have to vote against divestment. Right now, it's the best thing for the college. I'm sorry."

Cordelia was clearly shaken. "Oh, dear. Well, if you're sure . . ."

"I am. I'm truly sorry."

Harry was afraid his stark disbelief was evident as he and the reverend made and held eye contact. "Are you positive, Geraldo?"

The big man smiled a small, sickly smile. "Yes. I hope you understand too."

"Of course, but perhaps we could discuss it over dinner tomorrow, or—"

"No," Geraldo stated. "Thanks, though."

Cordelia straightened her shoulders and patted the big man's hand. "Of course we understand, Geraldo. I shall make every effort to change your mind, however."

"Yes. Well. Ah, I think I'll investigate the food."

As he headed one way, President Eckersley and his stunningly beautiful wife (if she had a name, Harry had never heard it) started up a conversation with Cordelia, who joined in out of reluctant propriety.

Harry's eyes followed the reverend. He decided to pry a bit, found another drink for fortitude, then he started after Geraldo. However, parties, like deep waters, contain strong currents and riptides, and Harry was swept into a succession of increasingly banal conversations with people whose names he could not for the life of him recall. Twenty minutes later, he could no longer find Geraldo's hulking form amid the crush, and pushed his way back onto the patio to search for him.

Harry was trying to remember how many drinks he'd had, when he realized there was an argument ensuing on the moonlit lawn, just beyond the patio. "I've never been so insulted," Irena Shoenborn-Eriksen was saying.

"Look, you can't push me around," Richard Llewelleyn's high-pitched voice came back. "If you weren't so damned busy trying to screw every last drop of money out of your husband, he wouldn't—"

"Enough!"

Harry twitched and his drink spilled into a hedge. Geoffrey Eriksen shoved his way onto the patio, until he stood before his wife and Llewelleyn. People were staring.

"Look, Geoffrey, I'm sorry—" the little man began.

"Shut up." Eriksen spoke softly, his teeth clenched, his English in tight control. "Get out."

"Now look, Geoff! Let's face facts. I've got—"

"Listen, you dirty little shit, get off my property now. If you ever speak to my wife in anything less than a civil tone, I will hurt you." Eriksen's words were clear and evenly moderated, each spoken with savage precision. Harry, pushed uncomfortably close to the action, suspected the toll it was taking on Eriksen to maintain both his temper and his English.

Llewelleyn, his pinched face ablaze, started to speak, studied Eriksen's face, thought better of it, and turned quickly, storming into the house.

"Ah, hey folks, let's break this up, okay?" Behind Harry, Lee Connar spoke up. "Mr. O'Malley, have I introduced you to our college president?"

With a few well-placed words and a light touch on an arm or two, Connar broke the dangerous dynamics of the moment. Neither Irena Shoenborn-Eriksen nor her husband had moved an inch, Harry noticed. They stared into each other's eyes, standing a few feet apart. Big Sam Broderick, Llewelleyn's boss, hustled into the house in Llewelleyn's wake.

All right, now the party's getting interesting, Harry thought, as he realized he was drunk.

SEVEN
❖

Harry was shocked to enter the Eriksen's living room and bump into Lyndon Johnson, whom he hadn't seen in more than twenty years. He was even more surprised to find Ingrid Bergman, dressed exactly as Ilse Lund Laslo, by Lyndon's side. They were arm in arm, and Lyndon punched Harry playfully in the shoulder and drawled, "Bishop, for a college boy, you've got some of the most chicken-shit notions I've ever heard."

Ilse Lund Laslo laughed uncertainly and said, "Harry, I want to get on the plane for Lisbon with you."

Oh, I see. It's a dream, Harry realized as the phone rang. His eyes dragged open. He was sitting in his old, over-stuffed chair, a copy of Michael Davie's *LBJ* open on his lap.

The phone rang again.

Dimly, Harry remembered being driven home by Lee Connar, Lee's wife following in their station wagon. He remembered feeding his cat, Niccolo, making a few moves in the ongoing chess game atop the old, empty aquarium (he played against himself), and picking up the Davie book. His memories ended there.

The phone rang again and Niccolo looked up from his spot on the mantel, imploring Harry to answer the damn thing. He struggled to stand but found his vertebrae had been fused into one long piece of bamboo, completely unresponsive to commands from his booze-shrouded brain.

The phone showed no respect for the dead and rang again. He leaned forward and grabbed the receiver. "Hullo." His own voice sound dull and lifeless.

"Harry? Tucker. I wake you up?"

"Yes. What time is it?"

"A little after five."

"Ungh."

"Harry, have you heard the news?"

"Hmm-um."

"Were you at that trustees' shindig last night?"

"Um-hmm."

"There was a murder this morning. Guy named Llewelleyn. The cops are questioning, lessee . . . ah, Geoffrey Eriksen. Get some coffee going. I'm on my way over."

EIGHT

❖

The Tuesday morning traffic was light, and Nelligan pulled his black and red Jeep CJ to a halt behind Harry's Datsun less than fifteen minutes later. He jumped out and jogged across the street, up the slanted cement walkway, and flung open the screen door. A yellow stick-um note had been slapped on the wooden door. It read: *TN. It's open. Help yrslf to coffee. HB.*

Nelligan ripped down the note and walked in. The front room of Harry's apartment was, as always, a disaster area. Approximately three billion books filled the dusty bookcase that lined one wall, were piled atop both endtables, lined the windowsill, and were stacked beside the threadbare Barcalounger, one of Harry's most prized possessions. The chessboard, thick teak with rough edges, sat atop the dusty, empty aquarium. Harry once claimed he had never owned fish and swore he had forgotten how he came to own an aquarium. Nelligan believed him. Niccolo gave Nelligan a blank look, saw no food, and returned to cleaning his tiger-striped tail.

Nelligan could hear a shower running and stepped into the kitchen, whistling some tune he'd heard on the Jeep's radio. He poured a cup of black coffee and unwisely took a sip before he remembered Harry's coffee possessed the flavor of plutonium.

He was sitting in the kitchen breakfast nook, reading his own article on college divestment in Harry's paper, when

Harry shuffled in. He wore his usual attire: gray suit, gray tie, black shoes. In the bright kitchen light, Nelligan could see Harry's socks: one blue, one brown.

"What in God's name happened to you?" Tucker asked. Harry poured a cup of coffee into a grungy mug and laboriously began adding the usual accoutrements. His hair was still damp, and hung low on his forehead. His skin was a poisonous gray and the bags beneath his eyes, though usually quite pronounced, stood out as if he had been punched.

"Nothing. Fine. Llewelleyn's dead?"

"No, seriously. You look like something no self-respecting cat would drag in."

"I'm fine, Tuck. Fit as a fiddle and ready for love. Would you like some breakfast?"

"Sure. What are you having?"

Harry studied an open cupboard. "Cap'n Crunch or Fruit Loops."

"Oh, my god. Thanks, no, I'll stick to stuff not made in a beaker."

Harry shrugged—the action took a lot out of him. He dumped some unidentifiable product into a bowl and added milk that was maybe a day or two away from cottage cheese, then slid onto the bench, opposite Nelligan. The sun shone brightly through the red and white checked curtains and Harry leaned over to tug the shade down.

"Tie one on last night?"

"Yes, a bit. About Llewelleyn . . ."

"Right." Nelligan radiated excitement. He dug into his tweed jacket and produced the omnipresent notebook. "Nasty stuff. Did you know this Llewelleyn?"

"We'd been introduced. I didn't like him. Don't you want some coffee?"

"I'd love some coffee. What I don't want is any of that sludge you make, thank you. Cops found Llewelleyn this morning, around two, smack in the center of Pioneer Courthouse Square."

"Downtown?"

"Right. He wasn't killed there, though, just dumped off."

"How was he killed?"

"Knifed. Repeatedly. Took one in the heart, it looked like."

Harry finished off the cereal and sipped his coffee. "You were there?"

Nelligan leaned against the window, his legs up on the bench. "Yeah. Marty and I had a bit of a fight yesterday. I was in no mood for a sermon, so I worked late, putting together some data on a guy I know who exports marijuana to military academies around the country. Anyway, I heard the squeal on the police band and remembered the name. Voilà."

"You and Martin are fighting? Anything serious?"

Nelligan spun his pen absently on the formica tabletop. "No. Domestic squabble. Anyway, I hustled down and got to talk to the medical examiner's people. It seems your friend Llewelleyn was beaten up pretty good, before he was knifed. But his wallet and watch weren't missing."

Harry slowly raised himself to his feet and rinsed out the bowl and spoon, adding them to the overloaded dishwasher. "Not a mugging, then?"

"Either that or an interrupted mugging, but that doesn't make a hell of a lot of sense, if Llewelleyn wasn't killed in the Square, but was dumped there later. Anyone hauling a corpse around would have time to grab the wallet, if that's what they were after."

He sat silently for a while and watched Harry open a plastic container and empty nine Bufferin into his palm. He replaced one in the container and washed the remainder down with the dregs of his coffee. Nelligan felt his hour-old bagel and cream cheese do a slow barrel roll in his stomach.

"Richard Llewelleyn," Harry mumbled. "That's terrible."

"Thought you said you didn't like him."

"I didn't. I also don't like apricots, but I'd hate to see an orchard on fire. Poor fellow."

"So tell me about the party last night."

Harry poured a second cup and turned off the percolator. "Well, it was your average academia affair—boring unto death. Though I admit that's usually figuratively, not literally. Llewelleyn was there, of course."

"Did you two speak?"

"Yes, briefly. He apologized for his comments to me at the board meeting. I once met a young woman outside the Lincoln Memorial, wearing sneakers and an electric-green boa. She told me I was the only man for her, with about the same sincerity generated by Mr. Llewelleyn's apology."

"Yeah? So what else happened?"

Harry sat again and stirred his spoon in the coffee. "Well, bit of this, bit of that. You know how these things go."

"Harry, don't muck around. What happened?"

"Really, Tucker, I'm not at all sure I should be discussing this with you. No offense, of course."

"Harry, buddy, please don't pull a Moral High Ground on me," Nelligan pleaded. "C'mon! This is my story, Harry! I was on it before it was a twinkle in the murderer's eye. Compared to the competition, I've been on this story for a light-year. Cut me some slack."

"Light-years measure distance, not time, though at those speeds they're very nearly the same thing."

"Harry, what the hell are you talking about?"

"Very well, Tuck. There was a row last night."

"Involving Mr. Llewelleyn?"

"Yes."

"All right! I told you the cops were talking to Geoffrey Eriksen, and you didn't seem surprised. Can I assume he was in on this brouhaha?"

"Don't quote me."

"Deal. You're deep background."

"Then yes, Eriksen kicked Llewelleyn out." Nelligan whistled. "But Tucker, it was a verbal argument, not pistols at dawn. I wouldn't make too much of it."

"Right, right. So what was the gist of the argument?"

Harry peered out through the red and white curtains at the making of another beautiful fall day. "I don't think I can tell you."

"Why not?"

"The police officer on my lawn probably wouldn't like it."

Nelligan leaned over the table to look out. A squat, American-made sedan with whip aerial was parked behind his Jeep. A squat, American-made male in a dark suit stood on the walkway, glanced at the two faces in the window, and stepped to the door, out of their field of view. The doorbell rang.

"Cheese it," said Harry. "It's the house dick."

NINE

❖

"Professor Henry Bishop?"

"Yessir. You're police?"

The smaller man looked surprised. He was short and black, with very dark skin, leathery and dry, with crags rather than wrinkles. Dinosaur hide must have been about that same texture. The man handed Harry a leather identification pouch. "Detective Sergeant John Wiley, Portland Police."

"How do you do, Detective Sergeant. Won't you come in." Harry held the door open and handed back the ID, unopened. Wiley stepped into the terminally cluttered room, his eyes sweeping casually and alighting on Nelligan who stood, arms crossed, leaning on the kitchen doorjamb.

"Hi. Tucker Bishop, Henry's cousin." Nelligan smiled and nodded, all country-friendly. "I'm just in for a few days. What's up?"

"Sergeant," Harry interjected, "may I introduce Tucker Nelligan, crime reporter for the *Post*. Tucker, Detective John Wiley, PPD."

Nelligan flashed Harry a look of mild panic and Wiley's eyes twinkled. He chuckled and stepped forward, hand outstretched. "Mr. Nelligan. I read your stuff. How do you do?"

"Uh," Nelligan ad-libbed, and grabbed the cop's hand. Nelligan had twice been decked by members of the Port-

land Police Department. He had been pushed and shoved
on various occasions and threatened with the business end
of a nightstick more times than he cared to consider. One
uniformed officer, wishing to offer constructive criticism
regarding a piece on police brutality, had once pointed his
service revolver at Nelligan's forehead and cocked the hammer. All of this was part of the business. Nelligan had never
had a cop offer to shake his hand or compliment his writing. It was unnerving.

"You're a friend of the professor's?" Wiley's voice was
high and soft, barely a whisper. He rested his hands on his
hips, pushing his jacket back to reveal a paging device but
no gun.

"Yes. We always play handball on Tuesday mornings. I
dropped by to pick him up."

Wiley digested the information, turned to take note of
Harry's hard-soled shoes, rumpled suit and tie, and turned
back, nodding once. "You told the professor about the
murder, I assume."

Harry winked at Nelligan over the shorter man's back.
"Yes, Sergeant. Tucker rang me this morning with the bad
news. May I assume you're here to ask me some questions?"

"Yessir." Wiley kept his gentle eyes on Nelligan. "I'm
pleased to finally meet you, Mr. Nelligan. Someone I know
said you worked in Angola for a while."

"Ah, no. Beirut," Nelligan replied, desperately trying to
figure the angle from which the cop's threat would come.

"That must have been fascinating. My parents came
from Ghana, and I've been reading up on that area. I don't
know much about the Middle East, except that it's war-rid-
den."

"Uh, yeah."

"I've never been overseas, myself. Well, sir, I wonder if I
could speak to the professor alone for a moment?"

Pummeled senseless by politeness, Nelligan shrugged,
nodded, and smiled. "Right. Okay. Ah. Harry?"

"I'll ring you up, Tucker."

"Right. Well, Sergeant, I'll, ah, call you later, about this
case?"

"Please do. We'll have an official statement in a couple
hours. Oh wait, here's my card. Home number's on the
back." Wiley fished out a plain white card, smiled, and

shook Nelligan's hand again. Nelligan took the card, smile, and hand, feeling like an absolute idiot.

When he was gone, Harry chuckled. "Tucker thrives on confrontation, Sergeant. I don't believe he knows what to make of you."

The detective shrugged. "I read the *Post*. He seems bright. So you know about Richard Llewelleyn being murdered?"

"Yes, and about your questioning Geoffrey Eriksen." Harry pushed back his sleeve and looked at the ancient, much-battered Timex. "I've got about forty-five minutes to get to work. May I offer you a cup of coffee or some tea, Sergeant?"

"Thank you, tea would be nice."

Wiley sat in the kitchen alcove while Harry boiled water and retrieved two clean cups. The sergeant asked questions, as cops are wont to do, but they were small-talk, polite questions: How long had Harry been at Astor? Is political science a growing field? Did many of his students go on to law school?

Harry set down the cups, minus saucers, and slid onto the bench. "What can I do for you, Sergeant?"

"I wanted to ask you a few quick questions about the Eriksens' party last night."

"There were perhaps fifty people there, Sergeant. I'm surprised you came to me for information."

"Hmm." Wiley sipped the tea. "Both the victim and one of our suspects are trustees of the college. You, on the other hand, are not. I thought you might give me some insight, as an outsider looking in."

"I see," Harry lied.

"Also, you were involved in those murders at Astor last year, weren't you?"

Bingo. "Well, I was only involved insofar as several attempts were made on my life, Sergeant. I take it you know about all that."

"Yes. Sergeant Clair DuPree is a friend of mine. She told me about it. I saw her the other day. She says hi."

Harry said nothing. Clair DuPree.

"She once mentioned you were very perceptive, that you have a talent for noticing detail. I wondered if there was anything unusual about the party last night that I should know."

"Yes. Geoffrey Eriksen probably didn't kill Richard Llewelleyn."

Wiley raised an eyebrow. He wrote nothing down. "No?"

"No. I assume you're questioning him because he kicked Llewelleyn out of his home last night."

"True."

"Sergeant, it was an argument, to be sure, but not the type of thing one murders over. Eriksen is, like myself, a displaced person—a European, with a bit of old-world machismo. Llewelleyn raised his voice to Irena Shoenborn-Eriksen, which is taboo. Eriksen asked him to leave."

"Told him to leave," Wiley corrected.

"Yes. Told Llewelleyn to leave, and Llewelleyn promptly left. It was one of those extremely uncomfortable situations. It was not, as I said, the stuff of murder."

"Do you know what Llewelleyn and Ms. Shoenborn-Eriksen argued about?"

"No. I was nearby and heard Ms. Shoenborn-Eriksen say she had never been so insulted. I missed the nature of the insult, I'm afraid."

"How did Llewelleyn react to this?"

"He said she couldn't push him around, and accused her of, ah, 'trying to screw every drop of money from him,' meaning Eriksen, I assume."

"You have a good memory, professor."

"I have a penchant for mixed metaphors."

Wiley smiled. "Me too. Did Llewelleyn mention her screwing anything else?"

"Ha! Now, that would have been a metaphor. No, Sergeant, he didn't mention any other impropriety on her part. He didn't even state any specifics regarding Eriksen's considerable fortune. What he said seemed rather silly to me, since I'm told Ms. Shoenborn-Eriksen is not without pin money of her own."

"You hear right, professor. She's quite wealthy. What did Eriksen say about all this?"

An elaborate shrug: "He ordered Llewelleyn off the premises."

Wiley nodded. "And?"

"And, that's about all."

"Did he threaten Mr. Llewelleyn in any fashion."

Harry waved his hand in the air, palm down. "After a fashion, yes. Geoffrey told Llewelleyn to get out, and said he, Eriksen, would hurt him, Llewelleyn, if he, Llewelleyn, ever spoke to her, Shoenborn-Eriksen, like that again. Confusing, isn't it?"

"A bit."

"You already knew Eriksen threatened him, didn't you?"

"Yessir, professor. You understand, I hope, why it's vitally important that I get the most accurate information available."

Harry offered more tea and Wiley declined. "Sergeant, how bad was it?"

"Llewelleyn's injuries?"

"Yes."

Wiley made a show of examining his fingernails and spoke softly. "Extensive. Gruesome."

"Tucker Nelligan tells me Llewelleyn's valuables weren't touched."

"Mr. Nelligan is very knowledgeable."

"Yes. He's good at what he does. It wasn't a mugging?"

"No, professor. Unless we have a lunatic loose here in Portland, which we're certainly hoping isn't the case. You can see why we're treading carefully around the press, I hope."

Harry nodded.

"Then I trust you won't tell Mr. Nelligan what we talked about."

"Of course not, Sergeant." Harry led the officer to the front room and opened the door. Wiley shook Harry's hand and smiled warmly, then dug out another business card, identical to the one he had given Nelligan.

"May I call you if I have any further questions, professor?"

"You will anyway. Yes, of course. Please let me know if I can help."

"We will, sir. Hope I didn't make you late for work."

"No."

"Well. Thanks, again. Good-bye."

"Sergeant?" Wiley was halfway down the walk when Harry spoke. The black detective turned and smiled expectantly. "Do you see Clair DuPree often?"

"Every month."

"Say hello for me next time, will you?"

"Yessir. Good day."

TEN

✤

Nelligan turned the key in the door and dashed into his home, whistling whatever had just been on the Jeep's radio. "Yo! Marty!"

"In the den," a voice came back.

Nelligan went straight to the bathroom and turned on the shower. He carried a small white bag, which he set down atop the toilet tank. He jumped into the shower when the water was near scalding and, once acclimatized, began scrubbing vigorously, humming. He washed his hair twice, quickly, and applied a conditioner. Finally, he turned down the hot water until the shower became chill and felt his nerve ends jangle beneath his skin.

He shut off the water and pushed open the curtain. Martin tossed a towel at him. "Good morning."

"Morning, Marty."

Martin sat on the counter by the sink, mug of coffee in one hand, *Wall Street Journal* in the other. The steam had curled the corners of the newspaper. He peered over the tops of his half-glasses at Nelligan. "Interesting night?"

"Yeah. We've got a murder."

Martin studied Nelligan's face. "You should have called and told me. I'd have dressed for it. What's in the bag?"

"Chocolate-chip cookie, from that place in Yamhill Market."

Martin set down his coffee, picked up the bag and peered in. "So it is."

"I'm sorry about yesterday, chief. I guess I was a little bitchy."

"A little?"

Nelligan finished toweling off and placed a hand on Marty's knee. "Yeah, just a little. I am sorry. Peace?"

Kady took a bite of cookie and returned to the *Journal*. He rested his hand atop Nelligan's for a moment. "It's stale."

Nelligan dashed off to the bedroom. "Sorry. I got it yesterday. Hey, guess who's involved in my murder?"

"Ray Charles?"

Nelligan returned, wearing pleated sky-blue slacks and black socks. "Close. Harry."

Kady looked up for the first time, concern etched on his long, thin face. "Harry is okay, isn't he?"

"Yeah." Nelligan lathered his cheeks and square chin. "Harry was at a party last night for trustees of JJAC, right? Anyway, one of the trustees, who was at this party, got himself knifed up, and another trustee was interviewed by the cops this morning. And which of Portland's famous crime reporters just happens to have a good friend at the party?"

"So you got the jump on the story?"

"Yes, Mr. Kady. Once again, Irish luck comes into play."

"Hmm. Lucky you. A murder."

"I know. It's too bad this guy got iced. But it happened on my watch, and I'm way ahead of the *Oregonian* and the TV guys, so I'm going to take full advantage of that lead." Nelligan made no effort to hide his smugness.

Kady folded the paper over and checked the Dow Jones. "Two of our stocks are down."

"So what else is new?"

"What's the word on Astor divestment?"

"What?"

"Divestment. Astor's trustees, divesting their South African holdings. Remember?"

"Oh, yeah. Nothing. They decided to form a committee to 'look into the issue.' But with the deceased and suspect both board members, I think we can assume divestiture is a wash."

"So where are you going, so bright and early? You haven't even been to bed yet. Or have you?"

"Now who's bitchy? I'm fine, I crashed on the couch in Joann's office. And I'm on my way to talk to the chief suspect. Wanna come?"

"Ugh."

From his closet, Nelligan chose a light tan shirt, a narrow knit tie in dusty rose, and his usual shoes; black and stylish, but with thin rubber soles. For sneaking around.

Nelligan checked himself in the full-length mirror, fiddled with his sandy hair, and walked to the dining room. Kady was sorting through piles of very tedious-looking forms: a sure sign he was scheduled to be in court that day.

"Marty? You in court today?"

Kady nodded. "Can you get away for lunch?"

"Doubtful, counselor. I'll call or leave a message on the machine."

"All right. Tucker?" Martin stood up and looked the smaller man in the eye. "Do me a favor?"

Sure.

"Don't write off the divestment story. It's important."

Nelligan shrugged. "To whom? It's make-believe politics, chief."

"Tucker, you can be an ass. It *is* important. It's important to lots of people."

"We're not going to relive those wonderful, reckless days of student protests at Stanford, with Gene McCarthy and Nixon and Vietnam and all that, are we?"

Silently, Kady left the room and returned with a raincoat and umbrella. He gathered up the essential piles of forms, leaving the rest on the dining room table.

"It's not supposed to rain." Nelligan tried to be civil.

Mutely, Kady clicked his briefcase shut.

"Okay. All right. Pax. I'll cover the student protests."

Kady grinned. "God, you're easy. Thanks, Tuck. Good cookie."

Harry arrived at John Jacob Astor College around eight-thirty. The morning fog was burning off, revealing a near-cloudless, perfect September sky.

He parked the little Datsun to the east of the football stadium, where it wouldn't pick up too much afternoon sun, and walked up through the campus. His knee creaked a bit, and he feared the heat and humidity might make a last-ditch attempt to rekindle summer. Thanks to his reassignment to the board of trustees, he didn't have any classes until well into Tuesday afternoon, and didn't actually have to be on campus until then, but he had other business to attend to.

His route took him past the ultramodern performing arts center and through one of Astor's countless thickets of pine and cedar. There were places on the campus that belied its urban setting, places so rustic and quiet that one could completely forget the city all around. Harry was neither a morning person nor a lover of the great outdoors, but the campus of John Jacob Astor had wiles and ways to soothe the grumpiest of souls.

He was even whistling a toneless facsimile of a Cole Porter number as he approached the chapel. From the rear, the graceful, curving architecture of the building seemed sullied by the garbage dumpster and rough gravel driveway. Harry entered through the rear door, noticed once again that Geraldo refused to lock any of the chapel doors, despite frequent thefts in the past years. He understood the point the chaplain was trying to make, although it seemed a trifle expensive to him.

Lights were off inside, and Harry moved from the glow of one window to another, listening for signs of life. Coffee simmered in the chapel kitchen, and dishes dripped in the plastic drainer beside the sink. Geraldo's office was empty. Harry racked his brain to see if he'd forgotten any important staff meetings that morning, but none came to mind. It hardly mattered; he had a policy of never attending meetings anyway.

He stepped back out into the sunshine and limped up the hill, favoring the arthritic knee. The campus was beginning to stir, and breakfast aromas emanated from the Student Union Building. He stopped by the Douglas Fir Room to grab a cup of coffee and two raspberry-filled doughnuts, which he wrapped in paper napkins and stuffed into his coat pockets. Across the cafeteria, he spotted Sandi Braithwaite, perched in a threadbare armchair in the study area.

Sandy sat with her butt hanging off the chair's edge, her head against the backrest, her stocking feet propped up on the windowsill, a textbook wedged between her knees and chest. Harry thought it must be the most uncomfortable position conceivable, something only a Tibetan holy man would do, and even then not for long.

"Hullo, Sandi." He sat on the edge of a wooden table. Sandi grinned and wriggled upright, blowing strands of hair away from her eyes. "Good morning, professor. I got that book on the union movement." She pointed to the massive text.

"Yes. You'll like that, I think. Some good interviews with surviving Wobblies. That was an interesting show you put on yesterday.

Sandi blushed. "I know it wasn't very ethical to sneak into that meeting, but I knew they wouldn't talk to me otherwise."

"True."

"And besides, the whole point of being a journalism student is learning how to do the job, no matter what obstacles you hit, right?"

Harry munched on a doughnut and did not comment. "I take it you've been talking to Tucker Nelligan."

"Yeah. He was here yesterday. Professor, I know you didn't approve of my sneaking in, but it made sense to me, and it wasn't illegal."

"Per se. Questionable ethics, but not illegal. To be honest, Sandi, I was a bit more disappointed in your dizzy female persona."

She frowned. "I thought I pulled that off pretty well."

"So did I. You looked for all the world like the stereotypical female newscaster, and no one took you seriously."

"That was the idea. Tucker says a reporter holds the upper hand whenever he or she is underestimated."

Harry wiped his hand on the napkin and nodded. He was familiar with the Gospel According to Tucker. "Well, I don't know much about journalism. I'm sure that works for Tucker, and he really is very good."

"He's the best."

"Of course, one can't help wonder whether this has an impact on all women in journalism."

"I don't understand," Sandi murmured, although she was beginning to.

"You have an excellent mind, Sandi. You're very bright, and a fine writer. But out there, beyond the college level, you'll discover people underestimating you, not because you can act dizzy but because you're a woman."

"Yes, sir. I understand that. I'm a feminist. But as Tucker says, being underestimated isn't always a bad thing."

Harry stood. "True. So long as the underestimating doesn't extend to pay scale, or hiring and firing, or who's granted interviews and who isn't, or access to higher level jobs."

"Well . . ."

Harry kindly changed the subject. "Have you been pulling an all-nighter?"

"Sort of. We just put the paper to bed a few hours ago. It's at the printer's now."

Harry thought it was probably silly and old-fashioned to think of a bright woman in her late teens as "innocent," but he couldn't bring himself to tell Sandi about Llewelleyn's murder. Let her enjoy her morning.

"Did you see my note about the class change? Will that be a problem for you? Having the class off campus?"

"Hmm? Oh, no, professor. That's fine."

"Good. I'll see you this afternoon, Sandi. Good morning."

"You too. Bye." He left her staring out the window at the elongated morning shadows.

The Werewolf searched slowly through the Sunday editions of the *Chicago Tribune*, reading each headline punctiliously. On page 13, Section B, he found a small article on a JJAC alumna who had been nominated to fill a judgeship vacancy on the circuit court.

Very carefully, the Werewolf brushed hair away from his eyes, selected the longer set of scissors, and clipped out the article. He cut slowly, keeping his lines straight and true, and connected at right angles. Done, he took the article and gingerly added it to a pile on his desk.

The counter bell sounded three quick notes. The Werewolf swore softly and stood, emerging from the darkened recesses of the Archives Department. He grabbed a set of dusty black plastic sunglasses from the front desk.

Even with the glasses, the bright light of the outer office made him squint. Archives was tucked away neatly in the basement of the college library in a cavernous area, kept dry and clean and under subdued lights. Here was stored the accumulated history of John Jacob Astor College and its employees, students, staff, and alumni.

The official college archivist was an indistinct fellow named Larson or Lawsen or something similar: he was rarely seen, and most faculty and staff had long ago forgotten his existence. It was the Werewolf, not Larsen or Lawsen, one saw if one needed anything from Archives. The Werewolf was a work-study student, and had worked in Archives since coming to JJAC, eight years earlier. He knew the endless files and photographs and scrapbooks and yearbooks better by far than anyone, because, for all intents and purposes, the Werewolf lived in the Archives Department.

He emerged now from his dwelling place into the Documents Room. The Werewolf was in his late twenties and stood approximately five feet four. His long black hair was a messy nest of tight curls surrounding a chubby face whose most distinctive feature was a nondistinctive beard. As usual, he wore blue jeans, a woolen sweater, and an endless striped scarf, wrapped three times around his neck. A *"Dr. Who"* button adorned his scarf.

"Yes?" He squinted through the Billy-Bob shades at the man behind the counter.

"Ah, is this Archives?"

"Yes."

"Are you the archivist?"

"Nope. Assistant." The Werewolf wondered how long they were going to play Twenty Questions. He had work to get done.

The man looked down at the queer little creature with his wild hair, beard, scarf, and sunglasses. "Well, do you have files on faculty members?"

"Yes."

"Ah. May I check the file on a professor?"

"ID?"

"Certainly." The man produced a leather wallet from his suitcoat pocket.

The Werewolf looked at the driver's license and Visa card and frowned. From behind the counter he produced the JJAC alumni directory and flipped pages, wetting the pad of his thumb with his tongue.

"Okay. Fill out this, please." He motioned toward a stubby pencil and a request form. When the man handed it over, the Werewolf shuffled back into the darkness.

He trudged straight and true for the proper aisle of dustless metal shelves. He didn't search about or check Dewey decimals to find the requested file. He knew where everything was in his basement universe.

Moments later, he emerged and handed across a manila folder. "Bishop, Henry, Ph.D. This is his curriculum vitae and clippings and list of on-campus positions held, and stuff like that."

"Wonderful," the man said. "I'll return this in about half an hour. Is that all right?"

"Yes."

"And, um, I was never here." Two crisp ten-dollar bills slid across the counter. The man winked at the Werewolf and walked away, the file tucked under his arm.

Normally, the Werewolf had no interest in anything that transpired out in the other world. But in eight years, no one had ever tipped him, not even a quarter. He picked up the bills and frowned at them.

Damnedest thing. He was so surprised he returned to his cavern and rolled his lunch joint an hour earlier than usual.

ELEVEN

❖

Nelligan stepped out of the Jeep and whistled two notes. He peered over the top of his aviator sunglasses. The spacious lawn inside the high shrub parameter of the Eriksen home was shredded and laced with waves of mud and tire tracks. A crew of five Philippinos were busy leveling the ground with a back hoe and laying squares of new sod.

"The rich are different from you and I," Nelligan mumbled, jogging to the double front doors. He rang the bell, waited fifteen seconds, and rang again.

The door was answered by a slim woman in a lavender and cream business suit, her blond hair piled up in a conservative—and expensive, Nelligan decided—fashion. "Yes?"

"Hello. Tucker Nelligan, with the *Post*. I wondered if I might speak to Geoffrey Eriksen."

The woman's eyes frosted, and she gave Nelligan a slow head-to-toe assessment. "My husband isn't home right now, Mr. Nelligan. And he doesn't speak to the press. His company has a public relations office for that."

"Yes, ma'am. I understand that. I'd like to talk to your husband about Richard Llewelleyn. And about the party last night."

The woman was taken aback. "How did you hear about this so soon?"

"I spoke to Sergeant Wiley about an hour ago. He told me," Nelligan lied.

She assessed the situation for a moment, then sighed. "I'm Irena Shoenborn-Eriksen, Geoffrey's wife. Please come in, Mr. . . .

"Nelligan. Thank you."

Irena Shoenborn-Eriksen led him into a tastefully appointed room. "Appointed" was the only word for it: Nelligan had never before seen a more uncomfortable room. The furniture was beautiful and unused. No head had ever rested against the back of the fawn-colored davenport, he thought. Delicate and obviously expensive antiques of porcelain and bone china balanced precariously on three-legged stands and endtables with etched-glass surfaces. His shoes sank almost beyond sight into the white carpet.

"Please have a seat." Shoenborn-Eriksen motioned toward an armless wooden chair about as old as England. Nelligan estimated its weight at seven ounces and sank down gingerly, absolutely positive it was about to transform into kindling.

Miraculously, the chair held. Shoenborn-Eriksen moved like a model on a causeway. Her every motion was stylized, theatrical. She sat on the davenport, her long legs crossed at the knee. "Would you care for some coffee or tea, Mr. Nelligan?"

No, I'd rather sit here over this incredible rug with a cigar and banana split, please. "Yes. Coffee, thank you."

"Davos?" The lady of the house spoke a fraction louder than conversational tones, and a henchman promptly appeared. Like "appointed," "henchman" was clearly the proper sobriquet.

"Coffee, please." Davos possessed the basic physique of a caribou. He digested the request and withdrew without a word. Nelligan wondered if Ms. Shoenborn-Eriksen was being a good hostess, or had simply wanted him to see Davos. He thought perhaps she was trying to intimidate him. He also thought she was doing a pretty good job of it.

"So, you spoke to the police?" Shoenborn-Eriksen uncrossed and recrossed her legs. Her calves were strong and tapered.

"Yes. I understand they also spoke to your husband."

"Correct. They wanted to know about the party last night, and who was the last to see poor Richard. I'm afraid he left the party rather early."

Nelligan opted to keep his notebook hidden. At this stage, a conversation might prove more valuable than an interview. "I see. Is your husband still with the police?"

"No, he's at work. This is a weekday."

"Let's see if I've got this. Your husband threw a party last night; one of the guests—a fellow trustee of Astor College—was murdered soon after. Your husband was called down to police headquarters before dawn, and now he's at work?"

Shoenborn-Eriksen flashed a genteel smile. "Yes, Mr. Nelligan. Cascade Electro is my husband's entire universe. We all feel terrible about Richard, of course, but life—and business—go on."

"So true."

She nodded appreciatively. "I'm glad you understand."

"Have the police spoken to you?"

She paused for a breath, then plunged in. "Yes. Briefly, this morning. *Very* early. They wanted to know about Richard and the party."

"I don't understand, Ms. Shoenborn-Eriksen. If Sergeant Wiley got that information from you, why did they want to speak to your husband?"

Davos shouldered his way through the door, bearing a silver tray and an ornate silver coffee set. He set it down between Nelligan and his host, glanced at the reporter with eyes like the marbles taxidermists use on moose heads, and left the room.

Shoenborn-Eriksen poured coffee, offered cream and sugar, then leaned back, cup and saucer on her lap, appraising Nelligan with beautiful, oval eyes behind curved lashes. He sipped the coffee and almost scalded his mouth. The woman made him feel off balance and he wasn't sure why.

"I didn't answer your question, did I? I believe the police wanted details of trustee business."

"I see. Aren't you a trustee of Astor?"

Her black eyes sparkled. "Yes. I am. Perhaps they wanted to know about Richard's business dealings or that SEC thing."

"The Securities and Exchange Commission That SEC? Was Llewelleyn being investigated by them?"

"Oh, I don't know, really. I'd heard something about an investigation. Poor Richard was a financial manager, you know."

"This would be the same poor Richard who wrote the almanac?"

That caught her off guard, and Nelligan felt a brief flush of triumph. For the first time he was operating on even ground. However, she quickly recovered her composure. "The senseless death of an acquaintance isn't all that funny, I'm afraid, Mr. Nelligan."

"My apologies."

She sat forward, setting down her coffee untasted. "Mr. Nelligan, you spoke to the police this morning?"

"True."

"May I speak off the record for a moment?"

"No."

She sat motionless. "Excuse me?"

"No. I don't think I can go off the record just now, ma'am." He smiled politely and cautiously sipped the scalding coffee.

Shoenborn-Eriksen frowned and brushed an imaginary stray lock of hair away from her ear. Solid gold bangles clinked on her wrist. "I've never heard of that before: a journalist refusing to go off the record, when someone wanted to speak to them about a sensitive subject."

"Ms. Shoenborn-Eriksen, 'off the record' isn't a constitutional right. It isn't like 'no comment,' which is within anybody's right, except in a court of law, and sometimes even then. Right now, I'm trying to find out everything I can regarding the murder of Richard Llewelleyn. I'm under the impression you have information that I could use. If I agree to go off the record, I'd be honor bound—not bound by law, you understand, but by my own set of mores—never to use the information I gain from our conversation, unless I could get someone else to say the same things. Right now, I don't know nearly enough about this murder. I can't afford to go off the record. It would be counterproductive."

She studied him, her teeth worrying her lower lip. Nelligan decided Irena Shoenborn-Eriksen was an amazingly attractive woman. When she was younger, she must have been utterly unforgettable. And she was one of those women who age well.

Finally, she nodded and sat back. "You answered my question, anyway. You said 'murder,' not 'mugging.'"

"It wasn't a mugging, ma'am."

"I see. And the police think Geoffrey is a suspect?"

Nelligan shrugged.

"Geoffrey didn't kill Richard. He was with me all night."

"Actually, I'm not looking for an alibi, ma'am."

"Well, the police will be. My husband had no reason to kill Richard. They were friends."

"And you?"

"Yes, I was his friend too. Well, not 'friend,' I suppose. We hardly ever spoke. But we were acquaintances and we worked together on the board of trustees at Astor."

"And you did fight with him last night."

Bingo. She studied him, smiling faintly, and finally nodded. "Davos?"

Davos materialized, his bulk filling the entranceway.

"Mr. Nelligan has to leave now."

Tucker set down the coffee and stood. "Yes, Davos. Mr. Nelligan leave now. Davos good boy."

Davos said nothing, but stepped into the parlor, clearing the doorway. Nelligan offered his hand and Irena shook it, a firm, dry grasp. "Nice meeting you, Mr. Nelligan."

"You too."

"Good day."

"Toodles. Coming, Davos?"

The massive man led the way to the front door, held it open, and shut it behind Nelligan, all without even a glance his way. A man the size of a compact car needn't bother with threats.

Nelligan was in seventh heaven. Any time a reporter can get kicked out by a thug, he's obviously heading in the right direction.

"Knock, knock," Harry shouted.

Reverend Avenceña turned from his work and grinned. The grin faded quickly.

Geraldo was in the combination workroom/storage room in the basement of the chapel, wearing a leather apron, leather gauntlets, and plastic goggles. He had been bent over an unfinished desk, electric sander buzzing away.

"This is going to be beautiful." Harry ran a hand over the beveled edge of the rolltop desk. "Did you build all the furniture down here?"

"Some of it," Geraldo replied, shoving the goggles atop his head. "This came from a kit, though. How are you today, Harry?"

"Fine, fine. You?"

"Fine."

"Good." Harry set down his doctor's bag and hitched himself up on the edge of the thick wooden workbench. "I didn't know you were a carpenter."

"It's cathartic. I used to be pretty good, but I don't get much chance any more. Do you build anything?"

"Bar tabs. I suppose you know what I wanted to ask you, Geraldo."

The big man removed the long gauntlets and slapped them together. Wood dust flew. "Yes. Harry, I really don't want to talk about the party. Do you mind?"

"Of course not. I understand. But you seemed awful worried about it yesterday, and you might want to talk."

"Thank you, Harry. I really do appreciate that. It's just a decision I thought I ought to make. I can't support divestiture."

"May I ask why?"

Geraldo busied his hands by peeling the sandpaper disk off the sander. "The economic situation of the college. I don't think the endowment campaign is strong enough to handle the stresses of divestiture. Besides, we're too heavily dependent on tuition dollars. I just don't think this is the right time to be making major changes in the school's stock profile."

Harry almost laughed. He leaned over and peered back behind the workbench.

"What are you looking for?"

"A pod. The real Geraldo Avenceña would never spout econo-babble like that."

Geraldo almost replied, reined himself in, and finally nodded. "Think what you like, Harry. Did you, ah, get a chance to talk to Cordelia after I left?"

"No. Things got a bit hectic, after our little talk. Did you stay long enough to see the contretemps between Richard Llewelleyn and our hostess?"

Geraldo went to the huge steel sink in the corner and washed his hands with generic soap. "No. I'm not surprised, though. I don't think Irena and Richard ever got along."

"You *have* heard about him, I assume."

"Yes." Geraldo dried his hands and smiled sheepishly. "I wouldn't worry too much about this, Harry."

"No?"

"No. He means well, I think."

The non sequitur took Harry by surprise. "Who means well?"

"Richard Llewelleyn."

"*Llewelleyn* means well?"

"Yes. Harry, are you all right?"

"Geraldo, I'm sorry, I don't know what you're talking about."

Geraldo hoisted himself up on the bench beside Harry, the muscles in his bare forearms bunching like a plugged high-pressure hose. "I'm talking about Llewelleyn's bid to become the new board chairperson. I'm, ah, supporting him. The elections are later this term, you know."

"No. No, I didn't." Harry felt his face redden.

"What were *you* talking about, then?"

"Geraldo, Richard Llewelleyn was murdered last night."

It took a few moments for the chaplain's face to reflect the news. Harry could see tension build across his forehead and eyes as he rubbed meaty fingers through his coarse beard. "Murdered?"

"Yes. His body was found in Pioneer Courthouse Square. I thought you'd heard. It's all over the campus."

"I just got here, about fifteen minutes ago. When did it happen?"

"This morning, about three, I understand. The police spoke to Geoffrey Eriksen and me at a rather hideous hour this morning."

"They wanted to talk to you? Harry, are you okay?"

"Yes, thank you. They just wanted a nontrustee's opinion of the banquet."

The two friends sat in silence for a while. Geraldo
rubbed his neck and nodded, as if in an internal dialogue.
"Richard didn't make it here last night."

"He didn't?"

"No." Geraldo remained in profile, not looking at
Harry. "I told you I was meeting with him, didn't I?"

"Yes."

"Well, he didn't show up."

"Ah."

"I just thought I ought to mention that."

"I see."

"In case you were wondering."

Harry had a sudden desire to leap down off the bench
and run for all he was worth. Instead, he climbed down and
gathered his blackstone bag, flashing Geraldo a lopsided
grin. "Well, the police may be around to talk to you. I suspect they'll be all over the campus for the next few days."

"Yes. Probably."

"Free for lunch?"

"Hmm? Oh, no. I've got to get some paperwork out of
the way."

"Fine. I'll see you later."

"Right. Harry?"

Harry turned at the door.

"Llewelleyn could be a royal pain. Almost everyone who
knew him thought so."

"So I'm discovering."

"But I'm sure no one on the board had anything to do
with his death."

"No. You're probably right."

"I mean, no one connected to the college at all."

The two men stood, facing each other, both fully aware
of the new tension between them.

"I'll call you later," Harry finally said.

"Okay. Bye."

Harry started to say something, then thought better of
it.

"Bye."

TWELVE

✤

"Securities and Exchange Commission, Seattle office. May I help you?"

"Bruno Kincaid's office, please."

"One moment, sir."

Pause.

"Kincaid."

"Bruno? Tucker Nelligan."

"Oh, hi, Tucker. How's Portland?"

"Fine. Seattle?"

"Getting cloudy. I think we've got a storm coming in. And this time of year, if we've got a storm . . ."

"Portland's due for one too. I know. I need a favor. Can you talk?"

"No. Can I call you back?"

"Yeah. I'm in the office. Do you have the number?"

"Yes. In about ten?"

"Fine. Thanks, man."

"You bet. Bye."

Click.

"Cascade Electro."

"Geoffrey Eriksen's office, please."

"One moment."

Pause.

"Mr. Erikson's office."

"Hello. I'm Tucker Nelligan, with the *Portland Post*. I would like to speak to Mr. Eriksen, please."

"I'm sorry, sir. Mr. Eriksen will be tied up most of today. If you'd like to leave your name and number, and the nature of your business, I'll see he gets the message."

"All right. Please tell him I'm calling in regard to Richard Llewelleyn—that's 'Llewelleyn' with four l's—and the Securities and Exchange Commission."

"I see. Um, can you hold for a moment, sir?"

"Certainly."

Longer pause.

"Hallo?"

"Hello, Mr. Eriks—"

"This is Eriksen."

"Hello, sir. Good of you to take the call. I'm with—"

"I know. What can I do for you?"

"Well, I'd like to speak to you, if I could, regarding Richard Llew—"

"Yes. I'm afraid I have no statement for the press. Did you say something about the SEC?"

"Yessir. I really would like to speak to you, about that, and about Detective Wiley. I spoke to him this morning."

"You spoke to Wiley? All right, Mr. Hannigan, I can squeeze you in late this afternoon. Five o'clock? No, wait. Five-fifteen. All right? Do you know where our building is?"

"Ah, five-fifteen is perfect, Mr. Eriksen. And no, I don't know where—"

"Go to Beaverton. Ask anybody. I'll see you then, Mr. Harrison. Good day."

Click.

"zamners fiss."

"Excuse me?"

"I said, 'Medical Examiner's Office.'"

"Oh. Good. Dr. Jonas Freemason's office, please."

"Okay. Hold on."

Click.

"Hello?"

"Hi, Dr. Freemason?"

"Hmm. Mumph."

"Pardon me?"

"Hode it. Hode on." *Pause.* "Okay, I'm back."

"Doc? This is Tucker Nelligan, *Post.*"

"Oh, hi, Nelligan."

"Hi. What was that all about?"

"It's about my lunch. I'm eating. What do you want?"

"I want to know what the official word is on that Llewelleyn murder, this morning."

Pause.

"Hello? Doc?"

"I'm here, Nelligan. We're not done on the prelim's yet. We'll let you know when everything's done."

"Did you run an autopsy on the guy?"

"'Course we did."

"No, I mean, did *you* run the autopsy?"

"Yeah. Look, I'm sort of busy right now, Nelligan."

"I know. Lunch really piles up on a guy. I just want to know the time of death."

"Sure. And we'll let the press know when we're done, okay?"

Shorter pause. "Doc, is everything all right?"

"What do you mean?"

"Forgive my abstract vein. I mean is everything kosher, regarding the Llewelleyn kill?"

"Well, not so's the corpse would notice. Everything's fine, Nelligan. I gotta go."

"Are you giving me a stonewall, Jonas?"

"No. Everything's fine. Really."

"Why don't I believe you?"

"Because you're an obnoxious snot."

"I mean besides that?"

"Good-bye, Nelligan."

Click.

"zamners fiss."

"Chief Medical Examiner, right away."

"Yessir."

Click.

"Lo."

"Jonas? We've got those fucking reporters upstairs. Did you release a statement on the Llewelleyn murder?"

"Hell, no. We got the word from homicide. Who is this?"

"Well, just checking."

"Nelligan? Is that you?"
Click.

"Nelligan."

"Switchboard. I've got a long-distance call for you. It's collect. You know we have a policy of not accepting collect calls, Mr. Nelligan."

"Switch it through, please."

"It's against policy."

"It's my mother, dammit! She's in the hospital!"

"Oh. Sorry. Here you go."
Pause.

"Tucker?"

"Hi, Bruno?"

"Yeah. I'm calling from a pay phone."

"Good. Look, we've got a homicide down here in Portland. Guy name of Llewelleyn. That's two *l*'s-e-w-e-two *l*'s-e-y-n. First name Richard. He's a financial consultant, with Broderick, Broderick, and Alphonsine. I hear you guys are investigating him. Can you confirm or deny?"

"Llewelleyn, Richard. Yeah, that sounds familiar. Don't know any details. I'll nose around and let you know."

"Listen, Bruno, I really appreciate this."

"No prob. I owe you. Hell, half the guys in the Washington State branch think that series you did on SEC bribery was the greatest thing to happen to us in a long time. Really cleaned house."

"And the other half?"

"Wanna kill you. I'll call you back today or tomorrow. I've got to run."

"Okay, Bruno. Thanks again."

"Tucker? No names, remember."

"No names. Right. Bye."
Click.

"Portland Police Department."

"Detective John Wiley, homicide, please."

"One second."
Pause.

"Hello?"

"Hi. Tucker Nelligan, *Post*."

"Yes. Mr. Nelligan. How are you?

"Fine, thanks. I'd like to ask you a few questions, regarding Richard Llewelleyn."

"I'm afraid we won't have an official statement ready for a few hours, Mr. Nelligan."

"Damn. Well, are you sure about the cause of death?"

"Yessir. Multiple knife wounds."

"Anything else unusual in the autopsy?"

"I haven't examined the ME's report yet, sir."

"Uh, right. Well, do you have any prime suspects?"

"No, sir."

"How about Geoffrey Eriksen?"

"Mr. Eriksen is cooperating with us at this time."

"And Henry Bishop?"

"Also cooperating with us."

"Did Llewelleyn have family in the area?"

"No, sir. He had a sister in Alberta, Canada. She's been notified."

"Is there anything you can tell me about the murder weapon?"

"No, sir. Not at this time."

"How about the scene of the crime?"

"No, sir. Not at this time."

"What's the capital of Paraguay?"

"Excuse me?"

"Just testing. Has your office put a hold on info coming from the ME's office?"

"Yessir, we have."

"Why?"

"Standard policy."

"No it's not."

"It is now."

"I see. Is there anything else you can tell me?"

"Asunción."

"Beg pardon?"

"The capital of Paraguay. Anything else, Mr. Nelligan?"

"No, Detective Wiley. You've been most helpful."

"I have? Oh. Good. Have a nice day, sir."

"You also, Sergeant."

"Thank you. Good-bye."

"Good-bye."

Click.

"Jackass cops."

THIRTEEN

❖

Harry pulled the Datsun into a parking slot facing the brick exterior of the Deco Penguin. According to his watch, he was only five minutes late, which was pretty good, considering his track record.

As he stepped out of the subcompact and swung his arms into his jacket, Harry's eyes strayed to a circle of chipped brick and mortar on the wall, five feet off the ground. It was the remnants of a shotgun blast that had been aimed at Harry and Tucker Nelligan, about a year earlier. It was the day he first met Tucker. Funny how you remember the good times.

Inside, the Penguin was relatively quiet. The lunch crowd had dwindled down to a few stragglers and Happy Hour wasn't for two more hours yet. The owner and barkeep, Dutch Rhodes, nodded once in Harry's direction, one corner of his mouth twitching. For Dutch, it was a warm greeting.

"Harry."

"Hullo, Dutch. No Scotch for me today. Where are they?"

The bartender, a cube-shaped black man with an eye patch and shiny, balding pate, nodded toward the back of the bar. "Put a couple tables together."

"Thank you, sirrah. Guinness, please."

Dutch produced a tall glass and a bottle of stout from a shelf beneath the bar. He kept a supply of the beer at room temperature for his sole British customer. Harry paid him and thanked him, and carried the Guinness, glass, and doctor's bag back into the well-lit interior of the Penguin.

"Hullo, class."

His eight students sat around two oval tables, half on wooden chairs, the other four in the red leather booth against the cool brick wall. A Marshall Rogers pen-and-ink of the Penguin—the Batman's nemesis, not the waterfowl—leered behind them.

Harry took a chair, set his blackstone bag on the hardwood floor, and produced a sloppy manila folder with papers and clipped newspaper articles spilling out. "Right. Welcome to Radical American Politics. How is everyone today?"

The students sat, shell-shocked. One young man giggled. Sandi Braithwaite, sitting opposite Harry, cleared her throat. "Uh, good afternoon, professor. Are you sure this is, you know, okay?"

"Is what okay, Ms. Braithwaite?"

"Our meeting in a bar. From the address you gave us, we figured it was some extra classroom at Portland State or Portland Community College."

"We're not meeting in a bar. Out there"—he waved toward the front of the building—"is a bar. Just yesterday our host, Mr. Rhodes, designated this alcove a public meeting hall. No alcohol is served back here." He sipped his beer. "We are *not* in a bar. Still, you're mostly seniors, so you know about our departmental quirks. I'd appreciate it if our illustrious department chairperson wasn't made aware of our location. Understood? Good. Would anyone like to order a cola or something to eat before we get started?"

While the students ordered their drinks and two large orders of onion rings—for which Dutch Rhodes was rightly famous—Harry set up Dutch's chalkboard on its tripod stand and beneath the word "Menu . . ." scribbled the class code and added *The Care and Feeding of Your Revolutionary.* "Radical American Politics, four-three-zero. By the bye, any sophomores?"

One hand went up tentatively. "Let me talk to you after class. You really should have Civil War to WWII and Federalism in the Twentieth Century before taking this class. Technically, they're not prereq's, but they are handy.

"Right. First things first. The name. Radical American Politics. Let's start at the end. What is, or are, politics?"

A young man raised his hand and drawled in a deep Louisiana accent, "The system for deciding what gets done by a govenment."

"Good. That'll work. Not only what gets done, but by whom and paid by whom. Paid. A very important word. I'm not an economic determinist, as those of you who've had me before know, but I do suggest that most things even vaguely political revolve around the question of who shall foot the bill. The cash nexus, if you will. All right, next: America. Definition?"

The class debated for five minutes about the use of "America" to define the United States only, a typically ethnocentric characteristic which always amused Harry. Two of Dutch's patrons, wearing orange sleeveless vests and baseball caps, edged their chairs around the corners and watched the debate, drinks in hand.

When the group reached a consensus on the colloquial use of "America," Harry cut in. "Radical: definitions?"

A tall girl with straight blond hair, purple running shorts, and a college sweatshirt raised her hand. "A radical is an extremely liberal person—someone outside the mainstream of, say, the Democratic Party, which is generally pretty leftist."

Harry beamed. "I have to take exception to your analysis of the Democrats. In 1986, Oregon's two Republican senators, Mark Hatfield and Bob Packwood, lost their committee chairs when their party became the minority, but they lost the chairmanships to two conservative Democrats. We'll get into party politics later in the term. Let's see, you are . . . ?"

The girl pronounced her name and Harry made a hashmark beside her entry on his class printout.

"Thank you. All right, do we, for the most part, agree with our young friend's definition, folks?" Harry's deep English accent was ideal for seminar classes. Kate Fairbain had once claimed Harry could reel off smutty limericks at a DAR meeting and get away with it, thanks to that voice.

There was a generally affirmative mumble from his students. "Good. Then riddle me this: why does the word 'radical' come from the Latin *radix*, meaning 'root'? According to most dictionaries, the primary definition is 'of or pertaining to the root' or fundamental. Hmm? Sandi, your arena is communications, what d'you think?"

Sandi slurped her Dr. Pepper and rubbed her eyes. She wore no makeup and her light brown hair had been crammed under a Buckaroo Banzai cap. As usual, she looked like an earthquake victim. "Ah . . . radical. Root. I don't know, that sound like diametrically opposite definitions to me. Unless . . ." Her voice trailed off and parallel vertical lines appeared between her eyebrows.

Harry moved on to others, who either had no answer or truly could not give a damn. "Well, it's something to think about," he said. "Especially since—"

"Unless a radical in the political sense is someone interested in changing the fundamental properties of a political system, and not just making Band-Aid type changes," Sandi blurted out.

Harry grinned. "Right. Right. Spot on, Sandi. That's a political radical. Someone who wants to change not only a specific aspect of the government, but the social processes by which that aspect is achieved. Generally, we think of a radical as making these changes to the left, or liberal, side. The opposite of a radical is—"

"A reactionary," someone contributed.

"Yes."

"Professor?" The blond student spoke up. "I'm an economics major. Is it true that you're pretty radical?"

The class snickered. Harry shrugged and finished the beer. "Ah, well, that's an interesting question. Am I a radical? Well, if I could be president for a week or so, we would lose the electoral college, political campaigns would be banned from the television upon pain of death, we'd reenter the World Court and stop the mindless militarism that has so dominated us in the eighties, the Pentagon budget would be cut in half the first day, then, in half again and half again and, ah, let's see now, anyone could rent Air Force One, for weddings and bar mitzvahs and that sort of thing. But am I a radical? Would I like to change the fundamentals of U.S. politics? Well, at the end of the term, I'll put that question on the final and let you answer it."

Harry knew his reputation as a fire-breathing anarchist and made no specific effort to dissuade the student. It was sort of nice being considered a Trotskyite or whatever rumors reached each new freshman class.

Harry went on with a quick overview of radicalism in the eighteenth century, focusing on the neophyte labor movement, and let the class go three minutes early. He stayed on for another twenty minutes and debated labor's stance with the two bar patrons, who bought him another Guinness.

Upon finishing the two-month-old *People* and last week's *Time*, Nelligan sighed, checked his watch again, and pondered whether to try the *Better Homes* or *Popular Mechanics*. He started thumbing through the latter when the receptionist behind the huge chrome-and-glass desk spoke. "Mr. Nelligan? Mr. Eriksen will see you now."

She led the way down a carpeted corridor to a massive door. Muzak whined softly from speakers in the ceiling. The walls were decorated in generic rural prints. In the middle of the hallway, in a lighted steel frame, was a diagram of a computer chip. According to the engraved plaque, the chip had revolutionized data processing, and had been developed by Cascade Electro. Nelligan thought it looked like an aerial photograph of Manhattan.

The receptionist opened the door at the end of the corridor. "Mr. Nelligan," she chanted formally. Nelligan half expected the queen's receiving line. What he saw instead was an office nearly the size of the *Post*'s newsroom. The carpeting here was thick and plush. A magnificent rubber tree dominated one corner, a combination mahogany bookshelf and entertainment center, with Bang and Oluf reel-to-reel, wide-screen TV, and a VCR, lined a wall to his left. Directly before him was a desk like a frigate, behind which sat a man in no way dominated by his elephantine furnishings.

"Mr. Eriksen?"

"*Ja.*" The man behind the desk set down a pen and removed reading glasses, but made no other effort at greeting.

"I'm Tucker Nelligan, *Post*." It took Nelligan almost a dozen strides to cross the office. He offered a hand across the great desk, and after a momentary pause, Eriksen accepted it with a quick, strong grasp.

"Hallo, Mr. Nelligan. Sit down." It was an order, and Nelligan chose to obey, sinking into a swivel chair cut in a futuristic design. Eriksen had clearly decided not to roll out the red carpet, so Nelligan took his cue from that and dug out his pen and pad. Fight formality with formality.

"I appreciate your speaking to me, sir. I have a few questions."

"I understand you spoke to my wife this morning. True?" The voice was commanding. It emanated from a face that had launched a thousand corporate decisions.

"Yes. Ms. Shoenborn-Eriksen was most helpful. I was wondering what you could tell me about Richard Llewelleyn?"

Eriksen steepled his fingers before his nose. "Not much. Nothing you don't already know. Richard was very good with financial matters, and he was a valuable trustee of John Jacob Astor."

"I see. Did he handle your finances?"

"The firm of Broderick, Broderick, and Alphonsine handle my personal finances, yes."

"But Llewelleyn actually did your books, I understand."

Eriksen shrugged, as if to say, *Believe what you will. I couldn't care less.*

"Well, can you tell me—"

A soft chime sounded. Eriksen touched a button on his state-of-the-art desk phone and the lush voice of his receptionist intoned, "Detective Kehough is here, sir."

"Show him in."

The two men sat silently, staring at each other, until the door behind Nelligan opened again and the receptionist announced the new arrival.

Nelligan turned in his chair and saw a big, blond man in a dark suit. He, too, tried to shake Eriksen's hand, and received the same lukewarm response as Nelligan. He turned to the reporter. "Kehough, homicide. And you are . . . ?"

"Nelligan, *Post.*"

With a curt nod, Kehough took the second, identical chair. His face was strong and chiseled, and his eyes were blue, so pale they were almost transparent. "Mr. Eriksen has been cooperating with us in this investigation, Nelligan. He told me of your interview, and I also needed to ask him a few questions, so I thought we'd kill two birds with one stone, as it were."

Nelligan smiled jovially. "That's logical enough. Except I don't want to run an interview with you here. I hope you understand."

"I'm sorry," Eriksen interjected. "I have only limited time, Mr. Nelligan. I can spare you ten or fifteen minutes right now, but probably not later. I should have told you the detective was coming by. It was inexcusable of me not to have my girl call you. If you'd like, we could simply forget the interview, and schedule it at a later date."

Eriksen flashed a quick smile at Nelligan. Detective Kehough did the same. Nelligan didn't understand what game was being played here, but he knew no subsequent interviews would be arranged. It was now or never, cop or no cop.

"Not at all, Mr. Eriksen. I don't mind working with the good detective here. I was going to ask you about the party last night."

"Ah, excuse me," Kehough broke in. "I'd really rather Mr. Eriksen not answer that question. We think that party is pretty important in the case. Best not to drag it through the newspapers. Sorry."

"I see. Well, how about your telling me about Llewel-leyn's movements after the party, Detective?"

Wide shoulders shrugged. "Again, Mr. Nelligan—sorry. Not till we know more ourselves."

"Mr. Nelligan," Eriksen broke in smoothly. "When you called, you said something about Richard and the Securities and Exchange Commission. Could you explain what you meant?"

The two men studied him intently. Nelligan grinned and put away the pen and pad. "Mr. Eriksen, I understood I was being granted an interview. Is that accurate?"

"Yes, but I asked you a simple question. Was Richard being investigated?"

"I don't know. Kehough here, would. Kehough?"

Kehough fiddled with the crease in his slacks. "No comment."

"I see." Nelligan nodded. "Well, that's fine. I've already interviewed others who were at your home last night. I was more or less just looking for confirmation from Mr. Eriksen."

"May I ask you who you've spoken to?" the detective asked.

"Yes. Detective Wiley, homicide. I'm surprised Wiley didn't tell you about our conversation."

He looked from one man to the other. Eriksen remained impassive, but Nelligan thought he caught a ghost of emotion on Kehough's handsome face.

"Mr. Eriksen, I really would like to talk to you about this, but I won't conduct an interview with the police present. May we talk privately, or shall we call it a wash?"

Eriksen sat quietly for a time, then nodded. Nelligan had gambled the direct approach would impress him. "Mr. Nelligan, I'm afraid I've been asked by Detective Kehough not to speak to the press, for the time being. I should have told you before you drove all the way out to the suburbs, but I was hoping perhaps you could tell me what you know regarding Richard and the SEC. As you say, Richard was handling my personal finances, as well as the finances of several friends. If he was acting incorrectly with our money, I have a right to know."

Nelligan swiveled to face the cop. "What say, Kehough? Can I talk to the man for a few minutes? I promise not to help him flee from justice, and I'll watch for cyanide suicide pills. What do you think?"

The big man was shaking his head before Nelligan had finished speaking. "This is a homicide investigation, Nelligan. We're playing it close to the vest. I hope you understand, but I'll tell you honestly, I won't lose any sleep if you don't. The word's come down from the top brass—no press."

Nelligan stood and buttoned his jacket. He reached across the desk, and this time Eriksen leaned forward, shaking his hand firmly. "Mr. Eriksen. Perhaps another time."

"Mr. Nelligan. Again, I apologize. Good luck on your story."

Nelligan smiled and sauntered out of the plush office. It wasn't until he was alone in the corridor that the look of utter incomprehension crossed his face.

FOURTEEN

✦

By six o'clock, a good-sized crowd had gathered for dinner or drinks at the Brasserie Montmartre. Harry wandered past the bar, searching the candle-lit faces clustered around tables. A smooth *a cappella* vocal trio was gliding through "Blue Champagne" when he saw Cordelia Applebaum wave.

Harry bent and kissed her cheek before sitting.

"Hello, Harry dear. How were the trenches?"

"Pretty fair, all things equal. I've got the makings of an exceptional seminar group this term. Really bright. Also a mix: at least two New Right Republicans and a kid who went to the Philippines in eighty-five to be a poll-watcher for Aquino. Nice cross section."

"That's lovely, dear. I always enjoyed seminars more than the larger classes." They chatted about Cordelia's years as a professor, and she ordered coho salmon and a Johannisberg Riesling for them both.

"It was lucky I got your note about dinner when I did," Harry said. "I left campus fairly early today. This is a pleasant surprise."

"Were you planning to eat alone?"

"I suppose so. Hadn't thought about it yet."

Cordelia sipped her wine and eyed him speculatively. "Harry, are you seeing anyone?"

"Romantically? No, not really. You?"

"Ha! I'm afraid I have little time for romance these days. And at my age, I probably don't have the strength for it, anyway."

Harry rested his hand atop her small, bony one. "Cordelia, you didn't ask me to dinner to find out about my love life. You're worried about divestment and the trustees and Llewelleyn, and you want to pump me for information. How do you plead?"

"Guilty, to all charges," she answered promptly. "You know about Richard's murder, I assume."

"Yes. Incredible thing to happen. I didn't know Llewelleyn all that well, of course."

Cordelia pursed her lips and spoke in a near-whisper, leaning across the table, her face bottom-lighted by the candle. "He wasn't a very good person, Harry. He had an almost mystical ability to make enemies. I must say, I'm hardly surprised someone did him in."

"I don't understand, Cordelia. How could a person so univerally disliked get on Astor's board of trustee? It's not like he's rich, is he? Nor an alumnus, nor even the senior partner of his financial management firm. How did he get on board the board?"

"Via Geoffrey Eriksen. Geoffrey nominated him about two years ago, and Sam Broderick seconded the nomination. I'd never heard of Llewelleyn before that. As you know, whatever Geoffrey wants, Geoffrey gets, and he managed to ram the nomination through."

"I know Llewelleyn worked for Broderick, but I gathered at yesterday's meeting Broderick didn't really like him."

"Oh, he doesn't. Or didn't. But everyone, myself included, has had to admit Richard is—or was—a financial sorcerer. His talent for making money was uncanny."

"If he's that good, why wasn't he the chair of the finance committee, rather than Irena Shoenborn-Eriksen?" Harry tried the fish, and smiled approvingly.

"Seniority, dear. Irena has been here longer. Moreover, Richard's forte was in taxes and investments. Irena is a champion fund-raiser. Richard, bless his soul, was a bit too rodentlike to effectively solicit endowments."

"Whereas Irena's class and looks—"

"And natural affinity to money."

"—make her ideal for raising funds. That makes sense, I suppose. I don't think Irena and Llewelleyn got along in the least."

"No, Harry. And last night's row was just one of many. Richard handled Geoffrey's personal finances, and I don't think Irena trusted him. One can hardly blame her."

"Then why didn't Eriksen change to another accountant? If his wife didn't trust Llewelleyn, I'm sure he could have found an alternative."

"Certainly, but as I said, Richard was very, very good. He did my accounting, you know."

Harry stopped in mid-sip of the white wine, studying Cordelia's warped image through the curved glass. "No. I didn't know that. Since when?"

"Oh, about a year ago. He's saved me a considerable amount, and he diversified my few, paltry holdings. I didn't like the man, but I'm forced to admit he was very good at his job."

"So it seems. Who else on the board used Llewelleyn, d'you know?"

"No idea, dear. I believe Sam Broderick—'Big Sam,' if you will—used Richard. And possibly Donal Patrick Cavenaugh, our illustrious once-artist."

They changed the topic and discussed college politics, but Harry's mind stayed on the incongruity of the ferretlike Llewelleyn as a financial genius. He simply didn't seem to fit the bill.

They both declined dessert, and Harry ordered two cognacs. He was playing with his cotton napkin, folding it into airplane shapes, when he finally mentioned the topic uppermost in his mind. "I was a bit surprised by Geraldo Avenceña vote-switch yesterday, weren't you?"

Cordelia's face darkened. "I don't know what to think of Geraldo, to be honest. I thought for sure he would vote for divestment with me. What did you make of all that last night?"

"I don't know, Cordelia. I was hoping you'd tell me."

"Well, I can't. I've never known Geraldo to flip-flop like that. He's usually so sure of himself, like many religious people. That's not to say he's preachy, dear. He isn't. But he's usually quite sure he's on the side of the angels. Literally."

"I know. I wonder if someone managed to convince him to change his vote."

"Probably. Either that or a voice from on high. Geoffrey may have called him, before the party. Or perhaps Richard. No, that's unlikely."

"Really? Why?"

"Just between us, Llewelleyn was genuinely disliked by everybody, but Geraldo probably stood at the head of the line. This last summer, Richard proposed a plan to shut down the chapel and break relations completely with the presbytery."

"But why? Astor and the church are only associated *de facto*, not *de jure*. The chapel doesn't affect federal funding any more. Why shut it down?"

"For a five-point-seven million dollar grant from the Catholic Church. Richard apparently had figured out some way to be the front-runner in a grant search, but said the college would have to break all ties to the Presbyterians first."

"My God. I had no idea."

"No? Well, we kept a fairly low profile on it all. To be honest, I think the board may vote to go along with it."

"You're joking!"

"I would never joke about five million dollars, Harry."

"And then Geraldo would be out of a job."

"Precisely." Cordelia sipped the cognac and studied him solemnly. "It's fortunate he's a man of the cloth, and completely above suspicion of murder, isn't it?"

Joann Dembrow read through the copy while it was still in the terminal, making almost no editorial changes. Nelligan's copy was often like that: crisp, concise, and punchy. Even his grammar and spelling were good. It annoyed her no end.

"Whacha think?" Nelligan sat on the edge of her desk and handed over a cup of Stash tea. Dembrow pushed her wavy hair off her brow and slowly raised her arms over her head, fists clenched. She could feel the muscles along her backbone protest to the stretch.

"Good stuff, Tuck. I just wish we could've gotten the official word from PPD. You're sure—I mean, absolutely sure—this Eriksen guy is a suspect?"

"Yes. There are two cops on the case. One, Wiley, mentioned Eriksen to me. The other, Kehough, was at Eriksen's office an hour ago. Kehough wouldn't let Eriksen answer any questions. Also, I was there this morning about three, before the ME's people and forensics arrived, and even then, the call went out to find Eriksen and bring him in for questioning. I talked to the prowl-car cops who picked him up, and they confirmed it."

"And the coroner's report?"

"Nothing yet. They're stonewalling, and I don't know why."

Joann rested her stocking feet on the desk and sipped the tea. "This is good copy. Who's your source in the SEC?"

"You're kidding, right?"

"Right. Can you assure me he or she is knowledgeable, and not just spouting off about Llewelleyn being investigated?"

Nelligan switched his view fron the VDT to his editor, his tired face stern. "If he or she wasn't knowledgeable, he or she wouldn't be in the story, Joann."

She sat up straight and rested a hand on his knee, squeezing. "I know, Tucker. I apologize. But you know I have to ask, because the brass upstairs will ask, and I have to have an answer. You understand that, don't you?"

"Yeah. Standard procedure. My sources are the best."

"Not good enough. You know the rules."

"My sources have always been good enough in the past."

Dembrow tapped the eraser end of her pencil against her teeth. "Okay. For now. You're sure I won't get my butt into any litigation on this?"

"Yes. Your shapely butt is safe." Nelligan rolled down his sleeves and began buttoning the cuffs. "I'm out of here. I'll keep hammering at the medical examiner till something cracks. I'm also going to take another stab at Sergeant Wiley. I got the impression he and Kehough aren't working together on this one. I wonder if there's a schism in the force regarding this case? How about you, what are you doing tonight?"

Joann watched him straighten his tie and slide into his jacket. She thought about getting a U-bake pizza from Papa Aldo's and going home to her cocker spaniel and spending the night alone watching a movie she had already seen twice on Showtime or maybe finally writing that letter she owed her father. She also thought about Tucker Nelligan and mentally kicked her own butt. "I've got a date. See you in the morning, hotshot."

"Night, boss." Nelligan squeezed her shoulder and headed for the elevator. Joann finished her tea and puttered around the office for a while, getting in the way of the night shift.

Harry's place was on a short side street that ended, one block later, in a cul-de-sac. There was usually very little traffic. His Datsun B210 fit in perfectly with the rest of the neighborhood's vehicles: two VW Bugs, a Pinto with mismatched right front fender, a dilapidated van with surfing decals, and Mrs. Abramowitz's shiny, 1962 Chrysler.

As Harry parallel-parked between the Bugs, he thought the classic Rolls-Royce looked as out of place as pâté de foie gras amid cheese puffs. A shadowy figure sat behind the wheel, unmoving. As Harry stepped out of his car, the gleaming driver's side door swung open and Geoffrey Eriksen climbed out. Before the door swung shut, Harry caught a glimpse of long blond hair in a mass of curls and white shoulders that belonged beyond any doubt to some woman, though not to Irena Shoenborn-Eriksen.

Eriksen strolled over, grinning broadly, and pumped Harry's hand. "Hallo, professor."

"Ah, hullo. What brings you to Sellwood? A bit out of your neighborhood, isn't it?"

"Yes, yes. I wanted to speak to you. Sorry I didn't set up an appointment. Do you mind?"

"Not at all. Please come inside."

Eriksen raised a hand, palm outward. "Thank you, no. I'm in rather in a rush. This will only take a moment."

"Very well." Harry rested the blackstone on the Datsun's hood and leaned back against the door. He could see Mrs. Abramowitz peek out between her curtains at the Rolls. A full spate of stars were out that night.

Geoffrey Eriksen was not a man suited for small talk. "I'm in real trouble, Henry. The police consider me a prime suspect in the murder of Richard Llewelleyn. I take it you know about that?"

"Yes. But why suspect you?"

"Please. You were there. You heard me threaten the man. As did many others."

"That was a domestic dispute; a man standing up for his wife. They can't possibly—"

Again the palm was raised in a halting motion. "They can and they do. I may be in very serious trouble, and I would like to ask for your help."

"My help? Certainly, but I don't know what I can do."

"I followed the situation very closely last year, when that student was murdered. I know you solved the crime, and I know the police were impressed with you. I have contacts in city government, you see."

"I'm not a detective, Geoffrey. I was very, very lucky that time."

"There is no such creature as luck. Trust me. I survived the war, I came to this country. I prospered. I know why some men succeed and some men fail, and I don't believe in luck. You have a sharp mind and an ability to perceive patterns that other men may miss. Now I'm asking you to help me."

"I'll do whatever I can, but I assure you, you've overestimated my skills. I'm an above-average teacher, an average thinker, and a way-below-average adventurer."

"You have your skills, I have mine. And mine is the ability to sense another's strengths and weaknesses. Henry, I want you to look around regarding this murder, find out what you can, and clear my name. I am innocent, Henry, and I can prove it."

"Wait a moment. If you can prove it—"

"I can, but I am unwilling to. I was with . . . someone . . . last night." He made a vague gesture toward the Rolls.

"Ah."

"Irena went to bed directly following her spat with Llewelleyn. I knew she would take a sleeping pill, she always does when upset. I have been . . ." He searched for a euphemism.

"Seeing?"

"Thank you, seeing a young woman for several months now. Last night, when everyone had left, I went to her apartment and stayed until about one-thirty or two. I arrived home about an hour before the call came from the police."

"I see." It was getting chilly, and Harry stuffed his fists into his pants pockets. "Geoffrey, forgive me, I understand this is a sensitive issue, but my advice to you is to tell Detective Wiley about your tryst. This is a murder investigation, after all, and if you can save the police from wasting time suspecting you, it could help them catch Llewelleyn's murderer."

"*Ja*, certainly, what you say is true." Eriksen brushed the suggestion aside. "But I will wait awhile before telling them this, yes? I am not yet their sole suspect, simply a prime suspect. And my relationship with this woman is supremely important to me. You are a man, you understand these things, eh?"

This was neither the time nor the place to question the man's sexism, so Harry merely nodded.

"Moreover, Henry, I shall strike a deal with you. I know how you stand on this divestment issue. Help me, and I promise to throw my support behind Mrs. Applebaum's committee. What do you say?"

"How about throwing your support behind Mrs. Applebaum herself? That committee is stacked against her, even without Llewelleyn, and you know it."

Eriksen studied him a moment, then grinned. "Yes. Of course it's stacked against her. Very well, I'll issue my support at the special meeting. We'll get together tomorrow or Thursday, to discuss Richard's death. Is it a deal?"

Harry rubbed his eyes. He desperately wanted to stay out of this mess, but couldn't for the life of him think of a polite way to say so. "Very well, Geoffrey. I'll ask around, see what I can see. I make no promises, and hope you're not disappointed if we find the detectives to be better detectives than I."

"Thank you, Henry." Eriksen again pumped his hand vigorously. "I owe you a debt. Remember, please, the young lady I mentioned is our secret. I've put more than forty years into this business. My primary client is the Pentagon, eh? They don't appreciate this sort of domestic situation getting into the newspapers."

"Of course."

"Good. I'll call you later, eh? Good night."

"'Night."

Harry stood in the glare of the streetlight and watched the big man climb back into the Rolls. Mrs. Abramowitz dropped her curtains and returned to the *PTL Club*. The Rolls pulled away silently, leaving him with his thoughts, which turned predictably to the warmth of his house and the bottle of Scotch in the kitchen.

"Hi, love!"

"Hmm," a voice hummed from the dining room. Tucker knew the sound well, and was sure he'd turn the corner to find Martin bent over a pile of briefs and legal-sized documents, half-glasses perched precariously on the edge of his nose, yellow highlighting pen stuck behind his ear.

Sure enough, Kady was there, pen in one hand, pocket calculator in the other. "How was court?"

"Good. I'm losing. How's your murder?"

"Great. I'm going to turn some of that roast into a sandwich, you want one?"

"Yes, please. What's happening?"

Nelligan went to the kitchen and started work on the sandwiches. "Well, I got booted out of a Better Home and Garden by a thug named—I kid you not—Davos. I caught the medical examiner on a cover-up. I got an informant in the SEC to confirm that our dead guy was playing fast and loose with his clients' funds. And I accused one of Portland's leading industrialists, on page one, mind you, of being a murder suspect. How about your day?"

"I bought into an office pool on the pennant races, and I made an appointment with Dr. Hazard to have our teeth cleaned. How do you spell 'fiduciary'?"

Nelligan walked back into the dining room and set down two sandwiches and two bottles of Smith and Reilly. He plopped down opposite Martin and dug into the beer and food, thumbing through the pile of mail. "I don't spell it. What's this?"

"What's what?"

"This." He held up a number ten envelope with his name and address typed in the center.

"I don't know," Martin replied. "It's to you."

"It's to me how? There's no postage."

The lawyer shrugged. "A real investigative journalist would open it and see what it says."

Nelligan set the envelope down on the table and ran the tips of his fingers over it.

"What are you doing?"

"Feeling for wires."

"Aren't we a tad melodramatic?"

"Laugh away, counselor. Remember, I covered the story on those letter bombs to that abortion clinic."

Feeling nothing out of the ordinary in the envelope, Nelligan ripped open one end. A single piece of paper fell out. It was a photocopy.

Kady peered at him over the half-glasses. "What is it?"

Nelligan read the single page over twice before answering. "It's the ME's report on Llewelleyn's murder." He took a deep drag from the bottle of beer.

"You okay, Tuck?"

He tossed the photocopy across the table. Martin only read a third of the way through before he stopped. "Oy vay."

"Yeah."

"That poor guy was *tortured*! Who'd do something like . . . something this *monstrous*?"

The telephone rang. The men looked at each other, as if the sound heralded the trump of doom. *Stupid*, Nelligan thought. *There's nothing melodramatic about a telephone.*

It rang twice more before he reached it. "Kady and Nelligan residence."

"Tucker? It's Harry."

"Harry! Hi. I'm glad you called."

"Tucker, when d'you have to be at work tomorrow?"

"No time, exactly. When I'm on assignment, my time is my own."

"Wonderful. May I come over? I know it's ungodly late, but I need to talk to you. About the murder of Richard Llewelleyn."

FIFTEEN

✤

It was nearing midnight when Martin pushed open the recessed doors to the study, pewter tray balanced on the tips of one hand's fingers.

"Here we are. Scotch, rocks for you." He handed Harry a square-cut glass with a healthy proportion of booze. "Vodka gimlet on ice for Clark Kent. How on earth you learned to drink those things, I'll never know."

"Thanks, Marty. I read about 'em in a Raymond Chandler novel. I forget which one."

"*The Long Goodbye*," Harry said, sipping his drink. "This is marvelous, Martin. Thanks."

"My pleasure. If you two will excuse me, I've got to be in court tomorrow. It's good seeing you, Harry. G'night, Tuck."

"'Night."

Kady slid the doors shut. Vivaldi played softly on the reel-to-reel. Over the years, Harry had grown accustomed to apartment dwelling, but the warm comfort of Nelligan and Kady's den made him nostalgic for a place he had owned in Chevy Chase, a thousand years earlier. "I love this room," he murmured, nestling into the wing chair.

"Me too." Nelligan swung his legs up across the couch and handed Harry the copy of the medical examiner's report. Harry read it through, stumbling over the medical terminology.

He took a healthy slug of whisky. "My."

"That's what Marty and I thought. Someone hand-delivered it here today."

"Did you see who?"

"No, but it'd have to be someone in the ME's office, or the cops. No one else would have access yet."

"Not even the district attorney's office?"

"Marty says no. When he was with the DA, they never received anything from the cops until an arrest had been made."

"Who knew you were on this story?"

"Lots of people. I spent most of today making a pain of myself."

Harry read the one-page report again and finished the drink. Nelligan refilled it from the decanter on the pewter tray. "Thank you. This stomach content is interesting, don't you think?"

"Stomach content? I'll tell you; I didn't really notice what the poor sap had had for dinner."

"Well, he was at the same banquet as I, which accounts for the mushrooms and the macadamia nuts. The Eriksens laid out a fine repast, which in any other setting would have been labeled 'munchies.'"

"So?"

"So, the report here says our Mr. Llewelleyn had a significant portion of caviar in his stomach. There wasn't any caviar at the party: I know, I adore the stuff, and I'd have noticed it."

Nelligan swirled his glass, watching the ice spin. "So he had some caviar. That could be important, if we can figure out where he got it."

"Well, we know where he *didn't* get it." Harry waved the ME's report. "According to this, he had been eating Russian sturgeon caviar, not cheap stuff. Probably beluga or Osetrova. He didn't get it at the 7-Eleven or Thriftway Store, and I somehow don't think he got it at his home. Llewelleyn didn't strike me as the kind with a cultured palate. This is the kind of thing people blessed with money might serve to him."

Nelligan made a zigzag pattern with his hand in midair. "Pretty thin, Harry. Could be something, I guess. Anyway, what'd you want to talk about?"

Harry frowned and tried to knead some of the tension away from his forehead with his long, thin fingers. "What I have to tell you is in strictest confidence. Regardless of the consequences."

"Done." It was not easy to become Tucker Nelligan's friend. The process involved bypassing an array of mental alarms to gain the young man's trust. However, once that trust was established, it was unshakable.

Harry rested his feet on a steamer trunk plastered with stickers from Marseilles, Copenhagen, and Lisbon. "I ran into Geoffrey Eriksen today, outside my place. It was just a little before I called you."

"Really? What did he want?"

"He says the police consider him a primary suspect, and he's innocent and has an alibi, which he can't disclose to the gendarmes, and would I be willing to help him, considering the wonderful job I did last year of catching David Wasserman's killer."

Nelligan grinned. "As I recall, it was a dramatic, last-second tackle by a brilliant young journalist that turned the trick."

"Hmm. Yes, I seem to remember something about that. Anyway, I told Mr. Eriksen I probably can't help him, but he insisted."

"And what is this wonder-alibi?"

"Herr Eriksen was with a Fräulein."

"Oh ho. I find that hard to believe."

Harry studied him over the rim of his glass. "Really? Why? Because Geoffrey's over fifty?"

"No, because I've seen his wife. She's a looker. Very sexy."

"True."

"In fact, I interviewed her this morning. You should have seen the English she put on her every motion."

Harry grinned. "Irena Shoenborn-Eriksen came on to you?"

"I forgot to wear my 'Kiss Me, I'm A Fruit' button today."

"Point well taken. Sorry. Anyway, I have no problem believing Geoffrey has a paramour. He's a bit of an old-world sexist. Probably thinks it's a sign of success to have one. The point is, until he absolutely has to, he doesn't want to go to the police with this bit of information. I told him he really ought to, and was rebuffed."

"So he wants you to look around?"

"Yes. Damned awkward, really. It's none of my business, and to be honest, I doubt Sergeant Wiley would appreciate my rooting around in this mess like a hog after truffles."

Nelligan frowned. "Wiley. How'd that go, this morning?"

"I'm not sure, really. Claims he was there to find out information regarding the party, but I wasn't able to add much to what he already knew. Seems like a nice enough sort."

"Yeah. Like interviewing Mr. Rogers. Did he mention a Detective Kehough, also on this case?"

"Kehough? No."

Nelligan replenished his drink and related the aborted interview at Cascade Electro, including the introduction of Detective Kehough. "That cop didn't want me anywhere near Eriksen. I tell you, I'll be surprised if they don't make an arrest tomorrow."

"Really? Eriksen?"

"Absolutely. Otherwise, Kehough wouldn't have shooed me off like that."

"Well then, we'd better get to work."

They talked for more than an hour and finally decided to split up and interview the members of the Astor board of trustees. It was Harry's opinion that the Monday-night party had been a catalyst of sorts. It was possible—maybe even probable—that the killer had been at the Eriksen estate. Or not. He or she could have been a transient, just off the train from Utah, looking for change, Nelligan pointed out.

"Granted," Harry conceded. "But if the murderer didn't know Llewelleyn, and this has simply been a case of very bad luck, then the police are best suited to discover the truth. If it has something to do with the board of trustees, then perhaps we do. I'll be honest: I don't believe for a moment any member of that board killed Llewelleyn."

"Yeah. Probably not. Still, you take the people closest to Astor, and I'll take the others."

"Fine. I'll also take Cordelia Applebaum. She's a friend."

"Applebaum? The old city council member?"

"Yes."

"Good friends, you two?"

"Yes. Why?"

"Conflict of interest, Harry. Better let me take her."

Harry smiled politely. "Thank you. No, Cordelia is a dear, dear friend, but I'm quite capable of being objective. All of which is academic, of course, because Cordelia is well into her seventies. I doubt she performed all that carnage on Llewelleyn." He motioned toward the ME's report.

They stopped talking and simply drank for a while. "You want some popcorn?" Nelligan asked at length.

"Yes, please."

Several hours later, having finished off one mixing bowl full of popcorn and an unspecified number of drinks, Nelligan was just finishing the tale of how he first met Kady. "So anyway, he won my case for me, the paper hired me back, and the rest is, as they say, history."

"You two are happy," Harry observed.

"Yep. He's a good man."

"Yes. He is."

"Tell me about the Mad Hatter, Harry."

A tired, lopsided smile appeared on Harry's otherwise saturnine face. Few people in Harry's life knew about his former occupation. When they had first met, Nelligan managed to dig up some information regarding a Henry Bishop who had been a member of the Central Intelligence Agency and liaison with the National Security Council for Presidents Kennedy and Johnson. Other than the code name, Mad Hatter, he had been able to find out precious little else.

"That was all a long time ago, Tuck. I really, truly do hate talking about all that."

"So tell." Nelligan propped his stocking feet up on the back of the couch and tossed the last half-decent popcorn kernel in an arc toward his mouth.

"Oh, nothing much to tell, really. I was a paper shuffler for the government."

"What was Kennedy like?"

Harry twirled his glass, listening to the ice clink. "Formal. A bit cold. A good man, really. I don't think he liked us much."

"'Us'?"

"The CIA. In some ways, like today, the agency worked outside the normal checks and balances inherent in the

American system. I think it bothered Kennedy that we were there. He treated us like a father with a loaded gun in the house, afraid one of the children would find it."

"What did you do?"

"Bit of this. Bit of that. I had a key to the executive men's room. We had one of the first, prototype Xerox photocopiers, but I jammed it first time out and they wouldn't let me use it after that. I was considered the Junior Birdman of the Council—far and away the youngest member."

"Why is your dossier still classified?"

"Is it?" Harry studied the condensation on the side of his glass.

"You know it is, Harry."

"Typical government paranoia. Tucker, please believe me. I wasn't a spy. Not in the cloak and dagger sense. I was a bureaucrat."

They were silent for a while. "Kennedy," Nelligan mumbled. "To have actually worked for him. Amazing."

"He was more or less what you've always heard. He was a politician. Lyndon Johnson, on the other hand, was the living definition of a riddle wrapped in an enigma."

"They say every American over a certain age remembers where they were the day Kennedy got shot," Nelligan mused. "I was in school. We were diagramming sentences. I hated it. I remember it like it was yesterday. Where were you, Harry?"

Harry finished his drink. "In a weekly debriefing."

"In Washington?"

"In a motorcade. In Dallas, Texas."

SIXTEEN

✤

It was nearing eleven on Wednesday morning when a bedraggled Harry Bishop, slumped in a window seat in Thadius' Pantry, finished a breakfast of Scotch eggs and a gallon of good, strong coffee. Sated, and with his mild hangover waning, Harry scribbled a list of things to do on a paper napkin. The list included interviews with Donal Patrick Cavenaugh, Cordelia Applebaum, and Geraldo Avenceña. Harry didn't know why he had failed to tell Tucker of his fears regarding Geraldo. Possibly because he, Harry, had yet to formulate the fear into anything concrete. Clearly, the chaplain was hiding something. Clearly, he lied about meeting Llewelleyn on the night of the murder. Equally clearly, he had motive, means, and opportunity to—

Harry folded the napkin over and ripped it in half. *I sound like Nick Charles*, he admonished himself mentally. Crazy. Geraldo Avenceña didn't kill Richard Llewelleyn. Not only was he a man of the cloth (which, in and of itself, was a powerful vote for Geraldo's innocence, in Harry's book), but he was also a calm, gentle, and philosophical fellow. A thinker, and a talker. Not a puncher. Especially not a stabber.

Stab. Harry ordered a last cup of coffee, feeling well and truly satisfied with himself. There was Geraldo's alibi, all right. Llewelleyn was stabbed. Reverend Geraldo Avenceña was six and a half feet of solid muscle. If Geraldo were driven to murder, he would simply fold a person in half, tie his or her torso in a granny knot, rip off his or her arms, and beat him or her senseless.

Fortunately for Harry's sudden good mood, the tiny voice in the back of his consciousness shouting "Quantum leap! Quantum leap!" was drowned out by the fading hangover.

———

At noon, the mortal remains of Tucker Nelligan slithered into the *Post* newsroom and poured itself into his chair.

"Tucker?" Joann Dembrow hurried over. "Are you alive?"

"Yah," Nelligan replied, and listened philosophically as the sound reverberated against his skull.

"You look like twenty pounds of guano in a ten-pound bag. What happened to you?"

"Joann. Please. Quietly."

"Ah-ha. Self-inflicted wound." She leaned over him, her hands kneading the muscles of his shoulders, bent her head low, and shouted, "HANGOVER, TUCKER?"

"Ghnaaaw," Nelligan replied.

"What's the matter, hotshot? This story too easy for you to handle with all your wits gathered? Need a handicap to make things interesting?" Dembrow sat in the chair by his desk, facing him. "Look, Tucker. This stinks. You want to drink? Fine. I had two glasses of wine last night. But if you *ever* waltz in here looking like this again, while you're on a story, I'll suspend you for a week. How in hell do you expect to function, looking like The Thing from Another Planet?"

"Shh." Nelligan put fingers to lips. "Softly."

"Damn it, Tucker! I'm serious!"

"The cops will arrest Eriksen today," he moaned.

"What?"

"The . . . cops . . . will—"

"I heard you. How do you know that?"

"I've got a contact who's helping Eriksen clear his name. This contact and I are working closely together."

"Is this a private investigator?"

"Sure," he lied smoothly.

Joann leaned back and ran a hand through her wavy hair. "I see. So you've got a direct link to the chief suspect."

"Yah."

"And can you get Eriksen to talk to you?"

"Probably not."

"How about the cops?"

"Yes."

"How?"

He dug into his jacket pocket and pulled out the ME's report. Dembrow read it through, wincing when she reached the description of the various wounds. "God."

"Yah."

"Who's your source?"

"Dunno. Doesn't matter. I'll go to the cops, tell 'em what we've got, and ask them to confirm or deny. I told you the two case officers—Wiley and Kehough—don't seem to be working together on this. I'll play 'em off each other, interview 'em separately, shake 'em up a bit, and see what happens."

Joann Dembrow had worked long and hard to overcome the sexism inherent in American journalism. She was a stick for hard work, long hours, and a certain level of propriety. It was the only way, in her opinion, to get the job done right.

It annoyed her no end to see Nelligan drag himself into the office, looking like the casting for *The Night of the Living Dead*, and announce major advancements in his story. "This is good work," she said through clenched teeth. "Keep at it."

"Ghaah."

"Hullo? Yes, I need to get a cost estimate . . . Yes, that's right . . . Carpeting, wall-to-wall. Yes, thank you, please tell me how much it would cost to clean the carpets in a townhouse apartment . . . What? Let's see, two bedrooms, largish living room, rather long entry hall . . . Mud . . . I said mud; large circles of muddy potting soil . . . That's rather a long story, actually . . . Yes. How much . . . Good Lord . . . Perhaps I've been unclear: I don't want you to knit her a new rug, I need the old one cleaned . . . I see . . . Yes, well, perhaps I'll call around a bit first . . . Thank you for your time."

Harry hung up the phone and rested his head on his arms. He moaned softly. Visions of large, brown ovals cemented into Kate Fairbain's carpet danced before his eyes. The nap of the rug had been frozen in waves and eddies of solidified soil. Beneath the plants that rested on windowsills, Kate's eggshell-white walls were plastered with the stuff. The only good news in his visit to her apartment was that the plants all looked relatively healthy. At least he hadn't damaged them. Harry tried to figure out why plants would reject water.

Well behind schedule already, Harry had moved the still-dripping plant out onto Kate's second-story balcony and tried in vain to clean the rugs with wet facecloths from her bathroom. Failing that, he wiped off the walls as best he could. His effort had been ineffectual, to say the least. He started to bring the plants back inside, but remembered the radio announcer saying the low temperature that night would only be in the low fifties. As far as the eye could see in Portland were plants that seemed not to mind a wee bit of chill. He left the plants on the balcony and locked up.

Now, a quick rapping on his office door brought him out of a reverie. "Come."

Sandi Braithwaite opened the door, smiling shyly. "Hi, professor! Um, can I talk to you for a sec?"

Harry sat up and swept a dozen textbooks aside. "Of course. Sit. Sit."

Trying not to stare at the Mr. Potato Head on his desk, Sandi set down her book bag and sank into the chair. "I'm doing the story on Richard Llewelleyn. I guess you've heard he got killed."

"Yes."

"Well, I wondered if you can tell me anything about last Monday's board meeting."

"Unfortunately, no, Sandi. But you knew that already, didn't you?"

"Sir?"

Harry smiled and rubbed his eyes. "Sandi, I know for a fact that you're well versed on journalism law, and Oregon's Open Meeting rules. The board meeting was executive session, and I'm not at liberty to tell you anything that happened therein. Correct?"

She grinned and shrugged. "Yeah. I know. But I'm hitting a dead end otherwise! I've talked to the police, and President Eckersley—"

"My condolences."

Introducing the first and only complete hardcover collection of Agatha Christie's mysteries

Now you can enjoy the
greatest mysteries ever written
in a magnificent
Home Library Edition.

Discover Agatha Christie's world of mystery, adventure and intrigue

Agatha Christie's timeless tales of mystery and suspense offer something for every reader—mystery fan or not—young and old alike. And now, you can build a complete hardcover library of her world-famous mysteries by subscribing to The Agatha Christie Mystery Collection.

This exciting Collection is your passport to a world where mystery reigns supreme. Volume after volume, you and your family will enjoy mystery reading at its very best.

You'll meet Agatha Christie's world-famous detectives like Hercule Poirot, Jane Marple, and the likeable Tommy and Tuppence Beresford.

In your readings, you'll visit Egypt, Paris, England and other exciting destinations where murder is always on the itinerary. And wherever you travel, you'll become deeply involved in some of the most ingenious and diabolical plots ever invented ... "cliff-hangers" that only Dame Agatha could create!

It all adds up to mystery reading that's so good ... it's almost criminal. And it's yours every month with The Agatha Christie Mystery Collection.

Solve the greatest mysteries of all time. The Collection contains all of Agatha Christie's classic works including *Murder on the Orient Express, Death on the Nile, And Then There Were None, The ABC Murders* and her ever-popular whodunit, *The Murder of Roger Ackroyd.*

Each handsome hardcover volume is Smythe sewn and printed on high quality acid-free paper so it can withstand even the most murderous treatment. Bound in Sussex-blue simulated leather with gold titling, The Agatha Christie Mystery Collection will make a tasteful addition to your living room, or den.

Ride the Orient Express for 10 days without obligation.
To introduce you to the Collection, we're inviting you to examine the classic mystery, *Murder on the Orient Express*, without risk or obligation. If you're not completely satisfied, just return it within 10 days and owe nothing.

However, if you're like the millions of other readers who love Agatha Christie's thrilling tales of mystery and suspense keep *Murder on the Orient Express* and pay just $9.95 plus postage and handling.

You will then automatically receive future volumes once a month as they are published on a fully returnable, 10-day free-examination basis. No minimum purchase is required and you may cancel your subscription at any time.

This unique collection is not sold in stores. It's available only through this special offer. So don't miss out, begin your subscription now. Just mail this card today.

☐ Yes! Please send me *Murder on the Orient Express* for a 10-day free-examination and enter my subscription to <u>The Agatha Christie Mystery Collection</u>. If I keep *Murder on the Orient Express*, I will pay just $9.95 plus postage and handling and receive one additional volume each month on a fully returnable 10-day free-examination basis. There is no minimum number of volumes to buy, and I may cancel my subscription at any time.   70110

Name_____

Address_____

City_____ State_____ Zip_____

QA 1
Send No Money...
But Act Today!

BUSINESS REPLY MAIL

FIRST CLASS   PERMIT NO. 2154   HICKSVILLE, N.Y.

Postage will be paid by addressee:

The Agatha Christie
Mystery Collection
Bantam Books
P.O. Box 956
Hicksville, N.Y. 11802

Sandi giggled. "Right. I'm going to be a week deciphering the notes I took in *that* interview! Anyway, I don't really have anything. Everyone on the board says I ought to talk to Geoffrey Eriksen, because he's the board chairperson, but he won't answer my phone calls. I just wondered if you have any suggestions on where I should go from here."

Her voice was pleading, and Harry thought he detected real anxiety in her eyes. "This is really bothering you, isn't it, Sandi?"

"Yes."

"But why? You always run into a brick wall when interviewing the board. They've been like that since before recorded history." He studied the intensity written on her round face. "Oh. I see. You read Tucker Nelligan's account in the *Post*."

She glowered. "Yeah, I saw it. Professor, his story is great! He's got all kinds of inside information. How does he do it?"

"Well, he doesn't take three classes a day, and he isn't preparing for a senior thesis. Beyond that, he's got about ten years' experience that you have yet to acquire. Oh, you *will*, eventually. I've no doubt of that. As for this specific story, all I can tell you is to keep digging. Dean Connar was there, you know. So was Reverend Avenceña."

"Okay, I'll try them next. Thanks."

"Nothing at all. Good luck."

Sandi was up and half out the door when she turned. "Oh, yeah. Um, this may be none of my business, but . . ."

"Something?"

"Well, yes sir. I mean, I don't want you to think I've been snooping, but . . . well . . ."

"Sandi, it's conceivable that whatever you have to say will seem like you've been snooping. If so, you're a journalist. If I didn't think you'd been snooping, I wouldn't think you were very good at your job."

"Well, it's just that the Werewolf said there was some guy down in Archives asking about you."

She didn't have to explain who she meant. The Werewolf had been registered as a major in almost half of the departments on campus at one time or another, and nearly everyone had had him in class. Harry felt a vague sense of dread. "What sort of guy?"

"The Wolf didn't recognize him as a local. Said the guy was an alum. He wanted to see your file, and since that's public information, Wolfie gave it to him. I don't want you to be mad at him, you see—"

"That's all right, Sandi. I understand the rules."

"Something else. This guy laid a twenty on the Wolf, as a bribe to not mention it to anyone!"

"Twenty dollars, eh? Isn't that odd." Harry tried to remember how one looked when one was relaxed and unconcerned.

"Yeah. Well, anyway, thanks for the help on the story."

"Thank you, Sandi."

"No problem, professor. Bye."

Before the door closed, he called her back in. "Oh, Sandi?"

"Yes, sir?"

"Call me Harry."

SEVENTEEN

✠

Big Sam Broderick crushed Nelligan's hand in his own. "Howdy," he bellowed.

Howdy?

"Tucker Nelligan, *Post*. I wondered if I could ask you a few questions regarding Richard Llewelleyn."

The big man had fat in places a normal human can't have fat. His eyelids looked puffy with fat, his ear lobes were fat. Even the checks in his tie were fat. He wore a chocolate-colored polyester suit with cream topstitching. He probably thought he was one of the Ewing Brothers, Nelligan thought. Or maybe both of them.

Nelligan shook the soft, sweaty hand and was ushered into the plush office of the senior partner of Broderick, Broderick, and Alphonsine. At least, Nelligan assumed this was the senior partner. "Which are you? Broderick or Broderick?"

"Sit, son." Broderick waved majestically to the chair opposite his mahogany desk. "I'm Broderick the first. Broderick the second is my firstborn, who was s'posed to join the firm and take care of me in my declinin' years. Kids often have other notions 'bout these thing. Alphonsine, in case you were wonderin', was my idiot partner who upped and had a stroke, about sixteen years ago. Never liked him. Liked the name, though. Looks good on the signs."

Nelligan looked around the office. One long wall was covered by a huge bas-relief map of the United States, with the Rockies bulging almost six inches from the paneled wall. An American flag rose behind the massive desk, flanked by the Oregon flag. For the second time in as many days, Nelligan sat in an office that deserved its own ZIP code.

"Broderick, Broderick, and Alphonsine is doing well for itself," he observed.

The fat man grinned in delight, showing a mouthful of uneven teeth, and waved stubby pink fingers as if prestidigitating. "Yes, we are. Yes, indeed! Times are good for accountants, Mr. Nelligan. Nobody—and I mean *nobody*—understands the new tax codes. They're five inches thick, pure and unadulterated horseshit." Broderick shook his head gravely.

"Yes, Mr. Broderick. I'm sure that's true. First, let me say I'm sorry about your junior partner, Mr. Llewelleyn."

"A tragedy. Truly. Richard was one hell of a financial counselor, Mr. Nelligan. A wizard with the almighty dollar, and you may quote me on that. We'll miss his revenue-generating abilities."

So much for grief. "Were you and Llewelleyn ... friends?"

"No."

"No?"

"No, sir. To be honest, Richard could be a mighty pain in the ass. He was annoying, and uncouth, and tended to talk whether or not he had anything to say. Personally, I couldn't stand being around the man for more than a few minutes at a time. Drink?"

"I—what?"

"Do you want a drink?"

The shockingly honest confession had actually managed to drive Nelligan's hangover into the background, but as his eyes followed the grand gesture toward the dry bar in the far corner, his stomach vibrated like a tuning fork. "Thanks, no. Ah ... Let's see ... you didn't like Llewelleyn?"

"Didn't I just say that?"

"Yes, sir, you did. But I've been covering homicides for quite a few years, and I've never heard anyone speak ill of the murdered. I mean, not to a reporter."

Big Sam pondered the thought for a moment, tugging on his thick rubbery lower lip. "Seems contrary to speak kindly of a guy just because he's dead. I didn't like Richard when he was alive, and I doubt his being dead's made him any easier to take."

"I see. Tell me, do you have a theory as to who killed him?"

"Yes."

"Who?"

"Somebody who's not on the board of directors of John Jacob Astor College, and who's not an administrator or faculty or in any way connected with the college." There was no doubt in Broderick's moon face, no hesitation in his drawling voice. He nodded once, for emphasis.

"Okay. Why do you think that?"

"'Cause I know those people, Mr. Nelligan. I've been a trustee at Astor for nearly fifteen years. I know the police think this murder had something to do with the board banquet we held at Geoffrey Eriksen's place, Monday night. Bull."

"Bull?"

"As in shit, boy. What if Richard stopped at a Union 76 station to get a fill-up? Would they assume the pump-jockey bumped him off? He could've stopped at Corno's for a pound of corned beef. Would they then arrest the stock boys? Sure, we had a party at Geoffrey's and Richard was there. Nobody from Astor killed him."

"If not, then who?"

"I've no idea. A junkie, a transient, an Iranian terrorist. An ex-girlfriend, a former wife."

"Had Llewelleyn been married?"

"Once. They got divorced six, seven years ago. Canadian girl, I forgot her name. Diane or Debbie or Denise. Della? Something like that."

"Do you know if he was seeing anybody currently?"

"I don't know anythin' about that," Broderick replied stolidly.

About what? "So, you wouldn't know if he was romantically involved with anyone?"

Thick fingers dug into Broderick's suitcoat pocket and pulled out a yellow bag of M & M's. He shoved the bag across the desk to Nelligan, who shook his head (chocolate being second behind liquor on his list of things to avoid that morning). Broderick popped a handful of the candies into his mouth and began chewing noisily. He neither confirmed nor denied.

"So the police suspect someone from Astor, huh?" Nelligan forged ahead.

"I'd say so, yes. They've been here already. I'm betting they've talked to a couple of the others. Geoffrey Eriksen and his wife, Irena, probably."

"Why them?"

"Party was at their home."

"Would you know which officer is handling the case?"

"Couple of them. Little black guy and tall white guy. Kehough—like the savings account—is the white guy, and . . ."

"Wiley?"

"That's him. He's colored."

Nelligan mentally crossed out one theory. The two homicide cops were working together after all. Still, that didn't mean it was a marriage made in heaven. He might still be able to shake them with the information garnered from his secret source in the ME's office.

"Well, that's about all, Mr. Broderick. You've been a big help. Tell me, I don't understand how a junior partner like Mr. Llewelleyn got to be a trustee at Astor. He wasn't even a graduate of the college. It seems a bit unusual, to be honest."

Even Big Sam's smile was fat. Now he pasted it on unskimpingly and hoisted himself out of his chair. "We're a pretty liberal bunch at Astor. Didn't hold it against Richard, just because his name isn't on the outside of the building. Besides, he worked hard and did a good job."

The big man came around the desk and hoisted himself up on the edge. The smile faded. "I tell you honestly, Mr. Nelligan, no one ought to mess with John Jacob Astor College."

"I don't understand. Is someone 'messing' with the college?"

"I mean you, of course. I don't generally like reporters, being carrion eaters, as you are. But I tell you, boy, I like reporters even less when they try and dig up dirt on my school. I love that college. I love the folks I work with."

"And if one of them is a murderer?"

Broderick laid a massive hand heavily on Nelligan's shoulder, their faces uncomfortably close. "Then *we'll* take care of him, Mr. Nelligan."

The secretary of Alumni Affairs looked over the tops of her half-glasses at Harry. "Nemo, did you say?"

Harry glanced again at the note made while talking to the Werewolf. "Yes. Nemo."

"Like the actor with those ears in *Lost in Space*?"

"*Star Trek,* and no: Nemo, like 'Little Nemo in Slumberland' or Jules Verne."

"And what year did he graduate, professor?"

"Jules Verne?"

"No, Nemo."

"Sixty-three."

"I'm sorry to break the news to you, professor, but according to our files, Thomas Nemo died nearly twenty years ago in Vietnam."

"I see."

"You want to see his file? I'll get permission from—"

"No, no. Thank you, though. Has anyone else requested Mr. Nemo's file recently?"

"N-no, I'm pretty sure not. It would have to be done through here, and we're not computerized yet, so these files have to be pulled by hand. I'm sure I'd remember that name."

"I see. Well, thank you."

Harry forced a smile and left the Alumni Affairs office. According to the Werewolf, an alumnus named Thomas Nemo, JJAC class of sixty-three, had pulled Harry's history from Archives. Yet Mr. Nemo had died close to two decades earlier. Harry put a Herculean effort into his inductive reasoning and decided the fellow in Archives probably wasn't Thomas Nemo at all.

So who was he?

Head down, hands stuffed into his pockets, Harry hurried uphill toward his office. Someone on campus was asking about Harry and doing so under an assumed identity. Yesterday morning, Tuesday, Harry had walked into the chapel kitchen and noticed dishes drying by the sink. Later, Geraldo Avenceña said he hadn't arrived on campus until much later in the day.

Harry changed tack and headed downhill, toward the chapel. His arthritic knee pulled sharply and he looked up, shocked to see a shroud of high, thin white clouds over the city. Where did they come from? It was still unseasonably warm, but the humidity was definitely on the rise. A storm was imminent, Harry decided. Good. What this city needs is a little less sunshine.

In the chapel, Harry found the college chorale practicing something he thought might be Berlioz. Geraldo was not in his office, and it took Harry nearly ten minutes to find one of the senior religious studies majors, who cheerfully informed him the chaplain wouldn't be back for an hour or so.

"Well, is he still on campus?" Harry asked.

"Yes, sir. He's at that special meeting."

"Meeting?"

"Yeah, some subcommittee for the board of trustees. I guess they called a special meeting regarding divestment from companies doing business with South Africa, 'cause one of the trustees got murdered. The meeting was supposed to start . . . oh, about fifteen minutes ago."

The birds were deeply unhappy to see Nelligan. As soon as he entered the foyer of the mammoth Queen Anne home in the Goose Hollow district, the entire ensemble of parakeets and cockatoos started in with a deafening cacophony. Some chirped, others hooted like owls. Gaudy tropical birds in blue and green attempted to fly through the bars of their cages and feathers flew. One large emerald-green parrot started chanting "We're Jehovah's Witnesses . . . We're Jehovah's Witnesses . . ." and cocked its head to stare with a frigid eye at the interloper.

"You must be Mr. Nelligan," said one of the two rather monumental women who greeted him. "I'm Mrs. Fenscher."

"And I'm Mrs. Feingarten," said the other woman. Individually, each woman outweighed Nelligan by perhaps a hundred pounds. Together, they looked rather like the Steelers' front line, he thought.

"Pleased to meet you." He smiled charmingly and decided he could tell them apart by their brooches: a massive cameo for one and ruby-studded oval for the other. "I hope you don't mind if I ask you a few questions regarding Richard Llewelleyn."

"Oh, of course not," said ruby-encrusted brooch.

"We're only too happy to help," affirmed cameo.

They ushered him into a large "best room," with open-beam ceiling, a huge braided rug in the center, and the most astounding collection of knickknacks, doodads, trifles, ornaments, miscellany, plaques, puffery, trinkets, trifles, baubles, gimcrack, gewgaws, bric-a-brac, bagatelles, bibelots, and nonsense he had ever observed. Every corner and open space in the room was cluttered with icons of memories-gone-by. The caged birds continued their ululation, as Mmes. Feingarten and Fenscher implored him to sit on the humpbacked couch with ball and claw feet. The women took identical chairs opposite the coffee table, which was laid out with a silver serving set.

"Would you like some coffee or tea?" asked the woman with the cameo.

"Thank you, tea, please," Nelligan said.

"It's all been quite terrible," stated rubies, pouring tea into a brittle bone-china cup. "Lemon?"

"No, thank you. How long had you known Llewelleyn?"

"Two years?" asked rubies.

"No, dear, closer to three, I believe," replied cameo.

"Are you positive? I could have sworn it's been only two."

"Well, of course I could be wrong, but I believe he joined the board during summer term, and that would be the same year your uncle Edmond passed away, wouldn't it?"

"Would it?"

"I believe so, dear."

"I think you may be right. Which would make it two years."

"Yes." Cameo turned to Nelligan. "Two years."

Nelligan sat throughout the exchange, pen poised above his pad. It had taken nearly a minute to get that answer. At this rate, the interview could take a week and a half.

"I see. How long have you two been with Astor?"

"Oh, forever!" cried rubies.

"Perhaps longer!" added cameo.

"I first joined in 1962, during winter term."

"Wasn't it 1961, dear?"

"Oh, I'm sure it was sixty-two. Wasn't it?"

"Well, I joined six months later, and I thought I joined in sixty-two, which would mean you joined in sixty-one, though of course I could be wrong about that."

"Well, ladies, that's all right, an approximation will—"

"I believe you're right, Olivia."

"Well, I've certainly been wrong before."

"Not this time, I believe. Mind the time you suggested the Lewis and Clark expedition ended up in Cannon Beach, rather than Seaside? You *have* been wrong before, but not this time, I think."

They turned as one to Nelligan and said, in unison, "Nineteen sixty-two."

Below *two years* Nelligan wrote *1962*. Courageously, he plowed forward. "I understand Mr. Llewelleyn was something of a financial genius."

"Oh, yes!" cried one of the women. "Would you like a cake?"

"No, thanks. Was he on the finance committee?"

"Yes, I believe so. Wasn't he, dear?"

"I believe so, as well. Of course, but that's dear Irena's committee, and not ours, so we would be remiss in speaking for her committee."

"Now, Helen, Mr. Nelligan didn't ask us to speak *for* the committee, but simply to comment on whether or not Richard was a member. Personally, I don't think we would be stepping out of propriety to answer that question."

"Of course, you're right, dear. Yes, indeed. Mr. Nelligan, Richard *was* a member of that committee."

Nelligan finally made a third note in the pad.

"And he was good with financial matters?"

"Oh, extremely!"

"Yes, indeed. Why, since he joined the board, our endowment campaign has increased significantly. Wouldn't you say significantly, Olivia?"

"Yes, that seems a fine term for it. Significantly."

"Er, how much is 'significantly'?" Nelligan asked.

"What would you estimate, dear?"

"Hard to say. As I say, it's not really our committee. We're on Activities and Graduation, as well as Physical Plant."

"Yes, that's our forte: activities. We love it so."

"But if pressed, I'd say the endowment increased by, oh, somewhere in the neighborhood of twelve million dollars."

Nelligan spilled tea on his lap and dropped the pad.

"Oh, dear, let me get a cloth for that," cried rubies.

"Oh, certainly that was my fault. Mother told me a thousand times not to discuss finances over tea!" admonished cameo.

"Twelve million?"

"Yes, Mr. Nelligan. I'd say that's a fair estimation, wouldn't you, dear?"

"Oh, yes, twelve sounds about right. Of course, to be honest, I thought it was closer to eleven and a half. Still, I never did have a sense for numbers."

"Tosh! You've a perfect sense for fractions and numerators and denominators and all that. I'm afraid I simply never grasped mathematics. How about you, Mr. Nelligan? Being a journalist, do you find much use for math?"

"Ah, well, sometimes. But—"

"Oh, dear." Cameo seemed most distressed. "I'm afraid Helen and I had a theory that mathematics simply are not practical for most Americans, and needn't be taught. But I've asked our lawyer, and the fellow who takes care of the Cadillac for us, and several people at Astor, and they all seem to use mathematics."

"Though not geometry and algebra, I still maintain," rubies assured him. "No, I don't believe those skills are used by anyone. Yet still we teach them to every student. Meanwhile, the roads are filled with drivers who don't understand the least thing about handling a car. Isn't that so, dear?"

"Beyond a doubt. *That's* a skill Astor should teach every student. When was the last time you saw someone properly use his or her turn indicator, Mr. Nelligan?"

"Indicator . . . ?"

"There, you see? I knew he would agree."

"Yes, journalists are so in tune with the ills of society."

"Llewelleyn increased the college endowment by something like twelve million dollars?" Nelligan struggled to retain the thread of his interview.

"Yes, though of course not single-handedly. Dear Irena is awfully good with fund-raisers, as well."

"Yes, certainly."

"Well, ladies, what is the endowment at now?"

"What would you say, dear?"

"Nearly twenty million, I would estimate, but of course—"

"That's not your committee," Nelligan finished. "How much of that increase would you accredit to Llewelleyn specifically?"

"Oh, I'm sure we couldn't say, Mr. Nelligan. Could we, dear?"

"No, certainly not. If I were you, I would ask Irena Shoenborn-Eriksen or Cordelia Applebaum."

"Now dear, Mr. Nelligan may be young, but we would be wrong to tell him how to do his job. He seems awfully competent."

"Er, thank you. Why would you recommend I speak to Ms. Shoenborn-Eriksen or Mrs. Applebaum?"

"Why, because Richard handled their private finances, as well," replied rubies.

"Yes, and I believe he helped them significantly," added cameo.

"Yes. Significantly."

Nelligan made note of that. Applebaum was on Harry's list of interviewees, but the reporter had hoped to get to Shoenborn-Eriksen later that day.

"Are you sure you wouldn't like a cake, Mr. Nelligan?" rubies asked again.

"Yes, thank you."

"Perhaps something else? Some caviar?" Cameo offered.

"Oh, yes!" Rubies nodded. "We do have some of that left, don't we. Terrible of us not to get it out. You should try it, young man. Wonderful, really. It's Russian, you know. That's the best kind."

EIGHTEEN

✤

Harry grabbed a cup of coffee with a lid and a Milky Way bar from the Douglas Fir Room, then checked with the work-study student behind the information desk in the Student Union Building, who stifled a yawn and informed him that Conference Room C had been reserved for the board of trustees' ad hoc committee on South African investments.

Harry hurried down the corridor and put his ear against the door to Room C. He heard muffled voices, and pushed the door open as quietly as possible. Inside, the room was furnished with a rectangular table with false wooden top, surrounded by chairs, and not much else. Irena Shoenborn-Eriksen sat at one end of the table, reading from a sheaf of perforated pin-feed papers. Cordelia Applebaum sat at the other end, her back to Harry. The only other board member present was also the newest: Elliot O'Malley, who smiled shyly at Harry and nodded.

Harry slid the door shut, and sat in one of three vacant chairs on one side of the long table. He sipped his coffee for ten minutes, while Shoenborn-Eriksen briskly read off a list of those companies currently doing business in South Africa.

"So you see," the finance committee chairperson concluded tersely, "there's really no way Astor can afford to divest at this time. Our stock portfolio is only now getting any sort of decent stature. These companies I've listed"—

she tapped the stack of reports with a bloodred manicured fingernail—"make up the bulk of public stock we own. We're talking about a quantum shift in our investment pol icies, if we were to divest, and that just simply isn't practical."

Irena Shoenborn-Eriksen tapped the reports once again and poured water from the plastic carafe that stood at her elbow. Cordelia, the chair of the ad hoc committee, nodded sagely and jotted notes with an old-fashioned, mono-grammed pen that required filling with ink. "Thank you, Irena," she said, removing her wire-rimmed glasses. "Hello, Harry. We're pleased to see you. What brings you around?"

"Ah, well, I thought perhaps, with Richard Llewelleyn's unfortunate situation, your committee might need an extra hand," he lied. "Since this is my free class day, I thought I might pop by."

"Well, we're always glad to get faculty input, and we are shorthanded. As you can see, Geraldo wasn't able to make it today."

Harry had, in fact, noticed the chaplain's absence.

"Very well," continued Cordelia, "I suppose the chair-person is expected to ask for comments after such a report. Elliot, since it's just the three of us, do you have anything to add?"

O'Malley sat up and cleared his throat. His face turned pink. "No," he said softly. O'Malley was unable to look at both women simultaneously, but turned his head to smile timorously at each. "No, nothing to add, except it sounded as if you, Ms. Shoenborn-Eriksen—"

"Irena."

"Thank you. Irena, it sounded as if you did a thorough job. Still, um, I think I should say, I'm . . . unconvinced the college's economic status is so dire. I think perhaps I'd like . . . well, I'd sort of like to take a look at those reports, if you don't mind, Irena. I mean, if it's not inconvenient."

Harry and Cordelia exchanged knowing glances. O'Malley was stepping on Shoenborn-Eriksen's turf, and he was clearly unhappy about doing it. Irena was equally un-happy. She nodded brusquely. "Well, if you want to. How-ever, we are on a tight schedule, Elliot, and I'm not sure the committee can afford too much time on this."

"Oh, I think we can afford the time," Cordelia inter-jected sweetly. "Elliot, I think that's a wonderful idea, since

I'm not too good with financial statements either. Thank you for the suggestion. Very well, any—"

The door opened again, and Geraldo Avenceña entered. "Hi! Sorry I'm late. Hello, Harry." He took a seat next to Harry and turned to Cordelia. "Had a little problem over in the chapel. Couldn't get away. Sorry."

"You just came from the chapel?"

The big man turned to Harry and paused before answering. "Yes. Just now. Anyway, sorry, everyone. Where are we?"

"We've just decided to give Elliot a chance to review Irena's reports, so more than one of us is familiar with the statistics. Irena, you don't know how bad I feel about making you handle all the financial aspects of the committee."

Shoenborn-Eriksen forced her mouth to smile, and looked to Harry as if she had just tasted something not yet dead. "Well, I suppose if Elliot feels he *must* examine my work . . ."

"Well, have we discussed how to vote at the next general meeting?" Geraldo asked.

"Not yet, dear, no."

"Perhaps we should." Shoenborn-Eriksen had heard about Geraldo's defection to her camp, Harry guessed, and was hoping to tie up the issue with a permanently split vote.

"I don't think that's a good idea, until Elliot has had a chance to absorb all the material you've provided him," Cordelia countered.

Unabashed, Shoenborn-Eriksen powered on ahead. "Well, I intend to vote against divesting. I've no doubt about that. Geraldo, how will you vote?"

"This may not be the best time—" Cordelia jumped in, desperately hoping to stave off a loggerhead.

"I'm going to vote with Cordelia," Geraldo said softly. "I think we should divest."

"What?" said Shoenborn-Eriksen, Cordelia, and Harry. O'Malley looked up from the reports and peered around like a startled hare.

"I said, I think we should divest."

Shoenborn-Eriksen blinked several times, her mouth wide. She had prepared to count coup against Cordelia, and clearly had not anticipated Avenceña's response. "But didn't you say, just Monday night, that you would oppose any move to divest?"

"Yes. But I've thought it over, and I think we should go ahead. Cordelia, I'm sorry if I've seemed wishy-washy on this subject." He made eye contact with no one.

Cordelia made a vain effort to keep a look of triumph off her face. "Nonsense, Geraldo. It's a weighty issue. I'd rather have someone seem unsure than intractable. Still, as I said, I think it's better to wait and make a final vote, say, next week?" The four committee members haggled over a convenient time and date, and Cordelia adjourned the meeting. Geraldo pleaded another important appointment and raced out. Without a good-bye to the others, Harry hurried out and jostled past students in the hallway and caught up with him just outside the SUB. The wind had picked up from the northwest, and the sky had darkened to an ominous gray.

"Looks like a storm," Geraldo observed.

"Geraldo, what's going on?"

"You mean with the committee? Harry, I just changed my mind. That's all."

"Nonsense."

"Harry, really, I have to get rolling—"

Harry stood close to the chaplain and spoke softly, lest students overhear. "Would you please stop looking so damned innocent, Geraldo, and tell me what's going on! If it's a problem, perhaps I can help."

"Look, it's nothing. I just changed my mind."

"Is that how the police will see it?"

Geraldo stopped, another protest half out of his mouth. He looked down and Harry and blinked. "What do you mean?"

"I mean the Portland Police Department, Homicide Division. I mean a murder investigation."

"Harry, good lord, you don't think I had—"

"No, of course not. You didn't kill Llewelleyn. But I'll tell you what I observe: you told Cordelia and me you would vote in favor of divestment. You met with Richard Llewelleyn Monday night following the board meeting—"

"Harry, he didn't make it to—"

"Geraldo, please shut up! You met with him Monday night, and later at the party, you shifted your vote to his side. That night Llewelleyn was murdered. Now, with him no longer on the committee, you switch your vote yet again. Irena Shoenborn-Eriksen seems to know about your Monday decision to vote with her. How? You arrived at Eriksen's, told Cordelia and me that you'd changed your mind, and left. I doubt Irena ever spoke to you that night. But she most certainly spoke to Llewelleyn."

"That doesn't mean I ki—" Two students passed by and turned their way.

"Everything okay, Reverend?" one inquired.

"Sure, Lonny."

When the students had passed on, he turned back to Harry. "I didn't kill Richard Llewelleyn."

"I don't think you did. What I *do* think is that Llewelleyn found a way to force you to change your vote, and with him now decidedly under the weather and unable to exert that same pressure, you're free to vote the way you always wanted to. Am I right?"

Geraldo stood and stared mutely down at Harry. Hands the size of coconuts flexed and unflexed at his side. Abruptly, he turned and walked away. Harry caught him in ten steps.

"Yesterday, someone on campus used a false identification to get a look at my dossier in Archives." That did it. Geraldo stopped and turned, thick eyebrows raised in surprise.

Harry took advantage of the moment and pressed on. "Yesterday morning, I stopped by the chapel to see you. The back door was open, and there were dishes draining in the sink. The doors downstairs were locked. You told me you didn't get to school till nearly noon. Who was in the chapel, Geraldo?"

After a pause of more than a minute, the giant grabbed Harry gently by the upper arm. "Harry, please—"

"What did Llewelleyn have on you?"

"Harry, leave it be."

"What the hell's going on, Geraldo?"

"Nothing. Nothing's going on. All right, Harry, I've gotten into a little trouble, but I can handle it. Leave this be, Harry, I'm begging you. As a friend. Let this go."

"Geraldo, I'd do nearly anything for you. But there's been a murder. I can't promise." The viselike grip tightened on his arm and Harry winced. The chaplain looked down suddenly at the hand and his eyes widened in shock as he realized it was his own. He pulled his hand back as if scalded. "I'm sorry," he mumbled, hurrying away.

NINETEEN

✣

Upon leaving the Colossus Sisters' cluttered home, Nelligan dropped by a Pay-Less Drug for a small bottle of Pepto-Bismol and some Extra-Strength Tylenol, and once again cursed his all-nighter with Harry. He sat in the cab of the Jeep, listening to Dire Straits and watching the sky darken, and sourly wondered why his body no longer allowed for such binges. Just a few years ago, he could have stayed up till three in the morning all week long and not felt the least weak-kneed. The thought was sobering.

Twenty minutes later, the Jeep had climbed the West Hills, its powerful engine humming. On a bluff just below the eastern edifice of Oregon Health Sciences University, Nelligan turned onto a private lane and parked behind a beige four-door. Standing to the right of the sedan was Detective Kehough. Stepping out from behind the wheel was Sergeant Wiley. Nelligan joined them on the blacktop.

"Nelligan," both men said, more or less in synch, then looked at each other.

"Gentlemen. How goes the war on crime?"

"Sometimes good, sometimes not," the black man answered, shaking Nelligan's hand. Nelligan wasn't sure, but he thought Wiley was the first Portland police officer to ever do that. "I read your piece in the *Post* this morning. Interesting."

"You think so?"

"Yes. Very."

"Where'd you get the info on Llewelleyn's injuries?" Kehough stepped around the car and joined them.

Nelligan had hoped to confront the two cops separately, and maybe rattle them a bit. That game plan shot to hell, he decided to try a little applied aggravation. He seriously doubted whether Wiley could be aggravated, so he turned to the big blond man and smiled his blandest smile. "Sources."

"Sources?"

"Sources."

"Like who?"

"Whom, Detective Kehough. It's an object."

Kehough punched Nelligan on the shoulder, just barely soft enough to be inoffensive. "That's good, Nelligan. Funny stuff. You wouldn't happen to be in possession of stolen police documents, would you now?"

"Kehough?" Wiley tried to break in, his voice barely more than a whisper.

Nelligan pretended not to hear Kehough's question. "You here to talk to Eriksen or Shoenborn-Eriksen, Detective?"

"Kehough?" Wiley tried again.

Kehough stepped closer to Nelligan. He stood a good eight inches taller than the reporter. "Nelligan, I understand you like boys. Is that so?"

"Kehough—"

"Look, I'm flattered that you're interested, Kehough, but you're not my type." Nelligan patted him on the arm. "Some other time, maybe?"

Kehough's cheeks darkened. Nelligan sensed the rabbit punch coming even before he saw the arm retract. John Wiley was between them suddenly, wedging them apart. He was shorter than either antagonist, but surprisingly strong. "Don't touch him, Kehough. We have work to do."

Kehough bristled, and for a moment, Nelligan thought the punch would simply be redirected at Wiley. Finally, reluctantly, the big man nodded and backed off.

"Would you go on ahead, please?" Wiley asked politely. "I'll be along."

Kehough dredged up the ghost of a grin for Nelligan. "I'll see you later."

Nelligan returned the grin serenely and leaned against the unmarked cruiser. Kehough loped up the wide steps to the Eriksens' front door. Sergeant Wiley turned to the reporter.

"I apologize for that, Mr. Nelligan. It was uncalled for."

"Are you for real?" Nelligan asked incredulously. "Of course it was called for, Wiley. I called for it. I was baiting him. Why'd you step in on my side?"

"Because you're a citizen. Would you tell me where you got the information on Llewelleyn's injuries?"

"No."

"All right. How's your investigation getting along?"

"Ah, okay, I guess. You?"

"About the same. We *are* going to find the person who killed Llewelleyn, you know."

Nelligan believed him, but chose not to comment. "Who are you here to talk to?"

"Ms. Shoenborn-Eriksen."

"Can I sit in?"

"No, but we won't be long. Please wait if you want to."

"You're a piece of work, y'know that, Wiley?"

The black man smiled shyly and turned away. He turned back after a step. "I don't condone bigotry, Mr. Nelligan. I am sorry about that."

"Okay. I believe you."

Wiley nodded once, then turned toward the ranch-style house.

Harry hustled back to his office, trying to ignore the dull ache in his bad knee. In almost miraculous time, the sky had regressed from clear and blue to a steely gray, with touches of yellow. The rainy season had hit for sure, and all around Harry, students in halter tops and running shorts, thongs and sundresses, T-shirts and miniskirts, raced from class to class, hoping for a chance to escape to dorm rooms for a change in costume before the deluge.

Harry had stopped by the campus post office and picked up his mail. Most of it looked official and important, and he tossed it unopened in a tall metal trash can. There was also a postcard from Kate Fairbain. On the front was a photograph of tall ships framed against the silhouette of Baltimore's skyline. On the reverse side were sixteen paragraphs, scripted in Kate's incredibly minute Cyrillic printing. Harry and Kate had been communicating in Russian for years, in an effort to maintain her fluency and his rustiness. He had stopped just outside the post office and read the note through, grinning.

Of course, thoughts of Kate led to thoughts of Kate's carpet, and the grin faded. Harry decided to return to his office and find a reputable—though not exorbitant—carpet cleaner.

Fate had other plans. He barely had his key in the door before Lyman Bledsoe, Jr., burst forth from his office, his pudgy face a deep and dangerous scarlet. "Henry!"

"Hullo, Lyman. How goes it?"

"Where were you yesterday?"

Harry opened the door, dumped his bag, and plopped into his chair. "Well, yesterday morning I had breakfast at home. I drove here in my car. I parked just below the football stadium. I—"

"No! Where were you during seminar?"

Uh-oh. "I was in class. Say, I'm glad you stopped by. Lyman, what's your analysis of the Eighty-eight senatorial race? Will Hatfield retire?"

"Henry! Please! I stopped by Lecture Hall Three yesterday and you weren't there!" Bledsoe's tubby body fairly vibrated with pique.

"How about Ron Wyden? Is he Oregon's Great Democratic Hope?"

"Nor were your students. Henry, I demand to know what you did with your seminar class!"

"Ah, is that all? Sit, Lyman. Relax. Would you like a Ho Ho?" He reached into a desk drawer and pulled out a box that had been there since spring term.

Lyman declined the seat. Harry formed his hands into a time-out signal. "All right, Lyman. Fear not. I didn't violate the Mann Act, I assure you. I simply took my students on a . . . field trip."

The effect would have been identical had Harry said, "I lined them up and shot them." Lyman's thick hands waved in the air in mute astonishment and he bounced on the balls of his feet. "Good God, Henry! Did you fill out a 10-L98?"

"Ah, well, that's hard to say. What is a 10-L98?"

"*Insurance*, Henry! Did you fill out the *insurance* forms!"

"Oh. No, but it was just a wee trip, so—"

"Did you use one of the campus vans! Political Science is only allotted three trips with campus vans per month! You could have put us over the top!"

"No, no. No van."

"Where did you go? How did you get them there?"

"We . . . are you sure you won't take a Ho Ho? No? Perhaps I will."

"Henry!"

"We . . . took a walking tour of the vicinity."

"A walking tour?" Lyman shrieked. Harry suspected Lyman had walked less than three miles, cumulative, in his life.

"Yes. I thought if would be valuable to show them the neighborhood."

"What does the neighborhood have to do with radical politics?"

"You don't know?"

That got him. Lyman's mouth flew open for a retort, then slammed shut. "Know?"

"Aaron Mullenhoff lived here for a short time. I thought perhaps it would put the students more in touch with history to see where such a famous anarchist lived. Ah, Lyman, you *do* know about Mullenhoff and the Kelso/Longview Bett'r Butt'r Dairy Uprising of nineteen oh five."

Bledsoe's tiny eyes fluttered as he searched his memory for a dairy uprising. "Vaguely. My specialty is the history of codified law and the Supreme Court, as you may remember. So. You took your students to see where Mullenhoff allegedly lived. But you didn't use a van?"

"No van. And what do you mean, 'allegedly'? Surely you're not one of those who claim Mullenhoff actually *escaped* the Kennewick mob? What about the trial, and the notes from Judge Weymouth? What about that solid, if ponderous, biography written by . . . oh, what'sisname, in the early fifties?"

"Yes, I remember the book, and I really do hope you're giving the students both sides of the story."

"Well, certainly."

"All right, then. Harry, I find it very difficult to believe you took our students off campus without filing a 10-L98. What would happen to *me* if a student was attacked by a Doberman or hit by a Tri-met bus?"

Harry bowed his head in shame. "Please forgive me, Lyman. I confess: I failed to think of you at the time."

"Yes, well that's just like you, Harry." Lyman turned and scurried away, still admonishing God and the universe on his lonely position at the top. Harry quickly filled his black-stone with a few texts and a tattered manila envelope with notes from past classes, grabbed his coat, and hurried out, taking the back door through the secretary's office. There was an off chance Lyman would attempt to look up the names Aaron Mullenhoff, the Kelso/Longview Bett'r Butt'r Dairy Uprising of nineteen oh five, Judge Weymouth, and the Kennewick mob. Harry wanted to be long gone before he did.

He wasn't out the door yet when Bledsoe reappeared, a dusty Northwest history text in his hands. "Oh, Henry. Mullenhoff, you say? I, um, can't seem to find the reference I was looking for."

"Oh? Well, good hunting. And may I say, I'm pleased you're taking this new social sciences department so well, Lyman."

Bledsoe's history concerns screeched to a halt. "Department?" Visions of competing with new faculty for capital outlays danced in his head.

"Yes. The one the board has been working on. You know; Undertaking Sciences. Oops, look at the time. Must fly."

"*Undertaking?*" The department chair visibly shook. "*Undertaking, Henry?*"

"Yes. Thought you knew. They're thinking of offering a bachelor of science in pathology, and a bachelor of arts in, um, taxidermy. It came from Dean Connar's office, is the scuttlebutt I hear. Anyway, you wanted to know about Mullenhoff?"

"Who? Oh, please, Henry! Not now. I'll—never mind, Henry. Barbara! Get me Lee Connar on the phone!" Lyman scuttled off to his office.

Nelligan dashed up the front steps as the first thick drops of rain began pattering on the sidewalk. His coat was thrown over his shoulder and his tie was loosened. His striped shirt clung to his chest.

"Marty?" he called, wiping sweat off his brow and pulling the damp material away from his back.

"In the den!"

Nelligan swooped down on the refrigerator and relieved it of a Smith and Reilly before heading into the den. "God! When did you get in? It must be eighty degrees out and just starting to rain. Humidity must be a thousand percent."

"Oxymoron," Kady replied. "We have company."

He sat in one wing chair, opposite Sandi Braithwaite, who, as always, looked like she just finished an ultra-marathon. "Hi, Sand. What brings you around?" Nelligan literally fell onto the couch beside her. "Geeze, it's muggy out there."

"Hi, Tucker."

"Sandi and I have been talking about education," Kady said. There was a hint of something—anger? disapproval?—in his voice that caught the attention of both Nelligan and Sandi.

"Oh?"

"Yes. You've been giving her quite an education, haven't you?"

"It's not like that," Sandi cut in, blushing. "Tucker taught me a few tricks for getting interviews and . . . ah . . ."

"Procuring," Nelligan mumbled into his beer.

". . . procuring information. I'm sorry, Mr. Kady, I know this is your house and I ought to shut up, but honestly, Tucker and I haven't been . . . you know . . . romantic."

Tucker spit beer across the shag carpet. A laugh erupted from Kady before he could squelch it. Sandi's bewilderment deepened. Her cheeks burned a deeper shade of pink.

"Thank you, Ms. Braithwaite," Kady said, regaining control and wiping a tear from his eye. "I wasn't accusing you two of having an affair. I'm accusing Tucker of teaching you the art of disposable ethics."

"Oh, come off it, Marty!" Nelligan grinned. "I wouldn't dream of telling you the law. Don't lecture me on journalism. Deal?"

Kady stood and offered Sandi his hand. "Nice to meet you, Sandi. Please don't listen to anything he says. Tucker: We'll talk." He left, sliding shut the oak paneled doors behind him.

"What'd I say?" Sandi whispered.

"Nothing. Never mind him—he's Andy Hardy, grown up. What're you doing this far from campus? I didn't think you drove."

"I hitched. I need to talk to you."

"Shoot. Want a beer?"

"Please."

Nelligan hurried out and returned, wearing a striped polo shirt and Reeboks. "Marty wants to know if you can cook."

"Cook? No."

"Then you're not invited to dinner. Neither can we. What's up?"

Sandi popped the beer tab on the can and collected her thoughts. "Tucker, I want in on whatever you're doing."

"Say what?"

"This investigation. On Mr. Llewelleyn. I know you're investigating this, and I'm betting Professor Bishop is too. I want in."

"I see. Well, look, Sandi—"

"No, *you* look, fella! I can't get anywhere! I'm a student journalist, working for the student rag, and the cops and everybody treat me like a kid!"

"Sandi, you *are* a kid."

"Bull. I'm a journalist. Tucker, how in heck am I supposed to learn to be a writer if no one will give me a chance? I want in on your investigation!"

"Well, I mean, that's sort of the way it is. Everyone's felt like that at one time or another."

"Look!" She slammed the can down on a coaster. "I know about the party or banquet or whatever last Monday. I figure Llewelleyn must've been killed just after that, right? I understand there were twenty people there, maybe more."

"So?"

"So, have you been able to run thorough backgrounds on 'em all? Of course not! Have you been able to check every alibi against a second source? Hell, no! Who has time?"

There was a faint glimmer in Nelligan's eye. Sandi caught it and fanned the flame. "You've got the experience, you've got the clout of a daily paper behind you. Fine. You be Perry Mason. Let me be Della Street!"

"Or Paul Drake?"

"That's it!" She almost burst from the chair and landed in his lap. "I'll do legwork for you. What say? The *Post* comes out before the *Pathfinder,* right? So we'll share whatever we find, only you'll get it first. I probably won't even get it before the local weeklies get it. But I'll be in on it. Please, Tucker, *puh-leeze!*"

Nelligan finished off his beer, set it down, and reached across the streamer trunk. "Deal."

"All right!" She pumped his hand furiously.

"On one condition."

"Name it!"

"Don't tell Harry. He'd kill me."

TWENTY

❖

Harry stopped at home long enough to dry Niccolo's paws and fur and pour fresh food in his bowl, then change into a dry shirt. He stood in the kitchen, healthy shot of whisky in one hand, telephone body in the other, the receiver cradled between ear and shoulder, and stared out at the deluge. It had started just as he left campus, first as fat, isolated drops of rain and then, within a minute or less, a maelstrom. Within minutes, visibility was down to a dozen yards. He was sure a miniature lake had already started to form in the intersection at the bottom of the hill.

"Hallo?"

"Yes, Geoffrey? This is Henry Bishop."

"Ah, how are you, Henry? How's the investigation?"

"Fine, such as it is. I was wondering if I could drop by later this evening and speak to you about that."

"Ah, actually, that may not be a good idea. I could perhaps come to your apartment? Around six?"

"Six is fine, sir."

"Good. Till then." Eriksen rang off quickly.

Harry hung up, set down the phone, and padded into the living room. He made one black and two white moves in the chess game, thought about it for a while, then rummaged around in his bookshelves for an alumni directory. The only one he could find was three years old and dog-

eared, but it would do. He returned to the kitchen and
called up the only alumnus rug cleaner in the listing.

"Avner's"

"Hullo, I'm a professor at John Jacob Astor. Do you still
have an alumni/faculty discount?"

"Professor Bishop?"

"Er, yes."

"Hi! George Avner! I was in your Intro to U.S. Foreign
Policy! About five years ago!"

"George! How are you?" Harry endeavored to echo the
unfamiliar voice's jubilation.

"Fine, sir. You?"

"Good. Good. So you're, ah, still in Portland, eh?"

"Oh, hell yes. Born and raised here. What can I do for
you?"

Harry outlined the problem in Kate Fairbain's condo,
leaving out the question of culpability, which wasn't truly
any of George Avner's—whoever he was—business. He
nearly spilled his drink when the effervescent voice blithely
gave him an estimate which, even with a ten-percent faculty
discount, was considerably higher than the estimates from
the day before.

"Ah. I see. Well. Thank you, George."

"So, when do you need us, professor?"

"Yes, well. This is for a friend who's out of town. I don't
know when she'll be back, but I'll have her ring you up first
thing."

"Great! Listen, if I can ask, who recommended us?"

There was a considerable pause while Harry stared at
the kitchen wallpaper and listened to the rain flow off the
edges of his clogged roof gutters.

"Professor?"

"I forget. Someone I was speaking to just yesterday.
Funny, isn't it? Has anyone from JJAC used your services
this week, George?"

"Yeah. Let's see, someone from over in Art History. A
prof or secretary or something: I don't know. A redhead.
And one of the trustees."

"Which one?"

"Oh, hell . . . what was that guy's name . . . Irish, I
think . . ."

"Cavenaugh? O'Malley?"

"Cavenaugh! That's him! Did he recommend us?"

"Yes, that's who it was, all right."

"Huh!"

Harry finished his drink, his hand trembling slightly. "You sound surprised, George."

"Yeah, a little. To be honest, professor, we weren't able to help him much."

"No?"

"No. Guy's an artist or something. Spilled turpentine on his wall-to-wall. Hell of a stain. We weren't able to get it all out."

"Really? Funny, he didn't mention that. Just said you charged a reasonable price."

"No kidding! Well, that's what we like to hear, even from a guy who had to buy a brand-new rug! Anyway, professor, if you recommend us to someone else, I can swing you an extra two-percent discount, on top of the alumni discount."

"Two percent. Wow. Sounds good, George. I'll be in touch."

"I salvaged the last of the roast," Kady called from the kitchen. "Want a sandwich?"

"I thought we weren't speaking?"

Kady turned to retort but stopped when he saw Nelligan, in his long waterproof coat and wide-brimmed fedora.

"This smells like mothballs. I can't remember when we've had a drier summer and fall."

"Where in God's name are you going?"

Nelligan flashed a smile. "Dropping Sandi off at school, then the office. I'll grab a burger somewhere."

Kady hoisted himself up on the counter. "You *do* realize there's a storm out there?"

"I'll be careful. Gotta go. Bye."

"Tucker!"

Nelligan stopped near the front door. "Yeah?"

"Where's Ms. Braithwaite?"

"Bathroom."

"Well, about what she said earlier, regarding you two—"

"Oh, I promise we haven't been romantic too."

"Truly humorous. A rib-tickler. I'm serious, Tucker. We spoke for about ten minutes. Ms. Braithwaite has a very worrisome and very . . . familiar outlook on the elasticity of journalisitc ethics."

"Could we talk about this later?"

"Have you been teaching her Tucker Nelligan's Variation on Machiavelli's Theorem?"

Nelligan sighed theatrically and hung his head. "Marty, please. Yes, some ends do justify some means. And yes, I've been filling her in on that. It's stuff she'll need to make a go of this business."

"I see."

"We'll talk later, okay? Promise."

"No we won't unless I bring it up again. About her denial, regarding the two of you . . ."

"What?"

"Tucker, you astounding flake, that young woman is in love with you."

"Get out of town!"

"Amazing. Tucker, you're the smartest stupid person I ever met."

"We'll talk."

"Drive careful."

"'Careful' is an adjective."

Harry sat staring at the chess endgame and rubbing Niccolo behind the ears and under his snow-white chin. He had played variations of that particular game time and time again, and had never seen it end quite like it had this time. The board had been decimated. He made a tactical shift in his standard middle game for white, which usually depended heavily on queen and queen's knight, and opted to lead the offense with his bishops. It made for an interesting game. White lost badly. Maybe the game was trying to tell him something.

Harry was actually looking forward to this meeting. He really wanted nothing to do with any murder investigations, and now he could—honestly—say he had done what he could for Eriksen. Hope I was of some service, old boy. Best of luck. Let me know how it turns out.

Harry was no detective, and his lack of insight into the murder would prove, if proof was needed, that he was better off in the classroom than the trenches. Surely Geoffrey would understand, thank him for his time and effort, and be off.

Three quick raps on his door broke him out of his reverie, and he slowly realized he had drifted to sleep. Niccolo was reluctant to move, and three knocks sounded again before Harry was able to reach the door. Geoffrey Eriksen, clad in calf-length coat and umbrella, stepped into the living room and created a puddle on the floor.

"Henry." He nodded curtly and scanned the chaos in the room.

"Geoffrey. Come in, come in. Let me take that." He took the drenched coat and folded umbrella and hung them on the coat tree, where they began to form a new puddle. Unbidden, Eriksen sat on the couch, adjusting the crease in his slacks.

Harry offered a drink which Eriksen accepted. When the Scotch was poured and Harry was seated in his favorite chair, Eriksen raised the tumbler in his direction. "To your health." He drained the liquor in one shot and set down the glass. "What have you learned?"

"Well, I learned that no one liked Richard Llewelleyn."

"True. He was a difficult person. The question, of course, is who disliked the little bastard enough to stab him repeatedly and dump his body downtown?"

"That I don't know. Sorry."

Eriksen looked at him blankly and readjusted the pants crease needlessly.

I'm not interested in being a detective, Harry reminded himself.

"Well, what is the next step?" Eriksen asked.

This is all none of my business, anyway. "I'm not sure. Perhaps you'd best play your trump. Tell the police about your paramour."

"Hmm. And that's your advice?" Eriksen's voice was brusque. He flicked imaginary lint off his sleeve.

"Yes. 'Fraid so." *Of course, I am mildly curious about one point. What harm is there in asking?* "By the way: You nominated Llewelleyn to the board. Why?"

Eriksen fiddled with the crease in the fine cloth again. "It was Sam Broderick's idea. Broderick said Llewelleyn was most skilled at raising funds. The college's endowment was quite shaky then—this was a few years back, you'll remember."

"I understood you nominated him, and Broderick seconded it?"

"Yes, that's right. Broderick came to me several times before the meeting and we discussed Llewelleyn. We both agreed he—Broderick—had little or no talent for forming coalitions, especially when trying to 'sell' someone as thoroughly unpleasant as Richard Llewelleyn. So I made the nomination and campaigned for him. Broderick seconded the motion and Irena voted with me. The rest of the board were easy."

"I see. Did it help? Is the endowment in better shape?"

"Oh, you know how it is, Henry. Times are tough."

Harry just sipped his whisky. It was standard practice at all schools to not tell the faculty how much money was on hand, for fear the union would demand wage hikes. If Llewelleyn had been unable to add to the college's coffers, Eriksen would have said so. Clearly, the murdered man had been a money-maker.

"I understand elections are coming up next term for board chairperson."

Eriksen scowled. "Yes."

"And Llewelleyn was hoping to replace you?"

The yellow eyebrows almost met above the nose. "You are joking. I had not heard this."

"Hmm. That's the skinny I hear."

"From whom?"

"Here and there."

"Ah. Well: no matter. The elections happen every two years, but they're a formality, a holdover from earlier days. I am always reelected as chairman. Fourteen years, now. I do the job better than anyone."

"Really?"

"Yes. Really."

Harry had only met one other human so absolutely positive of his superiority, that being Tucker Nelligan, of course, and he found the trait a bit unnerving in both men.

"Would you like another drink?"

"No."

"Okay. Mind if I do?" When Harry returned, he noted the look of annoyance on his guest's face. Harry reminded himself one more time that he was bowing out of the investigation, and was merely asking a few questions simply to be polite. "Tell me, were you seriously considering dropping

Astor's unofficial relations with the Presbyterian Church and accepting a grant from the Catholic diocese?"

"You know about that?"

"Yes."

"I see. Yes, it was under consideration. But no, I honestly doubt we would have done that."

"Why not?"

"Henry, if I am not being rude, please tell me what this has to do with proving my innocence."

"Forgive me, Geoffrey. It may have nothing whatsoever to do with you. At your request, I'm trying to find out as much as I possibly can regarding the board and Richard Llewelleyn. Truly, the only chance we have of figuring out this whole brouhaha is to look for a motive." *We?*

"Ah. That makes sense. And you think Reverend Avenceña may have murdered Richard?"

"What? No! What makes you say that?"

"This business about breaking off relations with the church. Avenceña opposed that most strenuously. That would give him a motive, eh? Because the entire thing was Richard's plan."

"Sorry, Geoffrey. I'm quite sure Geraldo had nothing to do with the murder. Tell me, why had you decided not to go after the Catholic grant?"

"Because too many of our alumni attended the college in the days when the ties to the Presbyterian Church were formal and official. Many alumni are members of the church, and would be reluctant to contribute money to us in the future."

"All right. I see that. Last point: Llewelleyn was your accountant, correct?"

"He handled my personal funds: yes."

"As well as those of your wife, Sam Broderick, Donal Patrick Cavenaugh, and Cordelia Applebaum. Was there anyone else?"

"No, not that I know of. I didn't even know he was doing Cordelia's books."

"Llewelleyn was being investigated by the SEC. Did you ever suspect he was playing fast and loose with your personal accounts?"

"No. Never. I read about that in the newspaper and could hardly believe it—*if* it's true."

"It's true. A journalist friend of mine wrote that. Tucker Nelligan—you met him yesterday?"

"Ah, yes."

"Well, anyway, if Llewelleyn was practicing insider trading or whatever, and using money from one of you five board members, that may well be a motive."

"Henry, excuse me, no offense, but you've simply found another reason to suspect me. That isn't what I wanted."

"Geoffrey, please. You must understand: I really would rather not be involved in all this. I'm not a detective, and to a degree, I resent people thinking that I am. You wanted information and insight. I've made an effort to provide that. I apologize if I haven't been able to find the Black Bird or the Thin Man."

"Bird? Henry, what bird?"

"Sorry. Nothing. Carry on."

Eriksen stood up suddenly and grabbed for his coat. "Henry, you're sounding foolish. You're doing a wonderful job. I understand how important it is to learn all you can about Richard. I have to run now. Did you have any other questions?"

Harry sagged. His delicate hints to have himself removed from the investigation had been for naught. "No. Thank you for dropping by. I'll call you later if I have any other questions."

"Er, yes. I'm not heading home just yet. I have some business to take care of." Harry translated the vocal intonations and arched eyebrows to mean a rendezvous with Eriksen's mistress. Eriksen extracted an embossed card from a slim metal holder and handed it to him. "If you need anything else, please call this number. It's my private line, at Cascade Electro. When I'm not in, a machine will record your message."

"All right. Drive carefully, Geoffrey."

"I am always careful, Henry. Thank you. Good night."

Eriksen stepped outside and touched a stud on the umbrella handle. The webbed tines popped open. Harry watched him navigate around the puddles on the cracked walkway and open the driver's-side door of his car. From his angle, Harry could see something on the passenger's side that looked like silvery fur (fox? lynx?), above a length of tapered leg. From the few glimpses he had been provided,

Harry was sure the entire package would be more than appealing.

He turned to Niccolo, who stared back dully. "I'm still investigating the murder," he admitted.

Niccolo shook his head in dismay and licked his paw.

Davos opened the door and peered out at the rain-slick coat and the water cascading off the brim of Nelligan's hat.

"Hi! Remember me?"

Davos said nothing.

"I need to see Mr. Eriksen, if I may. It's very, very important."

Davos closed the door. Nelligan waited, out of the rain but still shivering in the cold, for five minutes. He rang the bell again.

Davos opened the door and stared down at him.

"I talk to Mr. Eriksen, or I write what I've got. Mr. Eriksen wouldn't like that, Davos. Please tell him I'm here."

The door closed again, only to open a minute later. Irena Shoenborn-Eriksen stood before Nelligan, her tall, slim figure wrapped in a floor-length robe with padded shoulders. A dragon emblem twined from chest to hem.

"Hello, Ms. Shoenborn-Eriksen. I wondered if I could talk to your husband."

"No. Please go away."

"Ma'am, it's really important. I need some information regarding the Astor board of trustees."

"Mr. Nelligan, go away or I'll ask Davos to hurt you."

Nelligan grinned. "No you won't. That kind of publicity, you don't need."

They stared at each other for a moment, until Nelligan removed his hat. "May I come in? It's cold out here."

"No." Shoenborn-Eriksen sighed and nibbled her lower lip. Her arms were folded across her chest. She shivered slightly. "I'm a member of the board. Perhaps I could answer your questions."

"Perhaps, but I sort of need a quote from the chairperson. You understand, I hope."

"My husband can't see you now. He's not well."

"'Not well' is one of those excuses journalists come to hate, ma'am. Like 'my dog ate my homework' or 'sure, I'll still respect you in the morning.'"

"Listen, you obnoxious—" The anger burst forth before she could control it. Shoenborn-Eriksen gritted her teeth and trembled with the energy expended in quelling her rage. "Mr. Nelligan, I'll explain this only once. My husband had nothing whatsoever to do with Richard's murder. Please leave him alone. I'll tell you why he's clearly innocent, but you must promise me you'll go away and leave us alone."

"If I get the information I need, Ms. Shoenborn—"

"Irena."

"Irena, then I'll leave everyone alone. But this is front-page stuff. I can't just walk away. Those other reporters hanging around Cascade Electro won't just quit either. You *know* that. Them, you don't know. Me: you may not like me, but at least you've seen me. You can deal with me."

Shoenborn-Eriksen relaxed a bit, and brushed back a strand of hair that had escaped the otherwise severe style. She stepped aside. Nelligan stepped past her, into the foyer, and caught a delicate floral fragrance. When his hostess didn't move, he realized there would be no offer of tea or crumpets this time. They stood in the carpeted hallway, at the foot of the curved stairway.

"Very well. My husband couldn't have killed Richard because he was with me all night, from the end of the party until the police called."

"I see. You were asleep at the time?"

"Not really. I always sleep lightly." She paused, considering, then plunged ahead. "And I never take sleeping pills."

"Oh. Could you tell me what the fight was about? Between you and Llewelleyn?"

"Well . . . yes. Richard was suggesting some utter nonsense about Geoffrey's financial entanglements to Cascade Electro. My husband's company sells electronic parts to the South African government, you know, and with the JJAC board of trustees considering divestment, he intimated there was a conflict of interest for Geoffrey."

"Do you agree?"

"No. The college's investment portfolio doesn't include any Cascade Electro stock. The two things have nothing in common."

"I see. When you were arguing with Llewelleyn, did he mention anything about this SEC investigation?"

She paused, drummed her fingers nervously on her forearm, then shook her head. "No."

"I understand Llewelleyn worked on the investment portfolio for the college. Correct?"

"Yes. He worked on my finance committee."

"I'm told he helped increase the endowment by something like twelve million dollars."

She neither confirmed nor denied, which was confirmation enough.

"What are you trying to get at, Mr. Nelligan?"

"I'm just trying to find out exactly how honest Llewelleyn was, and how much of his financial razzle-dazzle was crooked. I thought your husband might know, because he has something of a savvy reputation in the business community."

"Yes. I see. Mr. Nelligan, I'll tell you what I can, but then I want you out of here. Is that understood?"

"Yes," he replied, agreeing to nothing.

"Richard's financial contribution to the college was . . . substantial. I happen to believe I contributed at least some of the hard work and diligence that increased our endowment from a slim and unproductive eight million to its current situation—nearly twenty-one million dollars. Still, I admit, he was very, very good with generating revenue. And I believed—I continue to believe—his systems were less than honest. He bought stocks with insider information, I'm almost positive."

"But you didn't stop him? Or bring your suspicions to the SEC?"

"No."

"I see. Llewelleyn handled your books, I hear. Was he as terrific with your funds as the college's?"

"Yes. I've been rich all my life. I'm richer now. I have him to thank for that."

"I see. Well, I guess you've answered my questions. Thank you."

"Thank you, Mr. Nelligan. Go away and don't come back. You suggested a while ago that I wouldn't have Davos hurt you. You were wrong. Good night."

The downtown streets were clogged with rush-hour traffic when Harry pulled into the underground parking garage beneath Cordelia's high rise. The guard in the basement gave him a visitor's pass and pointed to the intercom system.

He rang Cordelia's apartment and announced himself. The door buzzed open. Harry rode a glass elevator up to the fifteenth floor, watching the rain cascade off the thick panes.

"Cordelia, sorry to drop in on you unannounced."

"Not at all. Not a fit night for man or beast, as my father used to say. Come in and let me fix you a drink."

No one ever had that offer rejected by Harry. She ushered him into an apartment that took his breath away. One whole wall was taken up by windows, which on this night revealed nothing but a black-on-dark-gray silhouette of the city. Harry knew that on a marginally good day they would offer an incomparable view of Mount Hood's year-round snow cap. The front room was sunken and carpeted in a plush sea of browns and reds. On one wall hung a glass-framed Andrew Wyeth, carefully spotlighted. Harry had a distinct impression it wasn't a print.

"My lord," he whispered, as one might in the Sistine Chapel.

"Like it?" Cordelia asked, stepping to a wet bar that retracted into one wall. "I've been here for five years, at least. I thought you'd seen my place."

"Cordelia, this is gorgeous! I had no idea an old political hack could have such taste!"

"Who are you calling old?" She handed him the drink, her cheeks reddening. Clearly, she was savoring his reaction to the apartment. She ushered him to the ornate rust-and-gold davenport, where they sat at either end. "What is it, Harry?"

"It's about Llewelleyn."

"Have the police gotten anywhere in their investigation? I read in the *Post* this morning they suspect Geoffrey! Absurd!"

"I know. He's asked me to look around a bit, see if I can help him."

"Ah, because of what happened last year. Yes, I remember, Geoffrey was quite impressed with how you handled that situation."

"Thank you. I've always been shot at well. Cordelia, from what I can tell, virtually no one on the board of trustees liked Llewelleyn. True?"

"True." She adjusted her ruffled collar and sat in a most ladylike pose. "I'm afraid dear Richard was always something of a prick."

"Then how in hell did he get to be on the board? Llewelleyn was a junior partner in Sam Broderick's firm. Didn't it seem odd to you he would be on the board of trustees? No offense, my dear, but the rest of the board is, well—"

"Filthy rich. Yes, that's mostly true. Except for Donal Patrick Cavenaugh, resident once-artist, who's no longer rich, but still adds a certain social glitterati aspect to our little cabal."

"Then how did Llewelleyn get on board?"

Cordelia shrugged elaborately. "I don't know. He is—or rather, was—awfully good with finances. With his guidance, our endowment increased considerably, I believe."

"I thought Irena Shoenborn-Eriksen said the endowment was in trouble."

"Oh, Harry! Irena's job is to sound the trump of economic doom at all times. Oh, I understand your confusion. I heard her economic reports, both at the general meeting Monday and the divestment subcommittee this afternoon. But I know the sound of someone shouting 'Wolf' when I hear it."

Harry finished his drink, then eyed the cut crystal longingly. Cordelia stood and went to the bar to refresh it. On the glass-and-bronze end table beside Harry was a paperback novel, written by someone with the improbable name of Cassandra Angelique. The cover featured a buxom young woman with a bodice that desperately needed darning, sprinting along a windswept cliff. Harry shook his head.

"Here you go, dear." Cordelia handed him the glass.

"*Love-Flames of Pendarrow Castle?*"

"I don't ask you about the rubber chicken in your office, Harry. Or the Mr. Potato Head, or—"

"True. What made Llewelleyn so good with finances?"

"I don't know, really, except to say he was always shrewd, always looking for an inside track or a deal."

"Why let him handle your accounting? I gathered you couldn't stomach the man."

"Oh, I couldn't. He was loud and aggressive, and always vaguely prurient, if you know what I mean."

"Despite which you let him manage your books?"

"Harry, I have no sympathy or respect for Robert Vesco or Ivan Boesky. But if either offered to handle my investments, I'd jump at the chance. Ethics are nice. Money is better. My investment portfolio was quite useless until I met Richard. I'm old, and I've grown accustomed to a certain lifestyle."

"So I see."

"Judge not, Henry Bishop."

"Cordelia, you know this deal about a five million dollar grant from the Catholic diocese? I spoke to Geoffrey, and he claims the board wasn't seriously considering it. Is that how you perceive the situation?"

"Yes. It would mean breaking off relations with the Presbyterian Church, which would be a slap in the face to many alumni."

"Right. Geoffrey said much the same thing. Tell me— did Geraldo know the deal wouldn't go through?"

She thought about it, her eyes on the ceiling. "I don't know. Why?"

Harry finished off the drink and rubbed his eyelids, which were suddenly heavy.

"Good lord, Harry! You can't suspect Geraldo Avenceña of murder!"

"No. Of course not," Harry said, no longer completely believing his own words.

TWENTY-ONE

❖

The woman who used Nelligan's desk during the night shift was out of town for a week, so he had no trouble booting up the computer terminal and filing what little he had on the murder story. It wasn't enough for a second story, so he decided to go with the updated police report, just as the rest of the city press had. That finished, he started in on the piece regarding divestment, as a favor to Marty. Personally, Nelligan was sure no one would give a damn about student protests and a small yuppie private school's investment portfolio. Still, it was the story to which he had been assigned, originally, and he had a reputation for carrying out assignments, regardless of the difficulty, peril, or sheer boredom involved.

He was hard at it a little after eight, when the security guard called to tell him a Miles Archer was in the lobby, and requested admittance to the newsroom. Nelligan said okay, finished the story, and ran over to meet Harry at the elevator.

"Hi, Miles. Lucky for you I'm a Dash Hammett fan."

Harry shrugged. "A calculated risk. I called Martin. He said you'd be here. Do you have time to compare notes?"

Nelligan led him to the editorial board room, switching on two of the four banks of overhead lights. They sat on either side of the conference table, with Harry's coat hanging off a third chair and dripping water. "Still raining?"

"Worse. There's quite a bit of flooding now. The ground is so dry, the water's simply accumulating."

"Well, I've got a few things, Harry, and to be honest, I don't know if they help Eriksen or hurt him. Want to hear?"

"Certainly."

"First, I talked to those two ladies, Feingarten and Fenscher, which was a hell of an excuse for drug abuse. They tell me Llewelleyn increased the college's endowment from eight million bucks to twenty-plus million."

"Good God. I spoke to Cordelia and she hinted at that, but I had no idea we were so well-to-do."

"Also, Llewelleyn was handling the books for about half the other trustees."

"I heard that also. He was in fact doing a damned good job of it, at least for Cordelia."

"Shoenborn-Eriksen too. I gather he made her some serious coin on the investment market."

"Which lets the two ladies out, and Cavenaugh and Broderick as well, I suppose. I'm freezing. Could I get a cuppa?"

Nelligan already had the conference room Mr. Coffee going and dumped grounds into a plastic filtering gadget, atop a cup. "I disagree, Harry. I don't think we can write them off."

"If he was making them considerably richer, they wouldn't profit from his death."

"Yeah, and if he was buying stock with insider information, and the SEC was breathing down his neck, then none of them could afford to have the investigation continue. Surprise, Harry—the SEC was definitely investigating Llewelleyn like I wrote in my piece for the Wednesday edition."

"Llewelleyn's death would hardly stop a government probe. Especially a violent death."

"True, but what if the murderer was threatened by Llewelleyn, panicked, and killed him? Here." He handed Harry a cup, and a box of sweetener and creamer packets.

"Thank you. Your point's well made. Geoffrey Eriksen, Irena Shoenborn-Eriksen, Cordelia Applebaum, Big Sam Broderick, and Donal Patrick Cavenaugh all used Llewelleyn. If he was mishandling their finances, then each would be a suspect."

"Leaving who?"

"Whom."

"Whom? The reverend—"

"Avenceña."

"Right, and Elliot O'Malley."

"And the ladies collectively known as the Colossus Sisters."

"Your Colossus Sisters offered me some caviar today, Harry. Russian caviar."

"Come now, Tucker! Look at them: do Mmes. Feingarten and Fenscher strike you as the kind to organize a murder? A bake sale, yes. A spring pageant, probably. But murder?"

"They seem to care a hell of a lot about that school, Harry. All I'm saying is, we shouldn't be ruling anyone out too fast."

"Yes. That seems reasonable. On that subject, I discovered that Cavenaugh had his rug cleaned on Tuesday."

Nelligan arched an eyebrow. "So?"

"So, he told the cleaner he spilled turpentine on his rug. The stain wouldn't come out, and he was forced to replace it."

"Look, Harry, I'm really bushed. What's the point?"

"The point is, Donal Patrick is a sculptor, not a painter. Why have turpentine around the house? Moreover, Richard Llewelleyn was stabbed repeatedly, and not there in the Square. That medical examiner's report suggested he lived for quite a while, ruling out an assault in public."

"And the rug fibers in his hair and snagged on his wristwatch band suggest he was aced indoors, and there must've been a hell of a lot of blood, and bloodstains don't come out. Wow. Pretty good, Harry. How the hell'd you think to look for that?"

Harry preferred not to dwell on the condition of Kate Fairbain's apartment, and brushed aside the question. "There's something else, Tuck. I should have mentioned it earlier, but I thought it might not be germane."

He proceeded to tell Nelligan about his fears regarding Geraldo Avenceña, focusing on the reverend's twice-switched vote on divestment, his apparent falsehoods regarding someone hanging around the chapel, and the ersatz "Thomas Nemo" who checked out Harry's faculty file from Archives.

"Oy." Nelligan did his impression of Martin Kady. "I'll be damned. D'you think it's all connected? I mean, a guy like you probably made some enemies in his time—"

"Tucker!" Harry's voice was pleading. "I was never James Bond or Dereck Flint. There was and is precious little mystery in my life."

"Then why not tell me everything about the Hatter? Why keep your past shrouded?"

"Pay no attention to that man behind the curtain. Seriously, Tucker. I was as boring then as I am today."

"All right, already. Pax. It was just a suggestion. So anyway, the good chaplain is hiding stuff, huh? You think he had your file pulled?"

"No. The work-study student in Archives said it was an outsider. He's a career student and would know if it was someone from the campus. Also, I doubt it was someone Geraldo hired because, although he's a good friend and a dear man, he hasn't much sense of irony."

"Meaning?"

"'Nemo' is Latin for 'no one.' It was a nice touch, but not Geraldo's style."

"All right. Shall we concentrate on him for a while?"

Harry sipped his coffee, grimaced, and rubbed the back of his neck. "No. I don't think so, Tuck. Mind you, I'm not saying a man of the cloth is incapable of murder: no one is. But I think whatever Geraldo's playing at, he'll eventually tell me about it. Meanwhile, we need to find out what we can regarding Donal Patrick Cavenaugh and Elliot O'Malley."

Nelligan checked his Rolex. "Well, I've got an appointment with O'Malley scheduled for early tomorrow. I'd better get some sleep. You've got Cavenaugh?"

"Yes. I'll call him in the morning."

As Harry struggled back into his coat, they walked out to the newsroom. "Marty says you're to come over for dinner soon. How's this weekend?"

"Saturday's fine with me."

"Good. Bring wine."

"Oh, and Tucker, I'd like to look through your notes, if you don't mind. Something might jar a memory or two. One never knows."

"Sure, fine, but you won't be able to read them. I use my own brand of note-hand."

"Yo! Nelligan!" A sickly-looking man with heavy, dark bags under his eyes limped over to the elevator. "You the guy from cop-shop who asked the computer to pop out anything on a Geoffrey Eriksen?"

"Yeah."

"We just got a buzz from Portland Police. They just put out an APB on his car. Black Rolls, license is *Electro*. One of those vanity plates."

"An APB on Eriksen's car? Why?"

The heavy man shrugged. "I should know? You tell me; you're the gunslinger. All I hear is they got a homicide in Gresham, and they're lookin' for this guy's car."

TWENTY-TWO

❖

It was almost Friday by the time Nelligan and a staff photographer reached 238th Street, deep in the heart of suburban East Multnomah County. The rain continued to blast the city, aided now by a gusty west wind. Nelligan picked out a youngish sheriff's deputy in a yellow slicker and capped hat with neck protector and approached him from the west, leather identification packet extended. The shooter from the *Post* stayed well to the rear, outside the cop's field of vision.

"Hell of a night," Nelligan called out over the deluge. "Wiley or Kehough here?"

The young deputy glanced at the shorter man's trench coat and fedora, ignoring the ID, and nodded. "Yeah, the black guy is here. Inside."

"Thanks, buddy."

Nelligan hurried past the cordon and up the pathway, consisting of rain-slick, oval stones spaced a few inches apart. The path split in half and led to both halves of a duplex. To his left, Nelligan could see a window, with the image of a fat woman in curlers and four fat children shimmering behind a curtain of rain, staring out at the free show. The photographer joined him and they headed to the right.

Inside, the apartment was designed for ultimate simplicity. The front room was a box, with one entryway leading to a box of a kitchen and another leading to a short hallway and, Nelligan assumed, to boxlike bedrooms and a boxish bathroom. What the apartment's architect lacked in creativity was made up for by fashionable furniture and tasteful art. The living room was warm and comfortable with a couch and two chairs of black material with gold pinstripes, accentuated with blond wood. An expensive home entertainment center in a glass-and-maple cabinet dominated one wall, and a rubber plant loomed over one corner. The two paintings, one rococo lamp, and half a dozen *objets d'art* all suggested the feminine touch.

Two men from latent prints were dusting the room. A uniformed deputy stood by the kitchen door, shouting orders into a wall-mounted phone. Brief, white flashes of light erupted from down the hallway; the telltale sign of a police photographer at work. The *Post*'s shooter knelt and swiftly opened her shoulder bag, removing her camera body, lens, and hot-shoe flash. She took a measurement with her light meter and searched the room for the right shooting angle. Nelligan stepped over the kneeling forensics people, proving once again that if you look like you belong, you belong. On the entertainment center sat a glass and brass-framed picture of Geoffrey Eriksen.

"Hello, Mr. Nelligan." Tucker turned. Detective Sergeant Wiley was dressed in blue jeans, Nike tennis shoes, and a short black windbreaker, glistening with rain. The bottom third of his denim pant legs were soaked with rain. The lines under and around his eyes were deep, and he looked as if the squeal had caught him in bed.

"Hi, Sergeant. Do you know Sally Rojas? Sal, Sergeant Wiley."

Wiley turned to the shooter and nodded courteously. "How do you do, ma'am. Could you hold off on photographs for a moment or two? I'd certainly appreciate it."

The photographer cocked an eyebrow in Nelligan's direction, then shrugged and turned away.

"Thank you. Mr. Nelligan, care to come this way, please?"

Wiley headed down the carpeted hallway, Nelligan in tow. "Excuse me, Mr. Landsetter." The cop addressed a sheriff's deputy in the larger bedroom. "Are you finished in here?"

"Yessir. All yours. You city guys get the juicy ones, huh?" With a broad wink, the deputy sauntered out.

Nelligan stepped into the bedroom and whistled two notes. A huge brass canopy bed dominated the room, its frame draped with shimmering silk, the bedcover bearskin. Heavy red-and-cream drapes covered the window. Two ornate candelabra, unlit, sat on night tables on either side of the bed. Opposite the window hung an oil painting with garish, swirling bands of crimson and black in sensual and unsettling patterns. The rest of the furnishings matched the beautiful brass bed, with no extraneous household items visible and nothing out of place except for the corpse in the middle of the plush shag-carpeted floor.

It was a woman, young and truly beautiful, with a curly mass of blond hair outlining a face without makeup, and a diaphanous nightgown that made no effort to conceal her breasts and strong, flat stomach. She lay on her back, arms outstretched, one knee raised, the gossamer nightgown bunched up around her waist. A pool of blood had congealed in the layered material of the rug to the left of her skull. Four inches away, the edge of a mirrored night table was stained brown. Her right cheek was puffy and discolored.

"Hello," Nelligan said.

Wiley turned to him. "You've seen cadavers before."

"Yeah. Now and then. She's beautiful."

"Oh, yes. Jocelyn Sue Blaine. Age twenty-six."

"And she was Eriksen's lady?"

"No comment."

"I saw the picture out there."

"I know. No comment."

"How'd you find her?"

Wiley pushed his wire-rimmed glasses back up his nose. "Off the record. I've considered Mr. Eriksen a prime suspect from the beginning. He had lapses of time for which he could not, or would not, account. I had him followed. He led us here, just yesterday. Take a closer look at that bed."

Nelligan stepped forward and brushed back the silk curtains. Four oversized pillows were piled up at the head of the bed. He bent to look up at the underside surface of the canopy. "Oh-ho. Mirrored?"

Wiley knelt by the body and studied a thin gold bracelet around the girl's wrist. "Some of the men in vice knew her, vaguely. Ms. Blaine was a top-of-the-line tart." He stood and removed the glasses, rubbing his eyes vigorously. Wiley looked ten years older.

"'Tart'? I've heard cops call them tramps, whores, sluts, hookers, what have you. Never 'tarts.'"

"Trollop?" Wiley offered a fatigued smile.

"Do you have a statement for the press?"

"No. I wasn't expecting you this soon. You're awfully impressive, Mr. Nelligan."

"True. From the bruises and such, it looks like he hit her, she fell, clipped the dressing table, concussed and bled to death."

"Who hit her?" the cop asked, not putting much energy into his feigned ignorance.

"Uh-huh. Does this close the Llewelleyn murder investigation?"

"No. I don't suppose so. Please tell Ms. Rojas she can take ‚photos of the exterior and the front room, but not back here and not Ms. Blaine, all right?"

"He hits her, kills her, runs, but leaves his picture in her living room? This could be a frame, Wiley."

The cop sighed. "Yes. That's possible. Unlikely, but possible. Excuse me, Mr. Nelligan, I have some work to do."

Earlier, back at the *Post* building, Harry and Nelligan had agreed that Nelligan would head for Gresham to look into this latest homicide, while Harry would locate Eriksen. So it was, as Nelligan and Sally Rojas reached their destination, that Harry's dilapidated B210 pulled into the Eriksens' driveway and stopped beside a blue Plymouth with dual antenna.

Jamming his golf cap low on his brow and turning up his collar, Harry climbed out of the car and ran for the cover of the front porch. The bell was answered almost immediately by the human equivalent of a rhinoceros. Harry applied his kindest, least offensive voice. "I'm Professor Bishop. I need to speak to Mr. Eriksen, please. It's most important."

The monster stepped aside impassively and took Harry's hat and coat.

He was led to the den and was greeted by Geoffrey Eriksen, Irena Shoenborn-Eriksen, and a tall, blond man in sports coat and turtleneck.

"Henry! God, what are you doing here?" Eriksen jumped up. Shoenborn-Eriksen sat on a delicate wicker chair and sipped from an enormous snifter. Hers seemed to be the only glass in the room.

"Hullo, Geoffrey. Irena. Geoffrey, I thought you might need some help." Harry turned to the blond man. "You're Detective Kehough?"

"Yessir. You are . . . ?"

"Professor Bishop, from John Jacob Astor College. I'm a friend of the Eriksens."

"I see. How'd you know who I—"

"Antenna on your car. Tucker Nelligan mentioned your name. Detective, could I speak to Mr. Eriksen alone for a moment?"

"I don't think so, professor. I was just asking these folks some questions. May I ask what you're doing out at this hour, on a night like this?"

"Detective, please," Eriksen cut in. "May I have a moment with the professor?" Without waiting for a reply, he took Harry by the elbow and led him to the door. "I appreciate it. Thank you."

Irena had not looked up from her brandy snifter to acknowledge Harry's presence.

Eriksen led Harry out of the den and down the hallway to the front door. "Henry, I'm glad you're here. I'm in very big trouble."

"I know. A homicide just outside Gresham, I understand."

Eriksen struggled to keep his field commander's voice in a whisper. "You know?"

"Precious little. I know there's been another murder. I know the police were looking for you, and have apparently found you. May I assume the deceased in the suburbs is your lady friend?"

He expected pain in Eriksen's eyes, or perhaps even guilt. But Harry saw neither, simply a flash of impatience from a man with things to do and many obstacles in his way. "Yes. Her name was Jocelyn. Henry, she's dead."

"So I gather."

"They may think I did it."

"Indeed. I'd go so far as to say the police would have to be brain-dead to not think you did it."

"Henry, I didn't kill her!"

"Shh. Fine. Unfortunately, she was the star alibi for Llewelleyn's murder, the one you were saving for a rainy

day. Don't look now, Geoffrey, but it's raining forty days'
and forty nights' worth, and your alibi has become an al-
batross."

Eriksen dug a cigarette out of his jacket and lit it without
offering Harry one. "I know. This is very bad, Henry."

"True. You're taking it well. The young woman's death, I
mean."

Eriksen waved the cigarette in a small circle. "She was
. . . a pleasant diversion, Henry. I'm damned sorry she's
dead. Damned sorry. And it couldn't have happened at a
worse time, I assure you."

Harry said nothing.

"What should I do?"

"Were I you, Geoffrey, I'd tell our Detective Kehough
everything. The police are not the cardboard cutouts we
read about in mystery novels. Clearly they already know
about you and the young lady or they would never have put
an APB out on your—"

"What is it, Henry?"

"Hmm? Oh, nothing. Just had a notion. Geoffrey, is
there anything I can do for you?"

The industrialist inhaled smoke and searched Harry's
face. "No. Nothing I can think of. I also don't know why
you're doing as much as you are."

"Neither do I, to be honest. Getting involved is not my
trump suit, normally. I suppose a bit of my mother's Scots
stubbornness and father's military honor are swimming
around in my gene pool. Anyway, 'fraid I'm in this now, and
too damned curious to back out."

"Yes. Well, one way or another, I appreciate it. More
than you know. There *is* something you can do. I was going
to call a special, emergency session of the board for tomorrow, regarding Richard's death. I've scheduled it for four
o'clock. If you could inform the adminstration, Irena and I
shall handle the members."

"Certainly. Anything else?"

Eriksen gripped his arm and squeezed. "No, Henry.
Again, thank you."

"You're welcome. Geoffrey, you've asked for my help,
not my advice. Unfortunately, I've more of the latter than
the former. I think you would do well by telling the police
everything. It's the best solution to the problem."

"Very well. I'll consider it."

"Wait a minute. Did Llewelleyn know?"

For the first time, Eriksen avoided Harry's eyes. "Why do you ask?"

"Because the police will, of course."

"Oh. Yes. Of course. Yes, Henry, Richard knew about my . . . situation. In fact, he introduced Jocelyn and me. They were lovers for a time, last year."

"Oh."

"I'm not sure I like the sound of that 'oh,' Henry."

"And I'm not sure the police won't discover the link between your paramour and Llewelleyn. It may go better if they hear it from you first. Anyway, good night, Geoffrey."

Harry retrieved his damp hat and coat from the closet and opened the front door. Out on the porch, Eriksen shook his hand and stepped close. "Henry, few people in America ever stand up for their friends. Fewer still help acquaintances. That is my experience in this country, anyway. Thank you once again."

"See you tomorrow, Geoffrey. Good luck."

Eriksen withdrew into the house. Before the door could swing shut, it opened again and Detective Kehough stepped out, the collar of his sports coat turned up. "Professor, can I talk to you for a second?"

"Certainly."

Kehough opened his mouth to speak, stopped, and stared heavenward. "Good God."

"What is it?"

"Look! Stars!"

Harry did as directed. A dozen or so points of light were visible. "Orion's belt."

Kehough turned a bewildered gaze upon the professor. "Where the hell's the rain? The wind?"

"Looks like we're between fronts."

"Just like that? It was a fucking hurricane!"

"Welcome to the Pacific Northwest. Don't worry, I'm sure the rain will be back before dawn. And gone again and back again. I take it you aren't a native."

"No. Just transferred out here, from Chicago. Weird weather."

"Ah, Detective Kehough?"

"Hmm? Oh, yeah. I wondered what your connection is to Mr. Eriksen."

"I'm professor at the same college he—"

"Yeah, I know that. I mean his current troubles."

"What are his current troubles, Detective? Are you going to arrest Geoffrey?"

Kehough shrugged. "No. Not just yet, anyhow. I understand you're investigating the murder, on behalf of Eriksen."

"More or less; yes."

"Well, if I may, prof, two pieces of advice. One: don't get in our way or hinder our investigation. We're not crazy about amateurs muddying the waters. Two: if you do find out anything pertinent, I'd appreciate your telling us immediately. In fact, let's consider it a direct order. Withholding information or interfering with a policeman's duties aren't minor charges."

Harry mulled over the advice. "I understand, Detective. I promise to contact you if I figure this mess out."

"Yeah. You do that, professor. Good night."

He turned and reentered the Eriksens' home. Harry dug around in the various pockets of his voluminous coat until he found his key ring. As he reached the driver's side of the Datsun, an immense shadow separated itself from the overhang of the garage. The Eriksens' man—butler? majordomo? knee-breaker?—opened the door for him. Harry looked up at the simian face and tried to smile politely. "Thank you."

"Mr. Eriksen's been good to me," the human rhinoceros rumbled.

"I see."

"I owe him a great deal."

"Ah."

"It would pain me to see him hurt."

"Indeed. I'm trying to help him."

The monster nodded. "I find that a great relief, professor. I want to believe that you and I have interests that are conterminous."

"Er, yes."

"Because I would regret any contretemps between us."

"As would I."

"Drive carefully, professor." The monster's thick thumb depressed the locking mechanism and slowly closed the door. He rapped one hairy knuckle against the glass and bent low. "Use your seatbelt."

Harry quickly attached the seatbelt.

TWENTY-THREE

❖

Typical image of a Portlander: Tucker Nelligan drove to work Thursday morning wearing sunglasses and with the Jeep's windshield wipers activated. Oregon and Washington were between fronts at that hour, and the current heavenly cease-fire hadn't been long enough to affect the flooding. A few streets were still impassable, although the Jeep had a better time of it than many vehicles.

Nelligan parked in the *Post*'s underground lot, grabbed his attaché case and thirty-two-ounce cup of 7-Eleven coffee, and raced to the elevator. It wasn't eight yet, and the third floor newsroom was relatively quiet. Graveyard personnel were already gone or leaving, and day staffers were just beginning to straggle in.

Nelligan tossed his case onto his desk and headed for Joann Dembrow's. The news editor sat behind her terminal, her reading glasses perched on her nose. Nelligan turned her extra chair backward and straddled it, arms folded across the backrest. "Well?"

"Damned good stuff, Tuck." She squeezed his forearm affectionately. "When'd you file this?"

"About two this morning. I'm running on caffeine and Hostess Ding Dongs—it's all I could get out of that stupid Servo-mation machine. When can we go with it?"

Dembrow studied the story of Jocelyn Sue Blaine's murder and took a sip of Nelligan's coffee, unbidden.

"Epstein's on nights this month. He's been around. He saw it was good stuff and used it for the farm edition. It's already on the streets."

Nelligan chortled like a child on Christmas morning. "We scooped the entire mother-loving city!"

Dembrow leaned forward and ran a hand through Nelligan's hair. Nelligan flashed his canary-fed cat's grin and leaned forward, kissing his editor on the lips. "God, I'm good!" he cried.

As Harry applied pressure to his right leg, the water bubbled up and oozed around and into his shoe. He rubbed his eyes and tried to remember what he had done to displease the gods. He shifted his gaze slowly, taking it all in: the open sliding glass door leading to Kate Fairbain's balcony; the raindrenched curtains, splattered with mud; the lake of rainwater stretching from the balcony door to the formerly eggshell-white dining room wall; the sodden yellow leaves from the big oaks lining the condo's western boundary that were scattered throughout the room; the discoloration across the back of Kate's bronze and brown couch; the kaleidoscopic glitter from the shards of Tiffany shade surrounding the overturned lamp; the dozen receptacles on the balcony—wicker baskets, macramé hangers, ceramics, fire-baked earthenware—that now contained mud and sticks, but no sign of plant life.

A few days earlier, Harry had read about a job opening for a professor of agricultural sciences at the University of Riyadh, Saudi Arabia. He wondered how soon they would take him.

"Nelligan here."

"Tucker? Sandi."

Nelligan switched the phone to his other ear and spooned a gob of raspberry yogurt into his mouth. "Wumm."

"What? Hello?"

"Hi, Sand. Sorry about that. How's it going?"

"Pretty good. Listen, I've got Chem. in about five minutes, so I can't chat, but I've got some info for you."

"Info?"

"Yeah. Remember our deal?"

"Deal?"

"Tucker Nelligan . . ."

"Oh, right right right. Of course. You were going to do legwork for me. I remember. Sorry, kiddo, I didn't get much sleep last night. What've you got?"

"Well, for starters, Mr. Llewelleyn left no family, except an ex-wife in Calgary, Canada."

"Um-hum."

"You knew that?"

"Yes, Sandi. Anything else?"

"There's a new guy on the board—Elliot O'Malley?"

"Yeah, I know about him."

"Oh. Then you know he's from Calgary too."

Nelligan set down the yogurt and retrieved a pen and pad. "No. I didn't know that. How long ago did he live there?"

"Until four months ago. He moved to Portland last June."

"All right! Nice stuff, Braithwaite. Anything else?"

"Well, I don't know, exactly. Nothing specific."

"D'you have a hunch about something?"

"Yeah. I was asking around about Cordelia Apple-baum—"

"Hold it: asking around, how?"

"I told the people in the administration I was putting together a series of features on the board members. Nobody over in Savile Row considers us to be a real newspaper, so they didn't bother being evasive."

"Okay. Sounds good. What about Applebaum?"

"Well, I was talking to this guy who's in my Chem. class and work-studies over there, and he said Applebaum was pretty loaded."

"How'd he know?"

"I guess they keep a file on top financial contributors, and she's right up there. Thing is, she's only been contributing big for the past year or so. Before that: not a drop."

Nelligan scribbled the information in note-hand. "Anything else?"

"Well, she used to be a city council member, back in the early seventies."

"Yeah?"

"And that's the last job she had."

"What?"

"She hasn't been employed in the last fifteen years, Tuck. I don't know if she inherited big bucks or what. I found out her folks ran a leather tanning and upholstery place in Oregon City. I don't know—that doesn't sound like serious money-making to me."

Nelligan tapped the end of his pen against his chin. "That's interesting, all right."

"I suppose she could've invested her money, back when she was in city politics."

"Yeah. She plays the stocks, I understand. This is good stuff, Sandi. Really. What are you going to do now?"

"Now? Go to class and later work on my grad thesis."

"All right. Thanks for the legwork, Sandi. I owe you."

"That's right, Tucker Nelligan. You owe me the straight word on this story, for the *Pathfinder*. Right?"

"Right. We've got an agreement."

"You bet we do, Tucker. I'll call you later."

"Good enough. Bye." Nelligan hung up and began chewing on his thumb nail, trying to figure how best to circumvent this annoying agreement without actually *lying* to Sandi.

Harry rang the bell again and turned to look at the crystal-blue sky. It was nearly noon, and had already resumed raining in some parts of the city, so said the radio disk jockey on KMHD, but the air over Ladd's Addition was thin and cold and clear. According to the radio, the morning rush-hour traffic, which usually thinned out by nine, was still crawling through Portland. Flood stage had been reached and passed on almost every river, stream, and creek in the three-county metro area.

Donal Patrick Cavenaugh, artist, alumnus, and trustee, lived in a sprawling, three-story colonial house on a corner lot. The wide lawn in front was brown and unkept—more thistle than grass. The veranda was piled with boxes and crates, most covered by a cracked green tarpaulin. Harry rang the bell once more and the door creaked open.

"What!" Cavenaugh thrust his head out, his eyes narrowed against the sunlight. He had lost most of the hair off the top of his head, and the fine silver fringe hung down almost to his shoulders. Harry extended his hand and smiled. "Mr. Cavenaugh. I'm Henry Bishop, from Astor. Sorry to disturb you this morning, but—"

"Then bloody don't!" the little Irishman spat. "I'm working now, can't you see. What is it?"

"It's about Astor, and Richard Llewelleyn. May I come in?"

Cavenaugh held his position for a moment, his raw, red face a mixture of anger, frustration, and uncertainty, then stepped back into the shadows. Harry followed him in.

To refer to the area beyond the door as a living room would be a mistake. It had served that function once, and still contained a fireplace with brick mantel and hearth, and decorative window seats before the two spacious bay windows. But the room's furniture had all been removed, save for one tall bar stool. The hardwood floor was covered by a series of cheap, mismatched throw rugs. Four sculptures dominated the room, their sizes ranging from three feet high and tubular to at least eight feet high and the same width. Before this last, massive, arcane piece of twisted iron rested the stool and a Black and Decker standing tool kit. Various power tools and chisels stuck out of the kit at all angles. Nearby stood a large glass ashtray, filled to overflowing with cigarette butts and ashes. The room stank of cigarette smoke.

Cavenaugh fit the room perfectly. He wore an enormous, stained bathrobe, cinched at the waist, the wide sleeves hanging to his knuckles. His much-wrinkled chinos and leather thongs had seen better days. The little man looked every inch the eccentric artist.

"What do you want?" he asked unpleasantly, returning to the stool and perching, one foot on a dusty throw rug, facing away from Harry.

"To ask you a few questions."

"I'm busy, Bishop. Can it wait? That ass Eriksen has called another meeting of the bloody board for this afternoon. We can talk then, all right?"

"Alas, no. This won't take more than a minute."

Cavenaugh sighed a most theatrical sigh and spun around on the stool, arms folded across his sunken chest.

"Llewelleyn handled your books, I understand?"

"Aye. He did."

"Were you pleased with the work he did for you?"

"That'd be none of your business, Bishop. Who're you? You're some sort of professor, aren't you?"

"Yes. And faculty liaison to the board this term."

"And what right do you have coming around botherin' me with questions about my money? That's none of yuir business, I'm thinkin'."

The Irish accent was thick with a lower-class, regional dialect, which Harry found most interesting, since, if memory served, Donal Patrick Cavenaugh was born and raised in Cincinnati. Harry wondered what else about the man was affectation.

"Mr. Cavenaugh, with all due respect, there's been two murders. I've been asked to look around a bit, and I need a little information. I'm sorry if I interrupted you."

"Two murders? Who else got himself killed?"

"A young woman, whom I understand is only tangentially involved with the board. That's neither here nor there."

"Then why bring it up?"

"Point well made. Forgive me for digressing. About Llewelleyn . . . ?"

Cavenaugh ran a hand across the three days' growth of beard and nodded. "What the fuck. Yes, I was happy with Llewelleyn. He was a shit, o'course, but he was good with money and stocks and the like."

"Did you know he wanted to replace Geoffrey Eriksen as chairperson of the board?"

The Irishman grinned and dug a crumpled pack of unfiltered Camels out of the bathrobe pocket. Harry noticed for the first time the cursive logo of a posh Portland hotel on the robe pocket. *Certainly stolen.* "'Chairperson.' Good Christ, I hate those so-called feminist euphemisms. Did I know Llewelleyn wanted to be chairman of the board? Sure, I knew. He told me."

"And you were going to support him?"

"Again, none of yuir business. Time's up, Bishop. I've work to be doin'."

Was it the eyes? The twitchy, nervous energy of his movements? Something about Donal Patrick Cavenaugh sat wrong with Harry. The man looked like he was on a magnificent caffeine buzz. "Are you all right, Mr. Cavenaugh? You seem—"

"Bishop, why in God's name are ye rooting around in this? It's none of yuir business, man."

Harry just shook his head. "Truth to tell, I suppose I like Geoffrey Eriksen. He's refreshingly abrupt and honest. And he seems good at what he does."

Cavenaugh slid off the stool and flicked the half-finished cigarette toward the ashtray, hitting it dead center. "What's tha' got to do with me, boyo? I don't give a tinker's good God damn about you an' Eriksen. You can be fuckin' each other's brains out, for all I'm interested. I'm busy, man! Leave me be!"

"Geoffrey is the prime suspect in Llewelleyn's murder. I mean to prove he didn't do it."

"Good for you. You go do that, Bishop. You'll excuse me, now." The sculptor gently took Harry by the arm and motioned toward the door. As he did so, the robe's sleeve fell back, revealing bandages around the left hand and arm, extending at least to the elbow.

"What happened to you?"

"Ran into a bleedin' doorknob. Please, Bishop. I'll be at this afternoon's stupid meeting. We can talk then, if you insist."

At the door, Harry made a last stab at civility. "I'm sorry to disturb you, Mr. Cavenaugh."

"Fine, thank you. Good-bye."

"Also, sorry about your carpet."

That stopped him. Cavenaugh made eye contact for a fraction of a moment then started fussing with another cigarette and disposable lighter. The flame was adjusted for maximum output, and leapt up at least half a foot when Cavenaugh thumbed the wheel. "Carpet?" His query was overly casual.

"Yes, the one you spilled turpentine on. Nasty stain, that."

"Aye. How do you know about tha'?"

"Friend of a friend. That was Monday night, wasn't it?"

"I forgot. I'd love to share your enthusiasm for rugs, Bishop, but I've na' the time. Good day to you."

"Good day, Mr. Cavenaugh. See you this afternoon."

The door slammed shut. Behind him, Harry heard the dead-bolt lock tumble into place.

Nelligan rapped on the already open door. "Hel-lo?"

The tubby man waved from behind a cluttered desk, but did not look up. The desk was nestled in one corner of a room that was otherwise filled to overflowing with a jumble of boxes, crates, and cartons. A narrow corridor had been perilously carved into the mess, leading from the desk to the door that was jammed perpetually open.

Nelligan stood in the hallway on the third floor of the Governor's Building, a turn-of-the-century brownstone in the downtown historic district that housed a ramshackle collection of doctors, dentists, lawyers, and social organizations. The man inside the office sat with pen in one hand, tapping out digits on a calculator with the other, and with a slide rule clenched between his teeth. His eyes were magnified behind thick, round glasses. He was madly scribbling down notations, checking again and again with the calculator, then dropping the pen to measure something against the slide rule. After two minutes of this, Nelligan cleared his throat.

"Ah. Right. Hi." The man looked up and smiled shyly. "You're Mr. Nelligan, from the *Post*?"

"Yes. Elliot O'Malley?"

"Yes, sir. Sorry about all this. Please, ah, well, come in."

Nelligan squeezed down the aisle. O'Malley stood and removed his glasses, polishing them with the end of his tie. His eyes were very small and spaced far apart, Nelligan noticed. He smiled and shrugged and wiped his palms against his trouser legs before shaking Nelligan's proffered hand. "Please forgive the incredible mess. This isn't our permanent office, just a place to store things until we're ready to move in."

"'We'?"

"O'Malley Timber. I'm, ah, owner." He sounded like a schoolboy caught smoking in the lavatory.

"Well, I appreciate your giving me a few moments, Mr. O'Malley." Nelligan perched on the corner of the metal army-issue desk. O'Malley remained standing. "I'd like to ask you a few questions about Richard Llewelleyn and the Astor board of trustees."

"Ah. Well, okay, Mr. Nelligan, but I just joined the board this month. I've only been to one meeting, so far. I'm afraid I don't know much, actually."

"That's all right. You're an alumnus?"

"Yes. Class of fifty-four. It was, um, pretty different back then. The school, I mean."

"How so?"

"Smaller. Astor had less of a reputation as a high-class, liberal arts school. It was just a good place to get a degree without going Back East."

"Are you from this area?"

"From the Northwest, yes. Originally from Kellogg, Idaho. My father was in the timber industry up there."

"But you've just moved back, is that right?"

"Yes. From Canada."

"Calgary?"

"Yes." O'Malley eyes clouded over. "Um, may I ask—"

"Henry Bishop is a friend of mine. He mentioned you were from Calgary."

"Oh. He's in political science, isn't he?"

"Yeah."

"He seems nice."

"I suppose you knew Llewelleyn from Calgary?"

"Richard Llewelleyn lived in Calgary?"

"So I understand."

"No, I didn't know him there. Isn't that funny." O'Malley seemed unamused.

"Well, his ex-wife, ah . . ."—Nelligan flipped back the pages of his notebook—"Carol Jurgensen Llewelleyn, lives there still. Did you know her?"

O'Malley smiled and shoved his glasses back up his nose. "No. People from the States have funny notions about Canada. Calgary's a fairly big city, Mr. Nelligan. It's got about a half of a million people, now."

"Oh. I didn't know it was that big."

O'Malley shrugged, his face pink.

"And you didn't know either of the Llewelleyns?"

"No."

Nelligan justified his visit by asking a dozen more questions, discovering how and why the man had become a trustee, and his perceived role therein. It was just about noon when he finally closed the notebook and glanced around the storage-area-turned-office. "I noticed the door won't close. How do you keep this stuff from being stolen?"

"Oh, I've based my trust on the criminals of Portland."

"You have?"

"Yes. I'm assuming they're all smart enough to steal valuable things and won't bother with these boxes of trash paper."

Nelligan laughed, taken by surprise by the sudden glimpse of humor. "But you're moving out soon?"

"Yes. Three weeks, they tell me. We've got a place going up in Tigard."

"You're building? I'm amazed, what with land prices around here."

O'Malley blushed again and wiped his palms together. "Well, I thought we could splurge, instead of moving into preexisting space."

"I take it your company is doing all right, then?"

"Yes, sir. Not bad."

"Off the record, how much does O'Malley Timber turn in a year?"

"Oh," O'Malley said softly. "About a hundred to a hundred thirty million dollars. American."

TWENTY-FOUR

✤

As planned, Harry and Tucker rendezvoused at the Deco Penguin at one, late enough for some of the noon lunch crowd to dissipate. Nelligan was seated at the massive, hardwood bar with a cup of coffee and the latest issue of the *Columbia Journalism Review.* Harry hung his coat on the rack by the door, took the swivel stool next to Nelligan, and ordered a Scotch and a bowl of Dutch Rhodes's famous homemade soup (Swiss cheese and leek with mushrooms and a side of fresh garlic bread).

He took a first, solid sip of the whisky before getting down to business. "How'd the interview go with O'Malley?"

"Waste of time," Nelligan replied. "He's from Calgary, Alberta. Did you know that?"

"So is Llewelleyn's ex-wife: interesting. Anything to it?"

Nelligan looked crestfallen. "No. How'd you know about Llewelleyn's ex?"

"Last night, before we left the *Post,* you told me I could look through your notes. I did so after talking to Eriksen."

"You're kidding?"

"No. Tuck, I hope you don't mind. I *did* ask, you know."

"Harry, are you yanking my leg?"

Puzzled, Harry merely shrugged.

"You read my notes?"

"Yes."

"From my steno pads?"

"Yes. Tucker, I'm truly sorry. I didn't mention—"

"Harry, I write in code. It's my own personal form of note-hand. No one can read my notes."

"Oh."

Harry ordered another Scotch from Dutch, who reminded him he was teaching a class in the bar that afternoon. "Right you are. Coffee, please."

Nelligan grinned and grabbed a handful of popcorn from the bowl on the bar. "You cracked my code. Jesus."

"All right, I'll confess to a certain small knack for ciphers."

"Is that what you did for the CIA?"

"Sometimes. Please, seriously, don't make a federal case . . . let me rephrase that."

"So. The Mad Hatter strikes again."

"Aargh. Tucker, in all honesty, I've always hated that sobriquet. Let's drop it, shall we?"

Satisfied to snare even a hint of Harry's past, Nelligan obligingly let it go at that. "How's Cavenaugh?"

"Hurt. His left hand is bandaged, from palm to elbow, at least."

Nelligan dug out his pad and made a note (conscious that now, for the first time in his professional career, someone else could read the note). "Where's he live?"

"Ladd's Addition."

"Okay, nearest hospital would be, what? Providence Med. Center?"

"I suppose, yes."

"I've got a contact there, owes me one."

"Good thinking. You might also check Mount Hood Community Hospital, that's near where the girl was killed. By the way, I read your piece this morning. Very good."

"True. So d'you think our sculptor is a murderer?"

"Hard to say. He was damned secretive, and unhappy to learn I knew about his carpet. He was also quick to get me out of his house. Something of interest, there were four pieces he seemed to be working on."

"Yeah? Funny, I don't follow the local art scene all that close, but I gathered Donal Patrick Cavenaugh was in semiretirement."

"Exactly. I recognized all four pieces from a show he did, about 1982. I'd say he isn't working at all, and keeps a few pieces in his work room for unexpected guests."

"Harry, I'll level with you—I think this investigation became a foregone conclusion when Ms. Jocelyn Sue Blaine got herself iced last night."

Harry winced. "Her death does rather change the nexus of the problem, doesn't it? Even if it was chance-medley, and not premeditated. We were assuming the murderer was a board member."

"And now, it looks like one of two people: Geoffrey Eriksen or the Dragon Lady. They're the only two with possible bad blood toward Llewelleyn and Jocelyn Blaine."

"But that still leaves us with a bevy of questions, Tuck. For instance, what is Geraldo Avenceña up to in the chapel? Who requisitioned my résumé from Archives? Here's one for you: Llewelleyn knew Ms. Blaine. He even introduced her to Eriksen. Important or not? And the biggie: how did someone so universally unappealing as Richard Llewelleyn become a member of the board of trustees?"

"Here's another one, Harry. Your friend Cordelia Applebaum hasn't been employed since 1974. You told me last night her apartment is breathtaking."

"It is. Your point?"

"How does she afford the place? What's her source of income. I had . . . an associate . . . do a little digging into Applebaum's past. She didn't inherit her dough, and, like the ad says, she has no visible means of support."

Harry pondered the information while Dutch topped off his coffee. "So what do we do this afternoon?" Nelligan asked.

"Well, I've got class, for which I'm completely unprepared, and a board meeting this afternoon. Do you have plans?"

"Nothing hard and fast."

"Do me a favor, Tuck. Find out what's what with Geraldo. You have a sublime talent for intimidating people."

"Thank you very much."

"Not at all."

"All right, Harry. I'll rattle his cage. I think I'll also call on our vaudeville team, Wiley and Kehough, and see what they're up to. They may have found a lead on our ersatz Ms. Blaine."

Harry frowned. "Why ersatz? Don't you believe she was . . . ah, a sexual entrepreneur?"

"You sensitive male, you. No, I'm sure she was a pro. It's just that's probably not her name."

"No?"

"Harry, if you were a high-class hooker, would you go by Henry Bishop?"

"What does it pay, compared to education?"

"From what I understand almost all the topflight hookers use fake names, especially if they're working in the 'burbs, or more than one jurisdiction. Keeps the cops from pulling their rap sheets. The only thing you can bet is her initials. They're original, chances are."

"Oh. Cordelia."

"Something?"

"Yes. I'm an idiot. Initials. Don't let's worry about Cordelia Applebaum any more, Tuck. She's not our culprit."

"You're sure?"

"I am now, yes. I'll explain later."

Nelligan paid his tab and headed out, leaving his friend with barely an hour to plan a class lecture.

The rain was holding off again; the sun glinted off the myriad rain-soaked, reflective surfaces of the city. Nelligan drove to the college, shielding his eyes from the quick, painful blasts of sunlight that proved too dazzling for the sunglasses. Sure enough, upon reaching Astor he found the students and staff hustling from building to building, wearing sunglasses and carrying umbrellas, armed against the fickle autumnal weather of the Northwest.

Nelligan parked the Jeep illegally behind the chapel and hurried around the building, checking for open or uncurtained basement windows. There were none. If Harry was right, and someone had been using the chapel as a covert base of operations, then the basement was the best place to look.

He entered through the back door, moving quietly, his face set in its prepackaged smile of innocence. *Who, me? Lurking? Why, whatever do you mean?*

Geraldo Avenceña was in his basement office, debating with a student on the biblical basis of liberation theology. Nelligan listened to their voices from the hallway, testing each doorknob he came upon. With the exception of Geraldo's office and a broom closet/water heater/storage area, every door was locked. It was nearly three o'clock when the student raced out, passing the reporter without a glance. Nelligan rapped on the door, confident he finally knew something Harry Bishop didn't.

"Yes?"

Nelligan, who had never met Avenceña, wasn't prepared for the astounding mass of the chaplain, who rose from behind his desk to fill the room with his presence. "May I help you?"

"Ah, yes. Reverend Avenceña?"

"Yes."

"Tucker Nelligan, *Post*."

"Oh. Hello. I think I've seen your name in the paper. What brings you to John Jacob Astor?"

Unbidden, Nelligan took a seat on the chaplain's couch. "Harry Bishop and I have been working together, trying to figure out who killed Richard Lleweileyn."

Geraldo sat. His chair creaked in protest. "A terrible thing. I also read the account this morning, about the woman Geoffrey Eriksen was . . . oh, that's where I've seen your name."

"Yes. I wrote that."

"That seemed like an amazing accusation to make, Mr. Nelligan. You implied Geoffrey and that woman were having an affair."

Nelligan polished the lenses of his steel-rimmed shades against the inner lining of his jacket. "I didn't *imply* anything, and I'm not responsible for what people infer. I *said* Eriksen's picture was in her home and the police had a bulletin out on his car."

"I see. Well, if there's any way I can help—"

"There is, Reverend. Harry's told me all about his concerns regarding your switching positions on divestment."

Geraldo frowned and Nelligan held up a hand, palm forward. "This information was told to me in confidence. Harry Bishop is one of my best friends. I wouldn't print anything he told me without first digging it up on my own."

"My vote on South Africa has nothing to do with Richard's death, Mr. Nelligan."

"Harry thinks otherwise. You were planning to vote for divestment. Then, after speaking to Llewelleyn, you changed your vote. Once Llewelleyn was dead, you changed it back to 'aye.' Is that about right?"

"No! I mean, I know I wobbled a bit on the subject, but—"

"Did Llewelleyn *tell* you to vote against divestment?"

"Mr. Nelligan, please—"

"I don't think you killed him, if that's any consolation, Reverend. Neither does Harry."

"Oh. Well, that's a relief. If I may ask, what *do* you believe?"

"I believe Llewelleyn was one of those persons with a knack for finding another's weakness, and exploiting it. I believe that's how he became a trustee. I believe he was using his position to gain some sort of social clout and to line his pockets, by way of the endowment campaign. I believe he wanted to become chairperson of the board to further those ends. I believe he had something on you, and told you to vote accordingly. How'm I doing so far?"

Geraldo had picked up a pen and was tapping a rapid tattoo on his desk blotter. He thought about it for a while, then nodded. "Off the record?"

"All right. For now."

"You're doing very well, Mr. Nelligan. You seem to understand the late Richard Llewelleyn perfectly."

"Thank you."

"Have you figured out what he 'had on me'?"

"Yes, I think I have, now. According to these books on your desk and shelves, and the conversation you just had with that student, you're an advocate of liberation theology. As I understand it, that's the belief that the various churches of the world should work on behalf of the poor of every country, regardless of political situations."

Geraldo's lips twitched. "That's roughly accurate."

"Harry tells me someone was hanging out here in the chapel. I'd say that someone was an illegal alien, hiding out from customs and immigration people, right?"

"Go on."

"Nicaraguan? Mexican? Chilean?"

"Does it matter?"

"No, not really. Is he, or are they, still here?"

No answer. Geraldo's face revealed neither hostility nor fear.

"Okay. Fair enough. May I tell you, sir, that I think you're a flaming moron?"

Anger flared quickly in the jet-black eyes, and the pen snapped in two between Geraldo's thick fingers. "You don't share my theological or political views, Mr. Nelligan: that's fine. I don't ask you to."

"Oh, it's not that. I *do* share your views on this particular subject. But Harry Bishop is so liberal, he makes either of us look like William Rehnquist. And he's your friend."

Geraldo tossed the broken pen into the garbage can and attempted unsuccessfully to wipe ink off his fingers with a Kleenex. He avoided Nelligan's eyes.

"Harry's been so worried about you, he hasn't been able to think straight about the murder. He's damned good at figuring these things out, normally. You've been distracting him. There are also a couple of bright-as-a-penny cops running the investigation, and chances are they've twigged to your unusual behavior and mysterious goings-on. If so, you've been distracting them too."

"I see. What you say is . . . probably true. What are you going to do now, Mr. Nelligan?"

"About your little Underground Railroad? When the time is right, I'm going to badger and pester you until you agree to give me an interview. No names or locations will be used, I promise you. For now, I'm going to help Harry figure out what's going on around here."

Geraldo glanced at the clock above the couch and stood. For a fleeting moment, his passive exterior cracked and Nelligan saw absolute fatigue show through. Geraldo covered it quickly. "Mr. Nelligan, I appreciate what you've said to me. I've been acting irresponsibly. I've . . . probably been a flaming moron. There's an emergency meeting of the board in about ten minutes. I'll apologize to Harry first thing, and let him know what's been going on here at the chapel."

Tucker stood and offered his hand, which was engulfed in Geraldo's meaty palm. "Good plan, Reverend. Harry won't turn you in, I'm positive. Now, about that interview . . ."

TWENTY-FIVE

❖

As always, the Colossus Sisters arrived first, a good twenty minutes early, and staked out adjacent seats in the Karl W. Kneible Room. The newest trustee, Elliot O'Malley, arrived next, with Cordelia Applebaum and Donal Patrick Cavenaugh hot on his heels. As Cordelia and O'Malley started up a pleasant conversation, Cavenaugh sank quietly into a chair and lit up a cigarette. Big Sam Broderick entered promptly at four, all smiles and too-loud greetings for the group. Geraldo Avenceña stood in the SUB hallway, talking softly to Harry Bishop. The two men were seen to shake hands and enter the conference room, a few minutes past the hour.

"Has anyone seen our chairman?" Big Sam bellowed.

"Or his wife," Cavenaugh mumbled, his cigarette smoke drawing theatrical sighs of protest from the Colossus Sisters.

"Oh, I'm sure they'll be along shortly," Cordelia chirped amiably. "I believe I'll help myself to the tea while we wait." She and the Sisters moved toward the wheeled cart by the windows, the primary topic of conversation, of course, Richard Llewellyn.

"Hello, professor." Big Sam Broderick jarred Harry's spine with a tremendous slap on the shoulder. Broderick maneuvered his mammoth body between Harry and the rest of the group. "How's life?"

"Fine, thanks. You?"

"I'll tell you, professor, I'm mightily bothered." For once, his voice was held in check so no one else could overhear. Harry's curiosity was instantly piqued.

"Oh?"

"Yessir. I understand you've been nosing around in this damned business with Richard."

"Unofficially, yes."

"I see. I also understand the Keystone Kops are gettin' ready to arrest Geoffrey. Is that so?"

"Yes, Mr. Broderick, I think it is."

"I'll tell you right now, mister, Geoffrey hated old Richard. Hell, everyone in their right mind did. But he didn't kill him, and to suggest that he did is two things. First, it's asinine, and anyone makin' such an accusation is going to end up looking like a jackass. Second, it's slander. You understand slander, I trust, professor."

"Yes, Mr. Broderick. May I ask who told you I was looking into this situation?"

"You may not. None of your business."

"I see. Did that person also tell you I wanted nothing to do with the investigation, and only did so on behest of Geoffrey?"

Broderick's thick eyebrows bunched above his tiny eyes. "Yeah?"

"Yes. Geoffrey asked me to lend a hand, and I've been doing just that."

Broderick ran stubby fingers through his sparse hair. "Oh. Well, professor, I guess I've managed to look like a walkin', talkin' dildo once again."

Harry's laugh broke out before he could subdue it, and every eye in the room turned to them. "Fear not, Mr. Broderick. I understand whence your concerns."

"'Whence.' Never heard a man use that word before. Hangin' out with you educated types is helpin' my image." Broderick, his concerns abated, thumped Harry on the back. "James Samuel Broderick, Senior, rest his soul, didn't raise me to be a fool, but this time I jumped to conclusions without knowin' what was what. I apologize for that, sir."

"Forgotten."

"What the hell's going on out there?" Broderick peered over Harry's head at the open double doors leading to the corridor. Bright, white lights bobbed against the far wall and a low, frantic din began to rise.

Once more unto the breach, my friends, Harry thought. He had heard the sound before, and recognized it as a school of journalists in a feeding frenzy.

Geoffrey Eriksen and Irena Shoenborn-Eriksen burst into the room. Three campus security officers barred the door against the reporters, who tossed a last, futile volley of questions at the couple. One of the cops entered, closed the doors and bolted them into the floor with an in-built lever.

Eriksen, his square face set in jagged lines of determination, moved to the head of the table, set down his attaché case, and rapped his class ring three times on the wood. "Are we all here? Shall we get to business?"

Without a word, Irena took the seat to his right. She knew, and every person in the room knew she knew, that they had all read the *Post* article linking her husband to a dead call girl. Harry thought Shoenborn-Eriksen's coolness under fire was remarkable. After a brief, deeply uncomfortable silence, the other trustees and ex-officios took their places.

Due to the short notice for the emergency meeting, most of the administration contingent was absent. Even the faculty liaison was not obligated to attend this meeting, though Harry wouldn't have missed it for the world. When everyone was seated, Eriksen took command. "Very good. I apologize for the short notice. Thank you for coming. This meeting shouldn't take much time. We need to decide what to do about Richard Llewelleyn. He sat on three permanent committees, and we will need to redelegate his responsibilities."

The trustees stirred uneasily, taken aback by Eriksen's business-as-usual briskness. However, thanks to the chairperson's titanium force of will, and much to Harry's surprise, the board members soon got into the corporate swing of things. Robert's Rules of Order were unlimbered, and the nine trustees began jockeying duties and obligations.

Harry was in the perfect position. As liaison, he had no official duties, except to take notes and report back to the faculty. He was convinced, now more than ever, that the murder of Richard Llewelleyn was connected to Astor's board, as was, most probably, that of Jocelyn Sue Blaine. Harry sat back and watched the disparate group: the Colossus Sisters, with their nonstop chatter and apparently sincere feelings of love and duty toward the college; Eriksen, with his steely approach to running the organization. He was like a tank commander, Harry thought, ruling like a despot without alienating anyone. Irena Shoenborn-Eriksen sat quietly and responded only when spoken to. How different from her usual, cool-as-frost businesswoman's aplomb.

Unlike Shoenborn-Eriksen, and despite the chaotic events of the week, the rest of the board seemed more or less themselves—O'Malley was quiet and thoughtful, volunteering for some responsibilities but not allowing himself to be roped into others. Donal Patrick Cavenaugh sat slumped low in his seat, his bandaged left hand on his lap, his right hand drumming nonstop on the tabletop. From time to time, Harry thought he caught the sculptor staring at him. Tiny Cordelia was the aging, liberal Doña Quixote, forever operating behind a façade of genteel, old-world manners, but deftly blocking any actions with which she disagreed. Geraldo Avenceña sat beside Harry, silently drawing cones, circles, and squares on his photocopy of the agenda. Those who didn't know Geraldo would think, incorrectly, he wasn't paying attention. Big Sam sat on Geraldo's other side, and maintained his image as a living cauldron of bombast. Lee Connar and three other adminstrators—sans L. Charles "Chuck"—sat together. Connar threw Harry a couple of quick, hostile glances. Harry idly wondered what he had done this time.

Forty-five minutes after he entered the conference room, Eriksen made a small, precise check mark beside the final item on the agenda. "That should conclude this meeting. Further business? Anyone?"

"Yes." Cavenaugh sat up straight for the first time, and every head turned in his direction.

"Donal?"

"Yes, I've a motion to make. Can I see hands for everyone who's been questioned by a *Post* reporter named Nelligan regarding Llewelleyn's murder?"

There was nervous clearing of throats and quick glances around the room. O'Malley and Broderick raised their hands, as did Feingarten and Fenscher. Finally, Shoenborn-Eriksen nodded and flicked her wrist in acknowledgment. Geoffrey Eriksen did the same. "Your point, Donal?"

"Simply this, Geoffrey. I take it Nelligan didn't talk to you, padre? Or you, Cordelia, me love?" Neither trustee replied. "Nor I. But I'd wager my yearly bar bill that both of ye were interrogated by our esteemed faculty liaison here, the good Doctor Henry Bishop, Ph.D., no?"

Neither Cordelia nor Geraldo denied his charge.

"Me too." Cavenaugh thumped the desk with his right fist.

"Donal, if there's a point here . . ."

"There is, Geoffrey. Our inquisitive Professor Bishop, as you all may recall, was up to his ears in the murder of that lad, the Wasserman boy, last year. That story was covered by none other than Tucker Nelligan, ace reporter from the *Portland Post*. And now the two of them are messin' around this murder, and at our expense. I'd like to move that the board officially complain to the most honorable President L. Charles 'Chuck' Eckersley, idiot and all-around ass, as well as the dean of faculty and anyone else we can protest to, to get this amateur detective ousted from our midst. Seconds?"

At the outset of the tirade, Harry had smiled politely and borrowed Geraldo's pen. Now he scribbled a note on the back of his agenda, folded it in two, and wrote Cavenaugh's name on the outside. He passed it to his left, and the note went from hand to hand till it reached the sculptor.

"I'll be honest," Big Sam burst in, "I'm none to crazy about private investigations of a murder or murders. I spoke to the professor a little while ago and, er, he assured me his intentions are honorable. Still . . ."

"Still," Cordelia intervened, "and I mean no offense, Harry, it does seem a bit contrary to have a college employee investigating this situation. We all have great respect for Professor Bishop's abilities, but I'm afraid I'm forced to agree with Donal. Harry, forgive me. I second the—"

"Wait." Donal Patrick refolded the note, his bandaged hand above the table for the first time. Without looking up, he cleared his throat. "I withdraw the motion."

Eriksen overpowered the general murmur around the table. "Please, people! Order. Donal, none of us has the time or patience for games. If you want to withdraw your motion, you may, but that will be the end of it."

"Yes. Withdrawn." Eyes still on the table, the sculptor stuffed Harry's note in his jacket pocket.

"Too late." Shoenborn-Eriksen spoke up suddenly. "It's been seconded." She glared with undisguised malice at Harry.

Eriksen rubbed his chiseled jaw, contemplating his position. Four of the surviving nine trustees had expressed concern over Harry's investigation, and Robert's Rules aside, that sort of voting bloc was not to be ignored. "Before this goes any further, I would like to make a statement to the board."

"Geoffrey—"

The chairman barreled smoothly over his wife's protest. "The police have, of course, been investigating Richard's murder. From the first, I considered their chief suspect. I didn't particularly want word of this getting out, so I asked the professor to look around, unofficially. He did so, on *my* behalf. My reasons for asking his assistance are neither here nor there. I shall assume you all read the *Post* this morning? If not, it reported that I am, still, considered a prime suspect. That bit of information out on the table, I thought it best to let this group know of my request to the professor."

All of which left Harry in his least favorite position— smack in the center of the spotlight. He smiled bleakly at the sea of faces turned to him inquisitively.

"If I may?" Broderick spoke up. "I'd like to know what the good professor's found out. I think we've got a right to know that, don't you, Geoffrey?"

There was a general murmur of agreement. Harry cleared his throat. "When Mr. Eriksen asked me to lend a hand, I told him I wasn't much of a detective. That was an overestimation of my limited skills. So, as much as I would love to leap to my feet, point to someone, and shout 'There's your villain!' I'm afraid I can't."

"What *can* you say, professor?" one of the Sisters asked.

"I can tell you that the police know a great deal more than they're saying to the press. I can also tell you that Richard Llewelleyn was a gifted and hardworking blackmailer, but of course that's not such a surprise to many of you."

This statement was greeted by a volley of shouted questions, accusations, suggestions, and not a few unkind epithets. Connar groaned and rubbed his forehead. Geraldo alone was silent. He casually touched Harry's forearm in a sign of solidarity.

Eriksen's cool finally snapped. He slapped the table, open-palmed. "*Enough!* Quiet." His anger defused the angry energy in the room, and the cacophony ceased as suddenly as it had begun. "Henry, perhaps you could tell us what you mean by that?"

"Simply, Llewelleyn should never have been a trustee of this college. He doesn't fit the profile in the least. He also should not have been a serious candidate for the chair, which I understand he was."

"Well, he did make an awful lot of money for Astor," Cordelia interjected, fiddling nervously with a monogrammed handkerchief.

"True, and at least three people have cited that as the reason he was allowed on the board. But that happened after he was a member, not when he was a candidate."

"Meaning?" Eriksen demanded.

"Meaning, I submit that Richard Llewelleyn blackmailed several of you in order to become a trustee, and was diligently blackmailing others of you in order to take Mr. Eriksen's position. I might point out that this has already been confirmed by one trustee."

"Who?" Shoenborn-Eriksen's face was drawn and unhealthily white.

"Me." Geraldo faced the pallid woman. His voice boomed in the hush that followed. "Richard knew certain facts about me which I didn't want publicized. I'm not at liberty to say any more than that."

Harry took advantage of his friend's confession to study the faces arrayed before him. Very few showed any surprise. In fact, the only people apparently shocked were Mrs. Fenscher and Mrs. Feingarten, and Harry had never seriously considered them suspect anyway.

"I see." Eriksen resumed his seat. "Well. This . . . situation seems to be deteriorating. Henry, do you believe the police know more than they're saying?"

"Yes."

"What does that mean?"

"I haven't the faintest notion."

"Harry." Cordelia leaned forward. "Do you think one of us killed Richard and that girl?"

Yes. "Well, I'd hate to say that. I certainly don't have any evidence linking anyone in this room to the murders. Also, it may not be prudent to assume that the same person killed both Llewelleyn and Ms. Blaine. The police haven't decided on that, just yet."

A deluge of questions were hurled at him, and Harry realized, once again, that the illusion of his detecting skills was being perpetuated. "Please, ladies and gentlemen. I really can't answer most of your questions. However, I will be in my office this evening, following the meeting. If any of you wish to continue this, I'd be more than happy to tell you what I can. I will not, I should add, be slandering or indicting anyone. Right now, though, I would like to apologize to all of you for sidetracking this meeting. I'm sure we all have more important things to do than listen to the senile ravings of an aging political scientist. Geoffrey?"

The chairman checked his Rolex. "It is getting late. Once again, I thank you, professor. Is there any other business before this body? Anyone? No? Then I call this meeting adjourned."

The group began to disperse. Shoenborn-Eriksen, without a word or a glance at her husband, hurried off the dais and up the aisle toward the doors at the back of the seating area—away from the press.

Lee Connar came around the table and rested a hand on Harry's shoulder.

"How are things, Conny?" Harry tried to sound jovial.

"Bad, Harry." The dean shook his head gravely.

"Yes, yes. Nasty business, this."

"No, I was thinking about the long, long, very long conversation I had with Mrs. Feingarten and Mrs. Fenscher yesterday."

"Really? Regarding what?"

"Regarding some inane notion that we should be offering a class in pathology or mortuarial skills or some such drivel. Know anything about this, Harry, old buddy?"

"Pathology, you say? N-no, can't say that I do."

"Really? Or the hysterical call I received from Lyman Bledsoe this morning, about the new major department in taxidermy I'm allegedly proposing? Or the article in next week's *Pathfinder* on this subject, for which I was interviewed?"

"Ah, no, 'fraid not."

"Fine, Harry. Just asking. Tell you what, I'd really like someone to clear this mess up, with the Colossus Sisters, with the newspaper, and with your own darling Lyman Bledsoe."

"Junior."

"Junior. Otherwise, I may have to look into the rumors of a teacher offering a class in a tavern downtown."

TWENTY-SIX

✥

Harry hurried to the college library for some quick research, then returned to the political science office building in time to catch the department secretary leaving. They wished each other a nice evening and Harry left the front door unlocked.

Two minutes later, he sat behind his battered old desk, stocking feet raised, textbook in his lap, two fingers of Scotch in his coffee mug, his eyelids drooping dangerously low. A knock on his office door snapped him back to reality. "Come."

Donal Patrick Cavenaugh shoved open the door, which ricocheted off the wall and swung back toward him. He stopped it with the heel of one fist. His eyes were red and puffy, and his breathing erratic. Harry marked his page with an old parking ticket and slipped his feet into his shoes. "Hullo, Mr. Cavenaugh."

"You bastard! How dare you make accusations like this!" He tossed Harry's crumpled copy of the board agenda onto the desk.

"Care to sit down?"

"Take your bloody English hospitality and stuff it, mister! I'll have you know—"

"I'm not English. At least, not originally. Edinburgh, Scotland. A true Irishman would have known that."

"What does that mean!"

"Nothing, Mr. Cavenaugh."

"That note is slander!"

"No, actually it's libel. And it's only that if you can prove what I wrote *isn't* true: that you didn't burn your arm and singe your rug while freebasing cocaine."

"You can't prove I was doing anything of the kind, mister."

"True. I wouldn't want to try. Actually, it was only a wild guess, based upon your nervous behavior, as well as the fact you keep your cigarette lighter on its highest setting. Why carry a disposable flamethrower like that, unless you intend using it at times when your balance and depth perception are at their worst? You've the classic signs of drug abuse, Mr. Cavenaugh."

"You prove I was freebasing, asshole, and tell the cops! If you can't, I'll sue you for every cent you've got."

"That would just about pay for the cab ride to the courthouse. Actually, sir, I have no intention of proving you were using cocaine, although you may wish to."

Cavenaugh's eyes narrowed. "Meaning what?"

"Meaning Ms. Jocelyn Blaine was killed in a struggle, and the next day, you show up with a heavily bandaged arm. If a certain Detective Sergeant Wiley is as good as I think he is, he'll soon be asking you about that little coincidence."

"*What!* Bishop, I had nothing to do with that! I'd never even heard of the girl! How was I to know Geoffrey was getting a piece on the side!" The ersatz Irish brogue was nowhere to be heard.

"You didn't know about her?"

"Christ almighty, man! Of course I didn't!"

"Then what was Llewelleyn holding over you?"

"The drugs, of course! He was supplying—" Cavenaugh's waterfall of words abruptly halted, as he realized what he had said. "What—I don't know what you mean . . ."

"A bit late for that, don't you think? No offense or anything, but you did admit to it a moment ago."

A supernal calm, which was scarier by far than his earlier rage, overcame the little man. "How did you know about the blackmail?"

"I didn't. Not really. But I think everyone who was voting in line with Llewelleyn was doing so against his or her will; yourself included. Geraldo was. I was certain Llewelleyn was holding something on you. The drugs seemed a likely enough subject for blackmail."

"I see." He fumbled with a near-empty pack of cigarettes, holding it gingerly in his injured hand. "So now what?"

"Now, nothing. Mr. Cavenaugh, I'm not about to lecture you on your substance abuse. I've been known to take the occasional wee nip of whisky, myself, and any lecture from me would be fairly hypocritical. Nor am I interested in turning you in to the police. What you do to yourself isn't any of my business. Although I will admit a tinge of sadness at seeing your obvious talent wasted so."

"Talent." Cavenaugh snorted. "I haven't done anything worth shit in a decade or more. My muse filed for divorce, Bishop. It was an amicable enough settlement. I'm no more a sculptor than I am an adolescent. Both were true, once upon a time."

"Did you kill Llewelleyn?" Harry asked, although he knew the answer.

"No." Cavenaugh's angry energy was spent, and the hand holding the cigarette shook. He needed another fix. The store-bought accent seeped back. "I'm not sad he's dead, boyo. I don't know who did it, but it's not much of a crime, I'm thinking."

"Murder is murder, I suppose."

"You think so?" Cavenaugh actually seemed interested in the ethical ramifications.

"Yes. We have a system for dealing with people who deserve punishment. The system is flawed and creaky and way too big for its own britches. Nonetheless, it is our system, and it works for everyone or for no one."

Cavenaugh squinted through cigarette smoke at Harry. "You really believe that."

"Yes. I do."

Cavenaugh chuckled. "You stay well away from me, mister." It was an effort to muster the lasts dregs of his machismo. Harry merely nodded. The sculptor flicked his cigarette into Harry's trash can and stalked away.

Harry waited until he heard the outer door swing shut, then leaned across his desk and rapped in the wall. The door opened to the next office over, and Tucker Nelligan peeked around the corner.

"What do you think?" Harry asked.

"I think you were right—about the drugs, I mean. He wouldn't have backed down at the meeting if you weren't."

"And about his innocence?"

Nelligan cocked his head to one side and lifted a finger to his lips. "Hold on, Harry." He disappeared back into the office next door. Harry opened his text and took a sip of the Scotch. Cordelia Applebaum stopped just outside his door and cleared her throat.

"Cordelia! Come in."

Harry cleared his blackstone bag and a pile of old *Mother Jones* magazines off the extra chair and Cordelia sat, straightening her fawn-colored skirt.

"Quite the meeting," she said.

"Hmm. I trust they're not all that melodramatic."

"Harry, dear, I truly hope you understand why I voted to second Donal's motion to have you withdraw from any investigation."

Harry smiled. "Of course I do. And you're right, of course. As a college employee, I have no right to go poking around in this affair. On the other hand, when Geoffrey asked my help, I couldn't very well turn him down. I hope *you* understand."

She reached over and patted him on the knee. "I do. You have a noble heart, Harry."

"Ha! I don't know about that."

Cordelia fussed with her skirt again and pressed her lips tightly together. "Harry, mind what you said, about Richard blackmailing certain members of the board?"

"Certainly."

"Do you know which members he may have had under his thumb?"

"Yes, I think so. All those trustees who would've voted him in as chairperson. In other words, those people whose books Llewelleyn handled."

"I see. He handled my accounts, you know."

Harry nodded, his elbow on the arm of the creaky chair, chin in his palm.

"Henry Bishop! You don't think *I* was being blackmailed, do you?"

Harry said nothing.

"Henry Bishop! Really! At my age, what do you suppose Richard could have had on me? My wild sexual escapades?

The opium-smuggling ring? A planned coup d'état against L. Charles 'Chuck' Eckersley?"

Harry laughed. "No, no. Nothing quite so grand and exciting."

"Then what?"

"Does it matter, Cordelia?"

"Yes, Harry! It matters because you're wrong, he had nothing on me. There's nothing to be had."

"Did Llewelleyn know about your writing career?"

"The poetry and biographies, you mean? I suppose he did."

"No, the romance novels."

Cordelia's face flushed a deep crimson. She folded her hands firmly in her lap, stared him in the eye, and replied crisply, "Harry, I have no idea what you're talking about."

"Fine. Fair enough. It's none of my business, anyway."

"Sometimes I think you need to stay away from your beloved Scotch."

"You're probably right."

"Purest nonsense."

"Hmm."

Cordelia opened her mouth to continue berating him, but Harry's coy smile stopped her. She suddenly slapped her knee. "Damn you, Harry! How did you know I was writing those cheap paperback romances?"

"I didn't. Not until this afternoon. I was speaking to my friend Tucker, and he mentioned that most people chose pseudonyms using their real initials. We were, I hate to admit it, trying to figure out how you maintain a lifestyle of the rich and famous, with no visible income. Then I remembered the two romances I saw with you. Both were written by someone named . . . ah, Cassandra Angelique. C.A., my dear."

"Yes. I see. And you think I killed Richard because—"

"What? Good God, no! Cordelia, my dear twit, I don't for a moment suspect you of murder."

"You don't?"

"No. Not now, and not ever."

"Well. That's certainly a relief, Harry. May I ask why? Is it because I'm a bit past my prime to be stabbing perfectly healthy, middle-aged men?"

"Certainly not. You could have hired someone to do that. No, dear, I don't believe you did it, because I used to work with you when you were on the city council. I can readily believe you capable of slaughtering an enemy, but only with litigation, never with a knife."

"I see." She leaned forward suddenly and rested a tiny, veined hand on Harry's. "Will you promise to keep my secret?"

"About the books?"

"Yes."

"Good lord, dear, why? I think it's amazing you can write fiction. I never knew your talent was that diverse."

"Oh, hogwash! Harry, have you ever read any of Cassandra Angelique's novels?"

"No."

"Well, don't! They're trash, Harry. Utterly devoid of literary merit."

"I can't believe that. They're not my cup of tea, certainly, but—"

"Harry, you ignorant goat, I've only written one story! I stored the plot on my personal computer, and whenever I need another book, I crank out that hoary old plot, change the names, locations and dates, and rewrite the damned thing! Believe me, 'Cassandra Angelique' is an author the way Cap'n Crunch is part of the four basic food groups! And after all, I have a reputation as a poet and scholar of poetry to think about. I don't need the world to know about my . . . extracurricular work."

Harry cupped her hand in his and squeezed. "Very well, Cordelia. You're the boss, as always. Personally, I think you're wrong, and I intend to head over to the Multnomah County Library this weekend and check out one of your— or rather Ms. Angelique's—works, to see for myself."

"Whatever you wish, Harry. Let it be on your head if the stuff makes you nauseous."

"Forewarned is forearmed," Harry said serenely.

"Now, if you never suspected me of the murder, whom do you suspect?"

Harry shook his head. "Not a soul, I'm afraid."

Cordelia stood and, evoking some gentlemanly instinct in Harry, he did also. She raised on tiptoe and kissed him on the cheek. "Be careful, Harry."

"As always. Walk you to your car?"

"No, thank you. I parked right out front. Good night, Harry. Call if I can help."

When she was gone and a reasonable safety margin had passed, Nelligan returned to Bishop's Closet. "Seriously, do you know who killed Llewelleyn?"

"No." Harry fiddled with the clutter on his desk.

"Harry, are you leveling with me?"

"Certainly."

"Harry! You shit! You *know*! You know who did it!"

"I don't, Tucker. Honestly. Besides, even if I did, I could be wrong."

"You're never wrong about these things."

"That's true. For solving murders, I'm batting one-for-one. Eat your heart out, Monsieur Dupin."

"Har-ry!"

"Tucker, please. I went into today's meeting with lots and lots of unsolved questions and half-baked theories. Actually, what I had you couldn't even dignify as theories—notions, vague images, a rampant stampede of non sequiturs. Even now that we've eliminated Cavenaugh and dear old Cordelia, and you took care of Geraldo (and how the hell I missed *that*, I'll never know), we still have far too many good suspects."

Nelligan collapsed into the room's extra chair. "Ah, hell, Harry. I was sure you were going to pull the answer out of your hat, like you did last year."

"Sorry to disappoint you. Maybe next murder."

The two men waited fifteen more minutes, and when no one else showed up they wished each other a good night and Nelligan, sulking, headed for his Jeep.

Harry puttered around the office for another twenty minutes, forcing his mind to focus on American radicalism and what he was supposed to be teaching his seminar class. Once he had his notes for Monday's class in order he stored the loose pieces of paper, magazine clippings, and random photocopies in a manila envelope and stuffed it all in his doctor's bag. Rain began to patter against his window. Harry looked up the home number for Geoffrey Eriksen in the JJAC directory and tapped out the digits.

"Eriksen residence." a female voice answered.

"May I speak to Geoffrey, please?"

"He's busy just now. May I take a message?"

"Irena?"

"Yes."

"This is Henry Bishop."

Silence greeted his introduction. Harry waited until he heard her draw in a deep breath. "What do you want, professor?"

"I need to ask your husband a few questions. I promise not to take much time."

"Can it wait until Monday?"

"No. Honestly, it can't."

Another pause, then: "Very well, professor. But first, let me tell you I don't appreciate your digging into this matter. It's none of your business, and if you had a shred of dignity, you would have told my husband that you couldn't help."

"I see. Thank you for your honesty, Irena."

"Hold on." Outside Harry's window, the night crew shut off the lights in the history department building.

Geoffrey Eriksen's powerful voice came over the line. "Henry?"

"Hullo, Geoffrey."

"Henry, I'm glad you called. I'm sorry about that show today. I never expected Cavenaugh to speak up like that."

"Not at all, Geoffrey. No harm done. I'm sorry to interrupt . . ."

"Just packing. I'm off for the weekend."

That's not right, Harry realized. He forced his voice to remain neutral. "Out of town?"

"Yes. Electronics show, San Diego. I'll be back late Sunday, though, if you need anything."

"Geoffrey, excuse me, but does Detective Kehough know about this trip?"

There was a slight pause before Eriksen replied. "Yes. I'm not sneaking out of town, I assure you."

Harry had had a few vague notions about the whole contretemps. Now, with Eriksen leaving town, his schedules were useless. Cradling the phone between shoulder and ear, he replenished the whisky in his mug. "Geoffrey, listen to me. I don't think that's such a good idea."

"Why not? I told you, the police know about my trip. They don't mind."

"It's just . . . nothing. I guess I'm getting paranoid. I suppose getting away from town for a few days will do you a world of good."

"Yes and no. These things are usually chaotic. We're selling some new software to the Navy, and they're tough customers. Did you wish to ask me something?"

"Hmm? Oh, yes, but it can wait."

"Well, Irena will be staying home. If something important comes up, she'll have my number in California."

"Fine. Have a good trip."

"I will. Are you sure there's nothing I can do for you, now?"

"Not a thing. I'll call you on Monday."

"Fine. See you."

Harry hung up and finished off the Scotch, then poured more and finished that. Standing, he dug around his floor-to-ceiling bookshelves till found a Portland phone book. He looked up one more number in the blue pages and dialed.

"Portland Police Department."

"Detective Kehough, homicide, please. It's urgent."

"One moment, sir."

Harry dribbled the dregs of whisky into his mug and returned the empty bottle to his bag. No need to give the janitorial staff material for the rumor mill. "Kehough, here."

"Kehough, this is Professor Bishop."

"Good evening, sir. What can we do for you?"

"I know what's going on, here at Astor. I've figured it out, and I need to talk to you. It's urgent that we speak, tonight."

"Certainly, sir. Can you drop by headquarters, or—"

"No. I don't want Sergeant Wiley in on this, and neither do you."

Static crackled over the line as the latest storm closed in on Portland. When Kehough finally spoke, his voice was oddly subdued. "Right. When and where?"

Harry thought about it for a moment, then gave Kehough the address to Kate Fairbain's Lake Oswego condominium. "Thirty minutes?"

"Fine, professor. I'll be there."

TWENTY-SEVEN

❖

Harry arrived at Kate Fairbain's place and spent ten minutes figuring out how to make her state-of-the-art coffee maker work. The water had just begun to drip into the grounds when the doorbell sounded.

Kate's bottle of bourbon in one hand and two glasses in the other, Harry walked to the entry hall and called out, "It's open!"

Detective Kehough brought the gusto of the storm in with him. Rain dripped off his sports coat and pants, and his shoes squished when he walked.

"Good God, man. Here, drink this and take off that coat. I'll get you a towel."

"Thanks." The tall, handsome man accepted the bourbon with appreciation. "I thought the rain had stopped. I left the window of the prowl car down a couple hours ago and soaked the driver's seat."

"You *are* new to these parts," Harry replied, returning with a bath towel.

"Thanks again. I don't want to damage the rug, but . . ." Kehough's focus shifted into the living room. He stared at the muddy oval stains on the floor and the water damage to the rug, couch, and wall. "This your place, sir?"

"No. Belongs to a friend."

"Looks like Beirut."

"Yes, a bit. Coffee will be ready in a moment. Shall we wait in the kitchen?"

Harry took a seat on the swivel stools, facing the bar that separated the kitchen and dining area. Kehough stood in the kitchen and dried his blond hair, while a puddle formed around his shoes. He crumpled his jacket in the sink, where it would do the least damage to the apartment. Strapped across his shoulder was a holster and what appeared to Harry to be a damned big gun. "So. What can I do for you, professor?" His smile was pleasant.

"Refill?" Harry motioned toward Kehough's glass.

"No, thanks."

Harry added a few fingers to his own glass. He was beginning to feel the effects of the liquor. "Mr. Kehough, I believe I know what's going on, here. Please believe me, Geoffrey Eriksen didn't kill Llewelleyn or the young lady."

"Oh?"

"Yes."

"Coffee looks ready. Want a cup, professor?"

"Thank you, no. I'll stick to this."

Kehough found a china cup and helped himself. "If you'd like to make a statement, professor, maybe we should've done this at the station."

"That wouldn't be terribly practical, Mr. Kehough."

"No?"

"No."

"All right, sir. Suppose you tell me what you think you know."

"Certainly." Harry sipped the drink, feeling the warmth line his throat. "Geoffrey Eriksen was a Nazi, and you're not a police officer."

Nelligan pulled the Jeep into the driveway and reminded himself to pick up new wiper refills. It was coming down pretty steadily now, and the lights of the city glinted off the rain sheen on the streets and buildings. He snapped up the collar of his trench coat, hunched his shoulders, opened the car door, and made a dash for the safety of the porch overhang.

"Yo! Martino!" he shouted from the entryway. No one answered.

He kicked off his shoes and padded into the bedroom. His wet clothes were added to the already considerable heap in the clothes bin, meaning that it was his month for laundry. He added another mental note to get to that chore.

In jeans, a UCLA sweatshirt, and his old, comfortable Nikes, he made a beeline for the kitchen. After an unsuccessful rummage in the refrigerator (*my turn for grocery shopping?* he wondered), Nelligan noticed the red candle burning in its glass holder, atop the portable tape recorder on the counter. It was Kady and Nelligan's version of the candle-in-the-window, and meant there was a message. With an apple of questionable age and a Corona Extra beer, he hoisted himself up on the counter and flicked on the machine.

"Hey, love. Sorry I'm not home. Remember Michael Lund? Got himself arrested again. Anyway, I'm down at the courthouse, and I'll be home as soon as I can. Try to look presentable, someone named Ericksen called about sixish and said he'd drop by. Needs to talk to you about something. I'll be home before eleven, for sure. Love you." *Click, whirr.*

Nelligan shut off the machine and munched on the the apple. Eriksen. Interesting.

Mrs. Nelligan raised a few dummies in her large family, but Tucker did not count himself among them. He had written some very damning things about Mr. Eriksen, and it was entirely possible that gentleman was coming over to yell at him or punch him or shoot him. The man did seem to have a thing for killing people, Nelligan thought.

On the other hand, why call in advance? Surely you wouldn't do that if you planned violence.

On the other hand, why meet him at night, at home? Business is for business hours.

Nelligan gulped some of the pale Mexican beer and slid his butt along the counter until he could reach the telephone. He dialed Harry's number and let it ring ten times. He dialed it again, just in case he got it wrong, and let it ring some more. He finished the apple and dialed the *Post*'s number, but hung up before it was answered.

Marty keeps a gun in the bedroom closet, he remembered. He hopped down off the counter and threw away the apple core as headlights swung past the kitchen window and a car pulled up beside the Jeep.

He ran to the bedroom, grabbed the chair that rested in one corner, and plopped it down before the closet. He climbed up and began rummaging through the boxes, old sweaters, forgotten legal documents, one cracked bowling ball, and other flotsam generated by five years of half-hearted house cleaning.

The doorbell rang.

This is stupid, Nelligan thought. He climbed down, replaced the chair, and hurried out to the entryway. As the doorbell sounded again, he carefully slipped the door chain into its holder, then switched on the porch light and opened the door a few inches. "Yes?"

The fat, pasty face of Sam Broderick peered back at him from beneath the tines of an umbrella. "Mr. Nelligan?"

"Mr. Broderick? What can I do for you?"

"Wish I knew. Did you get a call from Geoffrey Eriksen?"

"Yes."

"Me too. Told me to meet him here. Can I come in, and if not, can I borrow a snorkel and some swim fins?"

Thoroughly confused, Nelligan closed the door, unhooked the chain an swung it open. Broderick squeezed his magnificent girth through the door and turned, holding the umbrella outside and shaking it. "Lovely night."

"Yeah. Um, look, do you know why Eriksen wanted to see us, Mr. Broderick?"

"Yes." Broderick turned again, the pistol in his hand arcing out from beneath his raincoat. Tucker snapped his head back, but too late, and the cross-grained wooden handle and butt caught him just over the eyebrow.

His head connected with the hardwood floor and bounced once.

TWENTY-EIGHT

❖

"Wow." Detective Kehough grinned and brushed damp hair off his forehead. He shook his head and leaned back against Kate's Formica counter. "Wow."

Harry sipped his bourbon. "I'm sorry to interrupt your operation, Mr. Kehough—d'you mind if I call you that? Kehough?"

"Not at all, professor. I picked the name myself. May I ask you a question, sir?"

"Certainly."

"When did you figure out about Eriksen's past?"

Harry splashed more bourbon into his glass. "Geoffrey let it slip."

"Eriksen *told* you he was a Nazi?"

"No, no. In fact, he'd be appalled to think anyone knew. No, it was just some things he said. When he came by my flat to ask for my help, he mentioned something about more than forty years of work with the federal government. That would mean he was working for the Americans as early as 1948, or perhaps earlier. But if he was with the Free French, he would still have been overseas at that time. Moreover, at the Monday banquet he reminisced a bit about the war—said he remembered watching the big guns firing across the Siegfried."

"So?"

"So, the Siegfried was an anti-invasion line, built by the Germans. The French anti-invasion line was the Maginot. For one to watch the guns firing over the Siegfried—"

"—one would have to be on the German side, firing into France," Kehough finished, squeezing his eyes shut. "Damn. We were afraid of that."

"Afraid Geoffrey would start babbling about his introduction to America?"

"Yes. You teach political science, sir. You realize this is a rough time for the U.S., internationally. It wouldn't do for the world to discover we brought a Nazi engineer over here before the war was over, to work on our bomb production."

"That depends, Mr. Kehough. I take it Geoffrey had a . . . colorful war record?"

Kehough sampled his coffee. "'War atrocities' is the favored phrase, sir. Eriksen was a coordinator at one of the buzz-bomb factories that used slave labor. I don't know how culpable he was, though I understand he worked with their heavy-water atomic experiments. Anyway, it's none of my business. All I know is, the Israelis wouldn't be too happy about our long association with him."

"Nor, I should think, would several South American countries, especially considering Washington's hard-line stance on war criminals. And the government couldn't very well claim to be ignorant of his status, since he was brought over to work on the Manhattan Project and has continued to make electronic parts for the U.S. war machine ever since."

"Exactly. All right, sir, so you knew Eriksen was an ex-Nazi. How in hell did you tumble to me?"

Harry sighed. "Really, Mr. Kehough, it was nothing you did, per se."

Kehough blew on his coffee. "Forgive my curosity, professor. It'd really help me if I knew what went wrong with the cover."

"Nothing. Truly. Once I realized who Geoffrey was, and knew Detective Wiley considered him his best-bet culprit for the murder, it seemed logical to assume a case officer would be sent in to help him out of trouble. The next day, you arrived on the scene."

"What made you suspect me?"

"Mr. Kehough, television cop shows aside, in real life it's extremely rare for anyone to transfer from one police department to another and maintain their rank. Traditionally, there are only two places one may join a police department: the bottom and the top. As rookie or chief of police."

"Ah. I didn't know that."

"Few people do."

Kehough lifted his cup off the saucer in salute. "Bravo. You know, when they told me the Mad Hatter was involved out here, I was hoping we'd meet. You live up to your reputation, sir."

Harry gulped some liquor. "That was a long time ago."

"We still use most of your old Wonderland Profile for internal operations, you know."

"Hmm. Yes, well, the past is, thank God, the past."

Kehough helped himself to another half cup. "And the future?"

"My future is a bit nebulous just now. As is Geoffrey's. That's why I asked you over tonight."

"And what do you see for that future, professor?"

"Not much, I'm afraid. I suspect—please correct me if I'm wrong—your orders were to get Eriksen out of trouble, or make sure he can no longer be counted a liability. True?"

"True."

Harry leaned on the counter, his eyes imploring. "Mr. Kehough, please believe me: Geoffrey did not kill Richard Llewelleyn!"

Kehough winked. "Ah, come on, sir. Sure he did. I'd hoped to razzle-dazzle that local yokel, Wiley, into looking for another suspect. At first, I even thought old man Eriksen might've been on the up-and-up. Even for a Nazi, it was vaguely possible. That's why I asked him to get you involved. I figured having the Hatter on our team, even in the double-blind position, would help."

"That was your idea?"

"Yes, sir. But then Eriksen aced his mistress, and I realized he'd gone over. He's beyond normal reconciliation."

"Kehough, Eriksen is redeemable." Harry winced as he realized how easily he had slipped back into the vernacular of the trade.

"I don't believe that for a minute. Professor, you understand my position. We can't have this former Nazi telling tales out of school or running around frying anyone he pleases. He *is* the only one who could've killed that whore, sir. I'm sorry, but my hands are tied." Kehough leaned back against the Formica counter. "And now you're in on this. Real awkward situation for me, sir. I hope you see that." He set down the cup and crossed his arms, his right hand resting easily on the leather holster.

"Yes. I realized that when Geoffrey said he was going out of town for the weekend. I couldn't imagine any reason you would allow that, unless you were planning an accident."

Kehough shrugged. "Well, you know how it is. They're always easier when the subject doesn't have a home-court advantage."

"Yes." Harry drained the remains of the bourbon and studied the bottom of his glass. "I know how it is. Heart attack? Auto accident?"

"Stroke. It's a favorite of mine. I'm sorry sir. You see my position."

"Mr. Kehough, I understand you. Truly I do. But I tell you again: Geoffrey didn't kill anyone."

"Then who did?"

"Sam Broderick."

"Broderick?"

"Yes. Llewelleyn had been blackmailing various trustees at Astor."

"So I hear."

"I knew what he had on Geoffrey, Mrs. Applebaum, Reverend Avenceña, and Mr. Cavenaugh, and what he was probably holding over Ms. Shoenborn-Eriksen—her husband's wartime allegiance, I'd guess—but not what he had on Broderick, his employer. I couldn't get that until Geoffrey told me Llewelleyn had introduced him to his mistress, Jocelyn Sue Blaine."

"So? Forgive me, sir, I'm not following."

"My friend Tucker Nelligan gave me a bit of fascinating trivia today. Most people, when choosing a pseudonym, use their real initials."

"Really?"

"I know: it's so ingrained in a professional never to do that, one tends to forget the folly of amateurs."

Kehough's eyes scanned the ceiling. "Um . . . there isn't anyone on that board with Jocelyn Sue Blaine's initials."

"Of course there is. Sam Broderick. He told me, just today, his father's name was James Samuel Broderick, Senior. Sam is his middle name: he's dropped the James."

Kehough mulled it over, then shrugged. "Fairly tenuous, sir."

"I checked in Archives. His full name *is* James Samuel Broderick, Junior. Also: he told Tucker Nelligan the second 'Broderick' in 'Broderick, Broderick, and Alphonsine' was for his 'firstborn.' Tucker assumed that to be a son. It's not a son, but a daughter, Jennifer Susan Broderick; who should be just about the right age for Jocelyn Sue Blaine, according to the Werewolf."

"Who?"

"The hirsute young man in Archives. The one you bribed to get my dossier."

Surprise flickered in the handsome man's eyes, but he said nothing.

"Forgive me, Mr. Kehough, we're getting sidetracked again. I think Broderick had a fine motive to kill Llewelleyn. And it should be easy enough to prove, with your help."

"Would if I could, sir. I think things are beyond that stage, now."

"Hear me out: you have two courses open to you. The first is the most obvious—assume Geoffrey Eriksen is mad as —"

"A Hatter, sir?"

"As it were. Assume that, and you must eliminate him as a threat. I'm aware of his real identity and I, too, must be killed. Tucker Nelligan has been working very closely with me, and he's a most tenacious young man. Kill Tucker, and the entire journalistic community of Portland will assume he was onto something big and will start dogging our most recent tracks. Are you with me?"

Kehough gnawed his lip. "Yes, sir. It's awkward, like I said. You mentioned a second option?" His hand never strayed from his holster.

"Yes. Simply put, at today's emergency meeting of the board, I let it be known that I knew the identity of the murderer. Whoever it is—Broderick or someone else—that person will undoubtedly feel me to be a significant threat to his or her plans."

"So now you're a target?"

"Yes. With the proper preparations, I'm sure that person could be tripped up. That's partly why I asked you to meet me here: so the murderer wouldn't find us talking before a setup could be hatched. Moreover, we'll . . ."

Harry's voice trailed off, and for a moment, Kehough thought the drinks had taken effect. "Professor?"

"Hmm? Sorry. Just had a thought." Harry leaned over the bar and retrieved the telephone.

"May I ask who you're calling, sir?"

"Yes. Tucker Nelligan. I made myself the primary target, but not necessarily the only target. Hope I haven't missed a trick, here."

"I'm afraid I can't let you make that phone call, professor." Kehough rested his fingertips lightly on Harry's wrist.

Harry kept his hand in place on the receiver. "Mr. Kehough. Please. You know who I was. Do yourself a favor. Trust me."

TWENTY-NINE

❖

Nelligan raised his fingers to his forehead and touched the damp cloth. "Ow," he whispered. A rhythmic pain pulsed sharply behind his eyes, which refused to open.

He thought he was lying on the couch in the den, but when he tried to raise his head, nausea swept over him.

"Beer?"

Nelligan fought down the bile and struggled to a sitting position. A damp facecloth fell from his forehead and, although he couldn't focus well, he realized it was dark brown. Nelligan touched his forehead lightly and held his fingers before his eyes. Blood.

Sam Broderick sat forward, the rocking chair protesting his shifting bulk with a groan. He handed Nelligan a cold bottle of Corona and the reporter took one cautious sip, not moving his head in the least. His vision still had not cleared and that worried him.

"Hope you don't mind, Tucker—I can call you that, can't I?—hope you don't mind I helped myself to the beer. How's the head?"

Nelligan tasted bile and was sure he had recently vomited. The beer tasted terrible. "You hit me."

"That I did. You don't have any American beer, I see. I always drink American beer. This ain't bad, though."

"Why?"

"It's what my daddy drank."

"Why did you hit me?"

"Seemed like the thing to do at the time. I'm also going to shoot you, once I've had another beer. I'll be honest with you, boy, I'm not very good at this violence stuff. I couldn't find your hard liquor or I'd helped myself to that. Fortifies the nerves."

Nelligan took a long swallow, tilting the bottle so he wouldn't have to move his head. He could make out the gun in Broderick's wide lap now. He didn't know much about guns, but knew that one was larger than police-issue. Maybe a forty-five. Broderick's thick, sausage fingers gripped the stock tightly.

Nelligan wondered what sort of weapon a bottle of Mexican beer would make.

"What is this, Broderick? Did you kill Llewelleyn?"

"Oh, yes."

"And the hooker in—"

The gun swung up, the barrel focusing on Nelligan's nose. Broderick thumbed back the hammer. *Oh shit oh shit oh shit . . .*

"She was a wonderful child, Jenny. Wonderful. You'll wanna keep your foul mouth shut about her, you hear?"

"Yes." *Jenny?*

The gun held its aim for a moment, quivering in his too-tight grasp. Broderick slowly returned it to his lap, still pointed at Nelligan, the hammer cocked. Broderick took a long drag from his bottle. Two more bottles in their cardboard carrier rested on the trunk between them.

"But you mean Jocelyn, that tramp of Geoffrey's, right? That's different. Sorry I yelled. This is very difficult, Tucker. Honest to God, I wish there was an alternative. Really I do."

Fear fought for dominance with nausea and won. Adrenaline began to clear Nelligan's vision and his head, and he made mental note of his options. Table lamp, three feet to his left: he could never hope to reach it in time. Bottle of beer: a possibility, but still not very comforting. How much fizz could he get by covering the opening with his thumb and shaking? He discarded the notion. Two throw pillows beside him, the *TV Guide* and a copy of *Willamette Week* magazine on the trunk between them: useless. The trunk itself?

"Why'd you kill Llewelleyn?" Nelligan asked, carefully raising one foot and resting it on the metal edge of the steamer trunk. Broderick seemed not to notice.

"Why do you ask?" The fat man took a deep drag from his bottle, emptying it.

"I'm a journalist. They pay me to ask questions." Nelligan sipped his beer, tilting his head slightly. The pain roared back in an instant, and the bottle almost slipped from his hands. He returned the damp, bloody cloth to his forehead.

"You all right?" Broderick set down one bottle, picked up a full one and slid it between his massive thighs. He produced Nelligan's kitchen bottle opener from a pocket and snapped off the lid.

"I think I'm concussing," Nelligan answered honestly.

Broderick nodded solemnly. "Could be. You wanna know why I killed that stinking little piece of rat shit Llewelleyn?" His tone never changed—the words were a statement of fact rather than an epithet.

"Yes."

The phone rang. The gun twitched violently and Nelligan was sure it would discharge.

It didn't.

The phone rang again, echoing violently in Nelligan's head.

"Who do you suppose that is?" Broderick asked conversationally.

Think think think. "Detective Wiley."

Broderick's ample stomach jiggled as he chuckled. "Could be. Probably not."

Ring.

"He knows I'm home."

"*Stop it!*" The gun reared up again, now shaking badly.
Ring.

"All right!" Nelligan winced away, jarring the pain in his head.

"*You stop your lyin'! I mean it! Just! Shut! Up!*"
Ring.

Nelligan sat as still as death, feeling his gorge rise into his mouth. He clamped his mouth shut. Broderick looked like he was enduring a grand mal epileptic seizure. The gun twitched violently, his face flushed red. The newly opened bottle lay on the rug, the beer gushing out.

Ring.

Nelligan sat and waited. Broderick's hand began to regain its control. His jowls slowed their quivering. The beer stopped running.

The phone didn't ring.

Harry stabbed the double tine, disconnecting the line. He turned the phone around and slid it across the counter toward Kehough. "Damn! Quick, call Wiley."

Kehough now had his gun unsheathed, but held it at his side, unsteadily, unsure of what he should do. "Um, what's going on?"

"*Just do it!*" Harry forced a normal breath into his lungs. "It's Tucker. He said he was going home. Please call Wiley. Now."

Kehough smiled indulgently. "Sure, but don't you think you're getting a little jumpy, sir?"

"No." Harry noticed his own hand was trembling. "I've been an idiot. I'm way too visible a target. Please call Wiley."

"Okay, but he's not in toni—"

"He carries a pager."

Kehough thought about it for almost thirty seconds, then reholstered the gun, picked up the phone, retrieved a note from his shirt pocket with the police department phone number. "Serious?"

"Yes. Extremely."

"Hello? Homicide, quick. Yeah, Kehough here. Connect me to Sergeant Wiley, now. Emergency."

Harry gripped the bar and held his breath, wondering how he could have made such a monumental error.

"I trust you know what you're doing, profes— Wiley? Hey, are you at home?"

Harry grabbed the phone from Kehough. "Sergeant, Tucker's home. So's the killer. Get him, please!"

Slowly, achingly, Broderick's gun hand returned to his lap. He reached out for the last beer, repeating the process of opening it, and downed a third of it in one gulp.

"He blackmailed me," Broderick said matter-of-factly.

Nelligan could feel his own muscles twitch as they relaxed. He nodded, not knowing what would set Broderick off next, and where it would end.

"Llewelleyn, I mean," Broderick went on conversationally. "You see, he was pretty good at what he did. Investment counseling, that is. Damned good, really. Made fortunes. But he was a greedy little pissant. Greedy. You ain't drinkin' your beer, Tucker."

Nelligan obediently raised the beer to his lips.

Broderick nodded, pleased. "Where was I?"

"Llewelleyn was greedy."

"Right. Right. Thank you. Llewelleyn was greedy. He wanted to be more'n a junior partner of Broderick, Broderick, and Alphonsine. *My* company. And one day, how in hell it happened I'll never know, he found out about Jenny."

"Jenny?"

"My daughter." He took a deep swig of the beer, his eyes losing their focus a bit. The aim of the barrel remained true. "Only had the one child. I'd hoped for a son: James Samuel Broderick III. Oh well. I kept the family initials and just changed the name. Jenny was such a pretty kid. Like her mama. Gorgeous. But she wasn't very good, Tucker. You got kids?"

"No."

"There ain't no better joy in the world, and no greater pain. I tell you that as a fact, boy. Children. After my Annette died, I tried to raise Jenny best I could. It's tough though, Tucker. Anyway, she turned kind of rotten. Hung around the wrong crowds, started doing all sorts of drugs and that sort of thing. You know how it is, don't you?"

"Yes." Nelligan placed the tread of his other shoe against the top edge of the steamer trunk.

"She was just plain bad. I threw her out. Couldn't take it any more. After a while, I lost track of her. Washed my hands of the whole situation. That sounds shitty, comin' from a father, doesn't it?"

Carefully, now. "I don't have kids. I don't know."

Broderick nodded, his chins multiplying. "I'll tell you the gospel truth here, Tucker. Jenny died a while back. Just died completely. In her place was this slut, this whore named Jocelyn. *Jocelyn Blaine.*" He spoke the name as if it tasted bitter. "She wasn't my flesh. No, sir. She didn't exist in my world and I never thought about her. Not once. A man can only do so much, you realize. There're limits, even to love."

"What happened?"

"Llewelleyn. He found out about her, about what she did. I don't know how he did it, but he did. I'm an important man in these parts, Tucker. My clients are the pillars of this town. News like that, that my own flesh an' blood was a slut, that'd ruined me. I couldn't let it.

"So I gave in. I did what he wanted. Oh yeah, he was a smart bastard. He didn't milk me for tens o' thousands, though he could'a. A few hundred dollars a week extra to the old paycheck, that's all he asked. That, an' to be put on the Astor board of trustees.

"I did what he said, and it wasn't long 'fore he was milkin' other board members too. He was so damned good at investments, people just opened up their books to him. Wrote him a blank check. 'Here, Richard, old son, look around my life. Go ahead. I trust you.' Shit."

"What did he have on Eriksen?" Nelligan's nerves twitched. What had he just heard? A sound? A creaking floorboard?

"Nothing. Not at first. Old iron-guts Eriksen's as clean as a whistle. No, there was nothin' there, so Llewelleyn created something. He introduced Geoffrey to . . . Jocelyn. Y'see, he had an arrangement with that whore. She and Eriksen started . . . fucking each other, behind Irena's back. An' she was takin' pictures of them, to use against Eriksen.

"After that party, Monday night, Llewelleyn met me at my place. He invited himself in, told me what he had on Geoffrey, an' told me he was gonna make his move for the chairmanship. See, on the investment committee of the board, he'd been skimming a tidy little profit. In the big guy's seat, he figured he could do a lot better.

"I told him to go to hell. I was tired of playin' his game, Tucker. Sick and God Damned Tired of It!" Broderick slammed his fist down on his thigh, the knuckle of the trigger finger dangerously pale.

"He acted like it was some kind of celebration, even brought champagne and caviar. There he was, sittin' in my front room, tellin' me about Jen—about her and Eriksen, and about how I'd better do what I was told or else people'd find out about my daughter, and *she was dead, Tucker! She'd been dead to me for years, and that shit was usin' her against me and I cut him! I cut him! And it took me two days to find that whore of Babylon but I found her and I got her, too, and I burned the pictures and she's dead, Tucker, and you and that stupid, boozy professor know way fucking too much and I can't have that, Tucker, I really can't."*

"Tucker? You okay?" Martin Kady rapped once on the door and stepped into the room. Broderick whirled in his chair and lightning flashed from the muzzle of the gun.

His ears roaring from the explosion, Nelligan jammed his feet into the truck, stretching his legs out till his knees snapped taut. The trunk smashed into Broderick, who was twisted around and leaning back in the chair. With a yelp, the huge body tumbled over backward.

"NOOO!" Nelligan screamed.

Kady fell back against the hallway wall, blood arcing up and away from his body.

Nelligan was up and over the trunk, landing with one knee against Broderick's crotch, the beer bottle smashing into the man's thick, rubbery lips. There was a flash of light to his left and the gun was back, cracking against his ear.

Nelligan toppled over, clutching his head, knees drawn up to his stomach, his vision a kaleidoscope of colors and hues with no pattern or shape.

Marty! he tried to yell but nothing came out, or maybe it did and he could no longer hear himself over the roaring, thundering passage of blood through his head.

The pain and the fear overcame the vertigo, and he forced his eyes to focus on the bleeding bundle in the hallway. He was dimly aware of Broderick crawling to his knees.

Nelligan groped around on the floor and found the *TV Guide.* He hurled it toward Broderick, but it fluttered astray. Broderick steadied himself on his knees and one hand now, blood oozing from his nose and mouth, and aimed the gun at Nelligan.

One of Broderick's empty beer bottles rolled within reach, and Nelligan grabbed for it.

Broderick fired. The bullet tore into the rug and wooden floor at Nelligan's shoulder, sending splinters into the air.

With a solid boom, the den window erupted. A sheet of glass shards spread out around the room burying themselves in Nelligan's back and Broderick's flank.

The fat man's necktie popped up and away from his chest as two of John Wiley's three shots hit home. Broderick landed hard on his back, air wheezing from his chest.

"*Martyyy!*" Nelligan cried.

THIRTY

❖

"How many?"

"One."

The doctor moved the carboard, covering Nelligan's other eye. "Now how many of me do you see?"

"One. I'm fine. How's Marty?"

The young doctor shone a light in the right eye and *tsk*ed.

"He's still all right, Tucker," Harry answered. He sat in the chair beside the hopital bed, his mammoth, threadbare overcoat across his lap. "He's out of surgery. He's going to be fine."

Nelligan nodded and bit his lip. A stretch bandage had been wrapped around his head, and a thick pad covered one ear. He was lying on his stomach, with the doctor kneeling by the bed, examining his eyes. Nelligan's back was exposed by the hospital gown, and thirty or more minor cuts had been swabbed and cleaned. A few had required stitches.

Nelligan reached out and squeezed Harry's hand. "Bastard shot Marty, Harry," he mumbled.

"I know. Marty's going to be fine. You sleep."

"He's crazy. Broderick's crazy. They've got to put him away."

"They will."

"Crazy bastard shot Marty."

The doctor stood and jerked his head toward the door. Harry followed him out.

"We bombed him pretty good. His adrenaline's going to wear off in a few moments and he'll be in never-never land. You a friend?"

"Yes." Harry replied, leaning against the wall, feeling short of breath.

"This Nelligan guy came in with PPD Homicide. You sure it was okay for you to be in there?"

"Yes. Detective Wiley arranged it. Where is he?"

"Don't know. Excuse me."

"Doctor? The other patient, Martin Kady. How is he, really?"

The doctor ground his heels of his hands against his eyes and he stifled a yawn. "Still under, I think. They've got a team of three chest-cutters in there, trying to see what can be patched together and what can't. I hear it's pretty messy."

"And Broderick?"

"Fat guy?"

"Yes."

"DOA. Tell your cop friend to stop bringing multiples into my ER, okay? I could use some sleep."

Harry found a machine that dispensed coffee, and bummed fifty cents off an orderly. He wandered for a time and found John Wiley sitting on a wooden bench outside Obstetrics.

Harry sat down and sighed. He passed the paper cup over and Wiley took a sip. "Thank you, professor."

"Thank you, Sergeant."

Wiley had aged fifteen years. He sat hunched over, elbows on knees, and Harry actually thought the gray in his hair had spread. The intricate lines and circles around the sergeant's eyes had grown like crystals.

"Had you ever had to do that before?" Harry asked at length.

"No. I wounded someone once, though. In 1977. I shot him in the calf."

"You saved my friends' lives."

"Kady is still alive?"

"Yes."

Wiley nodded and sat up. He accepted another swallow of the awful coffee. "That's good. The longer they're in, the better. My father says that, anyway, and he's a doctor. How did you know I was staking out Nelligan's house?"

"I didn't. I only guessed it."

"How?"

Harry thought about the question for a while, searching for answers. It all seemed like years ago, not mere days. "This imbroglio has had a strange . . . resonance . . . to it. I knew Tucker was pivotal, though for a while, I didn't realize just how. When his investigation slowed down, someone sent the autopsy report to him. Only someone in the medical examiner's office or police force could have done that.

"Later, when we had been floundering for a while, a radio bulletin was put out on Eriksen's car, in connection with the murder of that young woman. Why announce you were looking for Geoffrey's vehicle? Tucker told me the girl had been dead for quite some time. I arrived at Geoffrey's house less than twenty minutes after the bulletin and his vehicle was there, blocked by Kehough's car. It seemed obvious that the newspaper would have someone who listens to police band broadcasts, and who would notice Eriksen's name in connection with another murder. That put Tucker and me back on the scent."

Wiley nodded slowly. The wails of a newborn carried out from the obstetrics department into the tiled hallway.

"Why connect me to that? Why not Kehough?"

"I knew who Kehough was, and I suspected you would chafe at being partnered with a nameless federal agent."

"How did you know he was nameless?"

Harry finished the coffee and started peeling back the cup's wax layer with his thumbnail. "I used to have some working knowledge of that business. Long, long ago."

"Ah. So you figured I wouldn't trust my new partner, but *would* trust Mr. Nelligan, instead?"

"Yes. You'd trust Tucker to be thorough and persistent and dogged."

"And crafty."

"Yes, that too. And you'd keep tabs on him, perhaps even plant a transceiver on his Jeep, and let him do what you were unable to do."

For the first time, Wiley smiled. "There is a bug in his Jeep. I was just seeing Mr. Nelligan home for the night when Broderick showed up."

The man sat in silence for a while, listening to the babies.

"Will I ever see Kehough again?" Wiley asked.

"No. Kehough no longer exists."

"They brought Geoffrey Eriksen into Good Samaritan about thirty minutes ago. Dead."

"Stroke?"

"Yes."

"Oh."

Wiley stood and walked away. He returned in five minutes with two more coffees. "They think Kady's going to live."

Harry started to cry softly. Wiley waited before asking. "Did Kehough kill Eriksen?"

Harry didn't answer.

"Professor." The sergeant's voice was labored with fatigue. "You underestimated your hand, and made a mistake. But Broderick was probably more insane than you could have known. Someone was going to die, one way or another. You're not to blame. I saw him go in, and Mr. Kady too. I also underestimated the call.

"Kehough was given carte blanche. The word came down from as high as a word can get. And although he never said as much, it was clear Eriksen was to be found innocent of all charges. I couldn't just sit there, professor. I simply couldn't. That's why I used your friend and you."

"I know. I counted on that."

Wiley used his reflection in the infant observatory window to straighten his tie. "Are you still in that business, professor?"

"Not for many years, now."

"Good. I think I like you, sir. I honestly don't know what's happened here, this week, but I think I like you. Come on, professor. I'll give you a lift home."

EPILOGUE

❖

On Saturday morning, just after dawn, Sandi Braithwaite pleaded with the shop foreman at a small Milwaukee print shop, begging for a half hour on his presses. She and her photo editor had hacked together a four-page edition of the *Pathfinder*, with file pictures on the front of Geoffrey Eriksen, Sam Broderick, and Richard Llewelleyn, and a major story (by Sandi) on the murder with two sidebar articles. She filled out the fourth page with a stack of sports briefs and concert announcements. There was no time to negotiate for advertising, and she paid for a thousand copies with her father's American Express card. The minipaper was on campus by nine a.m.

The *Pathfinder* scooped the *Post*, the *Oregonian*, and all three local TV news programs. *Time*, *Newsweek*, and the wire services picked up the story of the murder and Broderick's death, as well as the story of the intrepid young journalist, and ran stories on her. The *L.A. Times* offered Sandi an internship, to begin the week after graduation.

Sandi sent a box of assorted chocolates to Martin Kady. Tucker Nelligan received a basket of flowers from FTD with a note that said, simply, "Gotcha!"

That next morning, as Sandi was handing out copies of the *Pathfinder* in the cafeteria, Harry Bishop and Niccolo were awakened by the telephone.

"Harry? Good morning! It's Kate."

"Kate?"

"Yes, it's me."

"Where are you?"

"In town. Portland. I wasn't getting anything done in D.C., so I came home to finish the book. I'm exhausted and, truth to tell, I've missed you, Harry. Never thought I'd say that. I hate to impose, but could you come get me? All I want to do is go home and relax. Would you mind, terribly? Harry . . . ? Hello . . . ?"

"I'm here. Kate, dear, fair Kate: when you look back on this day—and you will—be kind."

Kinsey Millhone is . . .

"The best new private eye." —The Detroit News

"A tough-cookie with a soft center." —Newsweek

"A stand-out specimen of the new female operatives."
—Philadelphia Inquirer

Sue Grafton is . . .

The Shamus and Anthony Award-winning creator of Kinsey Millhone and quite simply one of the hottest new mystery writers around.

Bantam is . . .

The proud publisher of Sue Grafton's Kinsey Millhone mysteries:

- ☐ 26563 "A" IS FOR ALIBI $3.50
- ☐ 26061 "B" IS FOR BURGLAR $3.50
- ☐ 26468 "C" IS FOR CORPSE $3.50

and coming soon:

"D" IS FOR DEADBEAT